War Memorials

Books by Clint McCown

War Memorials

A NOVEL BY

Clint McCown

A MARINER BOOK
Houghton Mifflin Company
BOSTON • NEW YORK

First Mariner Books edition 2001

Copyright © 2000 by Clint McCown
Reprinted by arrangement with Graywolf Press

For information about permission to reproduce selections from
this book, write to Permissions, Houghton Mifflin Company,
215 Park Avenue South, New York, New York 10003.

Visit our Web site: www.houghtonmifflinbooks.com.

Library of Congress Cataloging-in-Publication Data is available.

ISBN 0-618-12847-6 (pbk.)

Printed in the United States of America

QUM 10 9 8 7 6 5 4 3 2 1

Acknowledgments

Many thanks to the editors of the literary magazines mentioned below where the following chapters first appeared. "Exclusions in the Policy" was first published in *Hawaii Review*, Issue 47, Volume 20.2, 1996. "History Lessons" was first published in *Colorado Review*, Volume XXIV, Number 1, Spring 1997. "Cheap Imitations" was first published in *Colorado Review*, Volume XXVII, Number 1, Spring 2000. "Some Assembly Required" was first published in *Clackamas Literary Review*, Volume IV, Issue 2, Fall 2000.

Thanks to these friends for their support: David Milofsky, Kevin Stein, Keith Ratzlaff, Dean Young, Tom Mangan, Tim Knowlton, Tom McBride, Emilie Jacobson, Anne Czarniecki, Stephanie G'Schwind, Susan Canavan, and Gracie Doyle. Thanks also to Beloit College and to the Antioch Writers' Workshop.

for Tom and Doug Strong,
who know all the stories,
and for Cynthia, best reader

Contents

SUMMER 1992

Exclusions in the Policy

MY FATHER GOT KILLED TWO TIMES in the war. He was an eighteen-year-old bombardier and gunner with one of the B-24 squadrons based outside London, and the first telegram said his plane had gone down over France in January of 1945. There were no survivors. Then the second telegram had him dead on a different mission somewhere in Germany four months later.

This worked a double hardship on my grandparents. They'd been torn up enough the first time my father died, and when they heard about the second time they didn't know how to take it. Neither did anybody else, for that matter. The local paper had already done a big spread on him: *Jimmy Vann Killed in Action*. I've seen the clipping. His teachers all said what a polite student he'd been, his football coach praised him for his cheerful attitude on the field, and Flaps Pittenturf from down at the Elks Lodge called him the best baritone their barbershop quartet had ever had. "Good as Bing Crosby," he said. The whole county seemed to look on my father as a favorite son, and when the bad news broke, everybody spoke up to say how tragic it was that he was gone. Then they filed him away with all the other dead boys in town.

When he died the second time, nobody had anything left to say.

Of course, that didn't matter much in the long run, since he turned out not to be dead at all. In fact he was in perfect health, and when he turned up on his parents' doorstep a few months after the war, without so much as a wrinkle in his Army Air Corps uniform and completely in the dark about both of his recent fatalities, the newspaper played it up as big as D-Day itself:

Jimmy Vann Alive!

It was right then, when he read his story in the paper and saw the retraction of his own glowing obituary, that my father got his calling. The whole world, he claimed, became clear to him in that single moment, and he saw the path he was supposed to take. He rented an office above Willard's Barber Shop just off the square, bought a new suit of clothes, and opened his own insurance agency.

It was a smart business move. Sure, insurance is a pretty bland proposition—at least it always was for me, and I put in nine years at my father's agency. But the thing is, everybody buys insurance, and if there's something that sets you apart from the other outfits, some gimmick that makes your name come to mind before all the others, you can make a real killing. And that's how it was for my father. When he turned up alive after being twice dead, he became the man people wanted to buy insurance from. Veterans, war widows, even the old-timers at the Elks Lodge: everybody wanted a piece of his luck. He sold policies by the truckload. Pretty soon he got to be just about the richest SOB in the county.

And that's fine. I've never begrudged him his good fortune. How could I? He's put a roof over my head my whole life. I wouldn't be anything if it weren't for him, and that's the literal truth. But the thing is, his life and mine are two different cases. I never played high-school football, I never went to war, I never sang like Bing Crosby. True enough, I have sold a lot of insurance, but even that's more a credit to him than to me. Insurance was never my real calling—although I'd be hard-pressed to say what is. Maybe if I'd seen all my good points written up on the obituary page, like he did, I'd have somehow figured out my best direction. But so far nothing like that's ever happened, and lately I've started to worry about running out of time. I'm already thirty-three—old as Jesus. I'm underweight, with high blood pressure, and my hair falls out in clumps in a high wind. I've started to look old—unlike my wife, Laney, who was a perky cheerleader thirteen years ago and looks almost the same now as she did in high school.

She acts the same, too. For example, she recently acquired a new boyfriend. Steve Pitts. I used to play baseball with Steve. He was a good left-fielder. Laney's also pregnant with a baby she won't say much about.

Well. One thing Laney didn't know was that I no longer worked for my father. He fired me for forging his name on a backdated rider for my homeowner's policy. It was a good policy—dirt cheap and fairly comprehensive—but it had a proviso about notifying the company in the case of any structural improvements or built-on additions. All policies have exclusions of one kind or another, and, as a rule, the cheaper the policy the more exclusions you have to watch out for. You can always upgrade your coverage if your circumstances change, but most people forget to do that unless their insurance agent reminds them. Anyway, we did some renovation last spring, and somehow I forgot to update my policy. Then a couple of months ago a thunderstorm brought a 200-year-old oak tree down through the roof of our new family room. Smashed right through the beams and knocked out two plaster walls.

The next day I got Brady Pitts—that's Steve's brother—to come out with his junkyard crane to lift the tree out of the house, but he ended up knocking down the third wall and splitting half the floor joists. What it came down to was a total loss, and I hadn't bought a dime's worth of coverage. Laney didn't know that part either.

The third thing she didn't know was that I'd started a new job. Instead of walking down to my father's agency in the morning, I'd go over to Tump's Pool Hall Café on the west side of the square, order one of Tump's bad breakfasts, and wait for my cousin Dell to swing by and pick me up. Dell did repo work for Hometown Finance, and I was his new assistant. What we did wasn't anything at all like selling insurance for my father. There was still some paperwork, of course, but basically my job now was to break into deadbeats' homes and cart away whatever it was they hadn't kept up the payments on. I didn't even know if what we did was legal. But compared to what I was used to, it was satisfying work.

Anyway, a couple of weeks ago we made a morning call on one of the old whitewashed frame houses on Hill Street on the slope above the holding pens for the cattle auctions. The whole neighborhood was in pretty sad shape—always had been, for as long as I could remember—little cracker-box houses with blistered paint and broken-down porches. And there was the smell of the holding pens, which isn't really a bad smell at first—sort of earthy and green—although I think it might be hard to stomach over the long haul. But there was another smell, too, mixed in with it, like a rat had died in a wall somewhere. Even in my early insurance days, when I was peddling policies door-to-door, I never bothered with the houses on Hill Street. As far as I knew, I'd never even known anybody who lived there.

When we got out of Dell's pickup, he squinted along the row of houses and then focused on one a couple of doors down from where we were parked.

"That's it, Nolan," he said. "The one with the knocked-out window over the porch."

"How do you know?" I asked him. There weren't any numbers on the houses, and every place looked pretty much the same. The last thing I needed was to get arrested for hauling off the wrong stove and refrigerator.

Dell just shrugged and pushed his ball cap lower over his face. "I know all these houses," he said. Then he reached back through the window of the pickup and took his clipboard from the front seat. He stood there a minute in the quiet street looking over the papers, then frowned and tossed the clipboard back inside the cab. "Better watch yourself on this one," he said. "Rathburn don't go out much anymore. We might run into him."

Rathburn was a common enough name around town—the family had branches all over the county—so the name didn't mean much to me at first. It did bother me, though, to think that we might have to deal with another human being. The repo business was hard enough with nobody home, but when the clients were there to watch you take back their stuff, you never knew what might happen.

"How do you want to work it?" I asked, although I knew the answer. In my first few weeks on the job we'd made over a hundred house calls, and the drill was always the same. Dell would wait by the back door while I knocked on the front. If somebody answered, I'd tell them what I was there for, show them a claims sheet to make it look like we had some kind of authority, and give them one last chance to cough up the cash. They never had it, of course.

If it was a woman at the door, I'd explain that we'd have to take her washer, or the TV, or whatever the hell it was, and she'd let us right in. A woman won't bolt once you've spoken face-to-face.

The men were another story. Usually they'd tell me to wait a minute while they got the money, but then they'd lock the door and hightail it out the back. That's when Dell would make a sort of half-hearted grab for them, not really wanting to catch anybody but just trying to keep them preoccupied enough so they'd forget to lock the back door behind them. Dell is one stout sonofabitch, built like a grizzly, so he could put himself in harm's way like that and come out fine. Not me, though—I don't have the right bulk for real intimidation. That's one reason I was the front-door man. The other reason was that most everybody knows Dell by sight, and if he came knocking, no one would ever open up at all.

Anyway, Dell circled around through the neighbors' backyards and took his post at the rear corner of the Rathburn house. When I saw he was ready, I strolled up onto the front porch and rapped on the screen door. No answer, so I knocked again, hard enough to rattle the screen in the frame, and listened for sounds inside the house. Everything was quiet, so I hopped off the side of the porch and walked back to where Dell was pressing his face up to a dirty rear window trying to see into the kitchen.

"I don't think anybody's home," I told him. I rubbed away a patch of window dirt with the heel of my hand and tried to stare through the shadows, but it was no use, the sun was too strong behind us, and when I wiped away the grime all I got was a better look at my own squinty face in the glass.

"Maybe he went back to Mobile," Dell said. "He's crazy enough."

That's when I realized whose house we were about to break into. It didn't seem possible, though. "Is this *Jerry* Rathburn's place?" I asked.

Dell stepped onto the crumbling concrete stoop and jiggled the doorknob. "Well, I think it actually belongs to his brother Ned. But, yeah, Jerry's the one who lives here. When he's in town, anyway. He showed up at the office one day about four months ago. I told Ray not to loan him any money, but he and Rathburn go too far back. I might as well have been talking to a stump."

I'd seen Jerry Rathburn maybe three times in my life. The most memorable was fourteen years ago at Bryce Holman's high-school graduation party. I don't know why Jerry was there, because he was about eight or nine years older than the rest of us. I think he'd just come home from one of his hitches in the army. He wasn't all that close to Bryce as far as I knew, so he might have just been there selling drugs. That was the general word on Jerry Rathburn—that he'd got himself all screwed up with drugs when he was in Vietnam. Anyway, along about midnight the Harvel twins, Barstow and Jug, got into a fistfight. That was pretty normal for them—they were always trying to prove which one was boss. But this was the worst they'd ever been. I swear it looked like they were about to kill each other. Then somebody yelled, *Jerry, see if you cain't break that up,* I guess because Rathburn was the oldest one there and people figured he must know something from being in the army. So he walked over to where the Harvels were rolling around in the dirt and stood there for a minute like he didn't know quite what to do. Then he took a .22 pistol out of his army jacket and shot them both in the leg. That pretty much brought the party to a close.

"I thought Jerry Rathburn was in jail," I said.

"He was," Dell answered. "But he got out."

Jerry was a big local story last year. His wife—I forget her name, but she used to work at the Wal-Mart out on the Huntsville highway—anyway, she must've got fed up with Jerry because one night she just packed her suitcases and went to Mobile to live with her sister. Jerry drove down and fetched her home, which turned out to be the wrong thing to do, because the sister swore out a complaint. Pretty soon the FBI kicked in Jerry's door and hauled his ass off for kidnapping. Noreen—that was her name, Noreen—was tied to a chair in the living room, mad as hell. And it happened right here in this very house.

"I thought they gave him ten years for that last one," I said. "Why'd they let him go?"

Dell shook his head and smiled. "I didn't say they let him go. I said he got out."

I ducked clear of the window and pressed in close against the house. "Christ, Dell," I said, "no wonder nobody answered the door. He's probably in there right now with a goddamn shotgun." The siding felt hot through the back of my shirt, but I didn't move away. "And where's the sheriff in all this?" I wanted to know. "I mean, there's laws, for godsakes."

Dell just laughed. "Nolan, you need a more tolerant attitude," he said. "This ain't the insurance business—there's a lot more give-and-take. Not everything's written down."

"Dell—" I said. I meant to argue with him, but somehow the words just wouldn't collect themselves. I stared down at my feet. Even my shoes, I realized, were wrong for this kind of work. Cordovan loafers. What kind of moron wore loafers for hijacking furniture? And that's all this repo job amounted to, really. These weren't white-collar financial transactions we were negotiating; our job was to break down the door, shove people aside, and get the appliances up onto the truck. I should have been wearing sneakers— high-tops, with strong ankle support and good traction to help me hold my share of the load. Shoes I could run in.

Dell was right—this wasn't the insurance business, and nothing I'd learned selling policies was relevant anymore. If I belonged anywhere in repo work it was at a desk in the front office with Ray, filling out forms and explaining payment plans. I was comfortable on the fine-print end of things. Ironing out the black-and-white agreements. Outlining the rules people had to play by. Making sure we all understood what was expected and what the consequences were if somebody failed.

That was a system I could understand. My father understood it, too, and that's why he had to fire me. If I couldn't play by the rules, the system had no use for me. I could appreciate that.

But I never thought I'd drift so far into the fringes. The world I lived in now was not my father's. Here an escaped kidnapper could move back to the scene of his crime and take out a loan for a new stove and refrigerator. It was like being in a foreign country. I couldn't read the landscape. Back when I was selling door-to-door, I got to where I could walk into a house and tell just from the magazines on the coffee table what my chances were. But the people I dealt with now didn't subscribe to magazines. Their coffee tables were old ammo crates.

Dell hitched up his slacks and scanned the rear of the house. "You ready to go inside?" he asked.

"I don't know," I said. "The doors are locked. Maybe we ought to just leave this one alone."

"You're not worried about Jerry, are you?" He reached down and drew a brick out of the weeds beside the stoop and tested its heft. "You ever meet him?"

"Here and there," I said.

"Well, he's not near as bad as the newspapers made him out to be. Give you the shirt off his back if he likes you." Dell stepped up to the door and rapped the brick sharply against one of the small glass panes. Nothing happened. He tried again, harder this time, but the brick still wouldn't go through. Dell looked at me and then drummed his fingertips against the tiny window. "I'll be damned," he said. "It's Plexiglas."

"So can we go now?" I asked, though I knew Dell wouldn't give up that easily.

He stepped off the stoop and examined the kitchen window.

"This one's glass," he said, tapping his fingers lightly against it. "You go get the dolly off the truck. Door'll be open by the time you get back."

I still felt uneasy, but at least this time Dell would be the first one inside. That part usually fell to me, on account of Dell's size. If a window was too high off the ground, he couldn't hoist himself up well enough to shimmy through. This time, though, there was a gas meter just below the sill, so once he got the pane punched out he could step right into the kitchen.

I was about halfway to the pickup when I heard the window shatter. It seemed way too loud, and I looked around quickly to see if anybody else was there to hear it. But everything was dead calm. There were no kids, no dogs, no people on porches, no traffic in the street. Ideal conditions for repo work.

A minute later, as I rolled the dolly past the broken window, I could see Dell sitting inside at the kitchen table. He was alone, which was more than fine with me. I swung the dolly onto the stoop and started ahead through the open doorway, but one of the canvas belts snagged on a wheel and I had to stop to untangle it. I still couldn't see much of the kitchen, just the torn yellow linoleum and a painted cupboard on the far wall. But when I finally got the dolly inside, it was the smell of the place that nearly floored me.

"Holy Jesus," I said, "what's that stink?"

Bad smells are a normal part of the job, of course. Sometimes there'd be meat left in the refrigerators, and if it was at a house where the electricity had been cut off, the stench would be enough to make you gag. Dell just sat there, kind of staring at his hands like he didn't hear me, so I slid the dolly under the side of the stove and then pulled open the refrigerator door, just to check. It was chugging away fine, with nothing in it but a couple of old carrots and a six-pack of Pabst.

Dell pushed himself up from the chair like he was a hundred years old and then carefully looped the dolly belt over the top of the stove. "That stink belongs to Jerry," he said.

I glanced toward the table where Dell had been sitting, as if I thought Jerry Rathburn might suddenly be sitting there, too. Dell cinched the belt tight and buckled it, then wedged his work boot against the axle of the dolly. "I'll foot it while you tilt it into place," he said.

"Sure," I told him, but for some reason I turned the other way and walked straight through into the front room of the house, where the smell was so strong you could almost feel it against your skin. Jerry was there, all right, slumped in a big chair by the fireplace. He'd been dead long enough that you could tell it without having to look too close. I'd never seen a dead person before— except in funeral homes, where everything gets tampered with. But this was nothing like that. Nobody had closed Jerry's eyes, or combed his hair, or put color on his cheeks, or sewed his lips shut. Nobody had even kept the flies away.

Dell walked in behind me, but didn't speak.

"What do you think happened to him?" I asked.

"I think he died," Dell answered. "That's all." He handed me a half-sheet of yellow notebook paper. "I found this on the kitchen table."

It was handwritten. The letters were shaky, but big and loopy, the way grade-school kids write. *Anyplace but Arlington,* it read.

"Maybe he killed himself," I said, though I felt bad right away for saying it because it seemed too disrespectful. Besides, Jerry Rathburn wasn't anybody I could have ever second-guessed.

Dell took the note back and folded it away into his pocket. "Naw," he said quietly. "I just think he knew what was coming. Jerry'd been in and out of VA hospitals for the last twenty years. He got sprayed with that Agent Orange stuff when he was in Vietnam. Been dying ever since."

I wondered what the newspaper would say about Jerry Rathburn's death, if it would say he was one more local boy who got killed in a war. I knew it was unlikely. Newspapers look for easy labels. They'd do the story as a final chapter on his kidnapping case, since that was the way they knew him best.

One time I found an old camera in my parents' attic. It had a roll of film inside, and for all I knew it might have been there for ten or fifteen years, or maybe even longer, just waiting to be developed. I took it in to the Wal-Mart right away, and for two days I could hardly think about anything else. It was like I thought—I don't know—that when the pictures came back I'd really see something. Like some missing puzzle piece would finally be put back in place. I thought they might be pictures of my dead mother, or my grandparents, or even my father long ago, before he got swallowed up by his lucky tour of duty in the war. I thought that whatever was on that film would make me feel like I understood things a little bit better. But then I picked up the pictures: just a bunch of weird-looking double exposures of lamps and checkerboard linoleum floors. I don't know what the hell they were.

This was a lot like that, somehow. Looking at Jerry Rathburn sitting in that overstuffed chair, slowly caving in on himself, I felt like I was supposed to be seeing something, like I'd finally had this accidental look behind the curtain and all the mysteries were right there, laid out plain. Only no matter how hard I looked, I couldn't make sense of the picture.

"We'd better move on," Dell said.

I followed him back to the kitchen, where we rocked the stove onto the dolly and swiveled it toward the door. Stoves were easy—just big tin cans. I knew the refrigerator would be more of a problem, especially with no pavement between the back door and the street. The ground was still a little soft from all the rain we'd been having, so the dolly wheels were likely to bog down.

I wasn't worried, though. We always got the goods back to the truck, no matter how much ground we had to tear up along the way. I didn't even care anymore if anyone saw us, though I guess that could have meant trouble, under the circumstances. There's no repo manual to go by—or if there is, Dell's never showed it to me—so I don't really know how much we're allowed to get away with. But I guess we could have been arrested for not reporting a dead body, or breaking and entering, or grand theft, or any number of other technical violations. Trespassing, at the very least.

If that had happened, I wonder if my father would have come to bail me out. I suppose he would've, if I'd asked him to, as a matter of duty.

But maybe I wouldn't have asked him. Maybe I'd have given up my right to a phone call and just settled in for however long they wanted me to stay. Then he could've read all about it in the papers.

Or maybe I'd have used my call unwisely. Maybe I'd have rung up a radio station and asked them to dedicate a song to somebody. Like Jerry Rathburn, for dying in such a plain, straightforward way, no loose ends, no resuscitations. Or better yet, a song for Steve Pitts and Laney. A love song, something upbeat, something bubble-gum, wishing them a good life somewhere else, anywhere else, even as far away as Mobile. Wishing them a pink stucco house with chameleons skittering along the walls. Plenty of chameleons. I wonder what she'd have thought if I did that.

But then I wonder about a lot of things I'll never know the answers to. I wonder how the wind gets started. I wonder how clouds hold themselves together. I wonder how trees turn water into bark.

I wonder why we ever built our family room.

I guess it was just as well the police didn't show up, or the neighbors. I've figured out a lot lately about the way things snake together, but if somebody threw a question at me about how Jerry Rathburn and I fit into the same picture—which I know we do—I still don't think I could have said things right. I mean, it's like when you try to sell a whole-life policy to some kid fresh out of high school, and he asks what the fine print means. You start out saying, *Sure, sure. I can explain all this.* But then you see his puzzled face, and know you haven't got a prayer.

History Lessons

THE CORONER SAID NATURAL CAUSES, which probably surprised a lot of people, given Jerry's notoriety. A bullet or an overdose might have seemed more normal, or even a bashed-in skull. If he'd been stabbed to death by a church deacon in some smoky rented room some hot Saturday night, nobody would have thought it odd. But all he did was sit down in a soft chair and die, which was the one thing nobody would have expected.

The stories in the newspaper had always cast Jerry in a certain light. Standard stuff, really—live fast, die young, leave a good-looking corpse—the usual outlaw bullshit. In the end he missed on all three counts. From what I can tell, his life was just a slow stumble of mistakes, nothing fast about it; and he surely hadn't been young since his tour in Vietnam. As for the good-looking corpse part—well, if that sort of thing was important to him, he shouldn't have let himself die alone in summertime in a house so forlorn even the meter readers pass it by.

He got two final write-ups in the Wednesday morning edition of the *Observer*—first as a piece of front-page news, then inside with the obituaries. The obituary was hollow as a spent shell: *He was the son of . . . He is survived by . . . He will be buried in. . . .* The front-page version had more details, but it was hollow, too, boiling Jerry's life down to a simple record of arrests. Neither article mentioned his two years in the army, although the obituary did run an old photo of him in his uniform. Private Jerald Rathburn: dopey grin, panicky eyes, hair that looked scraggly even in a crew cut.

I studied all this over breakfast at Tump's Pool Hall Café, waiting for Dell to pick me up for the morning repo run. I felt comfortable hanging out at Tump's. My father used to bring me here for waffles when I was a kid, and as a teenager I played a lot of pool on the three warped tables by the back wall. There was something stable, something permanent about the place—mostly because Tump was too cheap to remodel. The wood floor was a little darker, maybe, from the extra generations of varnish, and the plastic checkered tablecloths had picked up a few more cigarette burns along the way, but not much had really changed. Tump hadn't even put in an automatic dishwasher. Except for the Formica counter with its built-in metal bar stools, the café had pretty much escaped the whole century.

Tump had just served me a plate of bacon and grits and was starting on his first load of dishes from the dawn rush. There were still a few Tuesday-nighters playing poker back by the pool tables, but otherwise the place was empty, which was typical for the time of day. Summer mornings, Tump's is pretty crowded from first light to about 6:30, when the old truck farmers gather to drink coffee and speculate about the weather. They leave their dusty pickups lined outside against the courthouse lawn in that first long shade of the day, clotting the south side of the square with half-loads of peanuts and sweet corn, snap beans and yellow squash, peaches and cantaloupes, cucumbers and tomatoes, watermelons and yams. I've loved the sight of that all my life. But anyway, by seven o'clock the truck farmers have finished their coffee and moved across the street to the stone benches around the monument to the county's Confederate dead, leaving Tump's place empty except for a few late-starters like me and whatever pool hustlers or cardplayers might be left over from the night before.

Tump left the first load of dishes to soak and moved down toward my end of the counter, smearing his gray rag across the countertop along the way, pausing here and there to scrub up a spill stain or a spot of dried egg. He guided the rag around my plate and pushed the pile of crumbs over the edge of the counter onto the dark wooden floor. A fat horsefly buzzed casually between us, and Tump waved it away with a single slow sweep of his hand. "How's the chow this morning?" he asked.

"Greasy," I told him. "You barely got the chill off this bacon." Tump's a nice fellow, but he's kind of erratic as a cook because he almost never cleans his grill and he treats every hot order like he's just warming up leftovers. Still, I liked being here—I liked that thick smell of breakfast in the air. It's funny, but in the long run I can get more comfort out of the way food smells than the way it tastes. Taste swallows itself away in a minute or two, but a good smell can hang in the mind forever.

Of course, so can a bad one.

Tump shrugged and looked past me to the table of poker players. "Hey, Morgan," he called, "I got another gripe about the food. Maybe you oughta investigate." Morgan Motlow is a health inspector with the state, but he was born and raised here in the county so the only places he ever cites for health violations are the fast-food franchises out on the highway. He runs the regular Tuesday night game; nobody sits in without Morgan's say-so.

He tipped his chair back and squinted toward us. The sun was high enough now to set up a glare through the front windows, so I guess he had trouble making us out. Or maybe he was a little drunk—there were three pint bags on the floor beside his chair. "Is that you, Junior?" he said. Morgan grew up with both my parents, and even though I'm not named after my father, he's called me Junior all my life. I could tell by the tone of his voice he'd had a lucky night.

"Yeah, Morgan, it's me."

"Well, how the hell are you, boy? Ain't seen you since Hector was a pup." He looked back down at his cards and slid a small stack of chips to the center of the table. The other four players all threw in their hands, and Morgan broke into a loud cackle. "You dumb sumbitches," he said. He had to be drunk. I knew a couple of the other players in the game—Buddy Pilot and Ricky Malone were two or three years older than me, but we'd all been in eighth grade together, and they'd been dangerous even then. They weren't the kind of fellows any sober man would laugh at.

Tump shook out his rag and draped it over the side of the sink. "Nolan says the bacon's greasy. Says you oughta close me down. Put me out on the street so I can get me some of them welfare checks."

"Hell, bacon's supposed to be greasy," Morgan said, raking the pot into his pile of chips. "Dish him up another bowl of grits. Grits'll soak up anything."

"No, thanks," I said before Tump could even offer. I'm not a picky eater, but you could patch a driveway with Tump's leftover grits.

Buddy Pilot suddenly stood up from the table. "I gotta go piss," he said, "but deal me in anyway, I'm coming right back." He swayed a little in place, looking around the room like he didn't know where he was. Then his eyes focused on the rest-room door and he tilted straight for it, ramming several chairs and tables along the way.

I turned back to the remainder of my breakfast. Tump was trying to scrape the last of the cold grits into the garbage pail beneath the counter.

"Looks like it's been a long game," I said.

Tump glanced past me to the poker table. "Too long. I wish they'd break it up and go home." He began to work the spoon edge against the inside of the bowl as if he were whittling a knothole out of a stick. When he'd gouged away all he could, he eased the bowl into the sudsy dishwater and picked up his old Timex from the back of the sink. He studied the watch face for a moment, then held it out toward me. "What time does that say?"

"Ten after eight," I told him.

He squinted out through the front plate-glass window. "Well, if Marty don't show up soon, he can kiss this job good-bye. I'm too old to be staying up all night and then work his shift, too." He frowned. "Hey, somebody told me you don't sell insurance no more."

"That's right," I said.

"Well, if you're looking for work, I think Marty's about to leave a vacancy."

"Thanks," I said, "but I've already signed on with Hometown Finance."

Tump rummaged through the dark water and pulled up several paring knives, which he rinsed briefly beneath the tap. "You'd be better off washing dishes," he said, dropping the knives onto the drainer.

I knew what he meant. When you work for the finance company, there's paperwork and neckties and a dozen other things to make it seem like a real office job, but the gist of it all is to be the bad news on somebody's doorstep, and that's a sad career for anybody.

It crossed my mind to tell him about finding Jerry Rathburn, but that would've got Dell involved, and Dell was already mad at me for reporting the body, even though I hung up when the dispatcher asked me for my name. Dell figures that whatever happens on the job is our business and nobody else's. Maybe he's right, maybe privacy is the least we can offer. Doctors, lawyers, preachers, undertakers—they're all supposed to keep the details quiet. Maybe repo men are, too.

Just then the front door creaked open, jiggling the tiny bell above the frame, and Tump and I both turned to see who it was, both of us, I suppose, expecting it would be Marty finally dragging himself in for work. No such luck. From where I sat the morning glare was at its worst, almost blinding, reflecting in from the bright chrome trim of the trucks across the square. But even through that white wall of haze it wasn't hard for me to recognize the trim silhouette of my father.

I suppose he must have spotted me, too, because he paused in the doorway like he had second thoughts about coming inside. We hadn't spoken in more than a month, not since he'd fired me from the agency, so I really didn't know exactly how things stood between us. I wasn't even sure I wanted to find out. He took a seat at the counter four stools down, just far enough away to make conversation optional.

Tump lifted the coffeepot from the warmer and fished out a clean cup from beneath the counter. "Well, look who's here," he said, smiling. Just about everybody smiles at my father; by now he must think it's the most natural expression on the human face. Tump filled the cup to the brim, still smiling, and eased it across the worn Formica. "What can I get for you today, Jimmy?"

My father brushed some crumbs from the counter and leaned forward onto his forearms. His limp gray suit was wrinkled and sweat-stained, as it always was by midweek. "What have you got that's good?" he asked, keeping his eyes focused on the wall above the fry vat like he thought there was a menu there.

"Not much if you listen to Nolan," Tump told him. "The boy thinks I'm trying to clog his arteries."

Ricky Malone let out a holler from the back of the room. "Buddy, get your sorry ass out here," he called. "We're dealing the hand."

I glanced around in time to see him hurl an empty pint bottle across the room at the rest-room door. It was plastic and bounced away into a corner.

"Here, now," Tump said. "We'll have none of that."

I could tell from his attitude that Ricky was having a good game, which was fortunate all around. I used to play cards with him myself, years back, before I realized the kind of risk I was running. Ricky gets impatient when he wins, like he thinks there's some kind of time limit on his luck. When he loses, he just turns cold. I've seen that happen, too. His face takes on an empty look, the kind you might see on a roadkill dog. Those are the looks to worry about, because you never know what they might lead to.

"I'll just have the coffee," my father said, tearing open a pair of sugar packets. "Cain't afford much restaurant food—I work for a living."

"Yeah, we're a real pricey place, all right," Tump told him. "I oughta have me a mansion and a speedboat."

"Tump, give the poor man a doughnut," I said. "Put it on my ticket."

My father looked at me like I was a face from his high-school yearbook he could only vaguely recollect. Then he nodded his head. "Make it corn flakes, Tump. Might as well take advantage of my wealthy relatives." Tump put a small unopened box of cereal into a bowl and set it on the counter with a half-pint carton of milk, then returned his attention to the sinkful of dirty dishes. My father stirred his coffee and took a careful sip. "I hear I'm in line to be a grandfather," he said.

That was nothing I wanted to go into, which he probably guessed. Laney and I shared a certain territory—twelve years of marriage will do that much, even for the worst couples—but we were like goalposts at opposite ends of a field. We hadn't yet said two words about her baby, or about Steve Pitts, or about when, exactly, she'd be moving out. More items on my list of things to do.

"I wouldn't go shopping for any baby rattles just yet," I told him. I folded the newspaper and tucked it back into the top of the menu holder for the next customer.

"Kids are a big responsibility," he informed me.

"Thanks for the tip," I said. "I'll be sure to pass it along." I don't think he understood what I was telling him—which was fine. In any case, I knew he wouldn't press it further, not without encouragement from me. My father is not the sort of talker who can hold up two ends of a conversation. Or even one. For him, talking is more or less a tool of the trade, a way to sell insurance. Outside of that, he rarely knows what to say.

Except, of course, when he fired me. He knew exactly what to say then: *Nolan, you're fired.* It was a real breakthrough for him.

The rest-room door swung open, banging hard against the wall, and Buddy Pilot came ambling back into the room, still zipping up his fly. "What's the game?" he asked.

"Seven-card stud," Ricky told him. "You're two rounds behind, but we made your bets for you. You raised us on the second round."

Buddy lowered himself into his chair. "What have I got?" he asked.

Morgan scrutinized the up-cards spread across the table. "From the look of it, not a goddamn thing," he said. "We all figure you're bluffing."

My father scowled toward the poker table. "There's sure no shortage of deadbeats in this town," he said. "I guess you got some job security after all."

"It's steady enough work," I told him.

He took another sip of his coffee and tore open the box of corn flakes. "So how come you're sitting here on a workday? Tump, I hope you don't owe this bloodsucker any money. Better watch your toaster if you do."

"I'm waiting for Dell," I explained. "We use his truck for pickups."

Tump wiped his hands on his apron and shook his head. "If you're waiting for Dell, you just got yourself a day off," he said. "Dell spent the night right over there." He nodded toward the poker game. "Went home about an hour ago, broke as a dead branch. You just missed him."

My father poured coffee over his corn flakes and reached for more sugar packets. "I guess the work's not as steady as you thought."

"I can live with the disappointment," I told him, though in fact I did hate to lose the money. Dell was on salary with Hometown Finance so it didn't matter if he took off a day, but I was just a jobber. They didn't carry me on their regular payroll.

My father scooped up a spoonful of the corn flakes I'd bought him and held them steady over the bowl, studying them through his bifocals. "What the hell's wrong with these flakes?" he said.

"You put coffee on them instead of milk," I told him.

Tump chuckled. "And here I thought you was just being exotic," he said.

My father lowered the spoon back into the bowl. He'd made a few other mistakes like that lately—not many, and never anything big, but they were starting to add up. He pushed the bowl away from him and wiped his mouth with his napkin like he'd just finished a big meal. "I'm too damn old," he said.

Tump snapped his fingers. "That reminds me." He took a clipboard from the wall above the cutting board. "Before you go slopping any more coffee on my counter, sign this petition."

Tump handed the clipboard to my father, who squinted down his nose at the top sheet of paper. "What's it for?" he asked.

Tump leaned across the counter and tapped his finger on the paper. "I'm trying to get the state historical society to register this place as a landmark."

My father took a pen from his shirt pocket and signed his name to the list. "Why do you want it registered?" he asked.

"So I can get a tax break when I have to put on a new roof next year," Tump told him.

"What's so historical about this place?" I asked.

Tump looked annoyed. "Didn't they teach you anything in school? In 1902 Frank James shot a man dead right here in this room."

I looked around the café, expecting, I guess, to see something significant, something I'd never noticed before. But it was the same worn-down place as always. No bullet holes in the tin ceiling tiles, no bloodstains on the tablecloths, no ghost of Frank James loitering by the door. Just the same three rickety pool tables, the same yellow lacquered walls, and the same pair of ancient ceiling fans clicking slowly overhead.

"How do you know it's true?" I asked.

Tump took the clipboard from my father and passed it to me. "Everybody knows it," he said. "It's common knowledge."

I signed my name below my father's. Even his handwriting looked old, full of sharp angles and tiny tremors. "What'd he shoot him for?" I asked.

"Hell, I don't know," Tump said, taking back his petition. "Maybe the guy complained about his bacon."

My father suddenly swiveled his stool in my direction and

smiled. "I've got an idea," he said. "I could do with a day off myself. How about you and me take a trip down to Horseshoe Bend. Tour the battlefield. See some real historical landmarks."

"That's a four-hour drive," I said.

I don't know what it is with my father and war memorials. When I was a kid, every family vacation, every weekend trip, even every Sunday afternoon drive took us to some kind of military park or battleground. I've eaten picnic lunches on the cement tables at Shiloh, Antietam, Chickamauga, Bull Run, Stones River, Cold Harbor, Kennesaw Mountain, Gettysburg, and a dozen other Civil War crossroads. I've stood where George Washington stood at Yorktown, where Campbell stood at King's Mountain, Morgan at Cowpens, Greene at Guilford Courthouse. I've seen the view Andrew Jackson had when he fought the Muscogee at Talladega, at Emuckfaw, and at Enotachopko Creek. I've hacked through the overgrowth where Red Eagle led the massacre at Fort Mims, and I've walked the wooded ridge at Tippecanoe. At my father's relentless insistence, I've read the inscriptions on a hundred small-town courthouse monuments honoring the dead from at least a dozen wars. I've stood before countless roadside markers commemorating where some distinguished troop of soldiers once set up camp, or stopped a retreat, or came down with fever, or rested, or surrendered, or died. I've climbed Creek burial mounds, and I've even paid my respects at the Fentress County homestead of Sergeant Alvin York, the conscientious objector who won the Medal of Honor. But in all our travels the Horseshoe Bend on the Tallapoosa River had inexplicably escaped our list.

My father started to say something more—some argument, I suppose, in favor of the trip—but a sudden commotion at the poker table cut him off. We both turned in time to see Buddy Pilot fling his chair aside and drag the big table awkwardly toward him. When he'd pulled it clear of the other players, he flipped it over, scattering cards and chips across the floor. "You rigged it!" he shouted. "You rigged it while I was gone!"

The other players seemed too surprised to react, and for a few long seconds Buddy just stood there, fists clenched, daring anybody to stand. But nobody did—they just stared back at him, calm but interested, like he was a sideshow act from the carnival. Finally, Morgan leaned forward in his chair. "So what's your point?" he said, and everybody except Buddy started to laugh. Buddy might have done something then, he was mad enough, but by that time Tump had come up beside him. Tump's a pretty old guy, nearly seventy, but he was some kind of Marine MP in the South Pacific, and he still knew how to handle himself. He stuck his leg behind Buddy to trip him, then grabbed him by his shirt collar and jerked him straight over backwards. Buddy hit the floor hard and vomited all over himself. I guess we all winced at that, and a couple of the other players edged their chairs away to make room for whatever Buddy might try when he got up. But he didn't get up, he just lay there on his back, groaning. Tump leaned down across him and shook a finger in his face. "Don't treat my furniture like that," he said. Buddy gurgled something, and then Tump hoisted him up by his belt buckle and walked him to the back door. "Now go home," he said, shoving him gently through the doorway into the alley. Then he walked back to his stack of dirty dishes, giving Morgan a hard look along the way.

Morgan stood up and stretched. "Y'all clean up this mess," he said. "And watch how you divvy up those chips—I know what I had in front of me." Ricky Malone muttered something I didn't catch, but for once he did what he was told, getting down on his hands and knees to rake the chips together into a pile. He dropped the first handful noisily into the battered Christmas-cookie tin Tump stored them in.

"The hell with this," one of the other two said. "Ain't none of my money on that floor." As he stood and headed for the door I got my first clear look at him. He was short and skinny with a pockmarked face, and it seemed to me I'd maybe seen him operating one of the carnival rides at the county fair. The Tilt-A-Whirl, or the Scrambler. I don't think he was a local.

Morgan didn't waste any breath calling him back, but turned to the other one I didn't know, a pale-looking moonfaced man in a blue-checked shirt. "What about it, Rolly?" he asked.

Rolly rubbed the side of his face and frowned toward the door. "Yeah, okay," he said. He squatted in front of his chair and began to gather up the mingled decks of cards.

Morgan stepped around the overturned table and joined us at the counter. "Still just a bunch of kids," he said, shaking his head.

But he was wrong. I don't know the story on Rolly or the carnival guy, but Buddy and Ricky had never been kids, not for as long as I'd known them. Although I couldn't say why. Their parents are all decent, upstanding people—Ricky's dad owns a furniture store just off the square, and Buddy's folks have a good-sized farm south of town. I've sat with both families at church picnics, Little League games, and Lions Club bingo. On the surface of it, there's just no reason why Ricky or Buddy should be any meaner or wilder than anybody else. But they are.

Maybe they got bad treatment somewhere along the line—I know a lot of people think that's how it works, that we only turn out bad if bad things get done to us first. But I don't think that's the whole answer. When a lizard or a snake first cracks out of its shell, it already knows what to do in the world, and it won't ever change. Maybe some of us are more like that, born with something we can't ever get rid of, some basic knowledge that right away makes us who we are.

Morgan eased himself onto one of the stools between my father and me. Tump handed him a roll of paper towels and a spray bottle of cleaner. "We cain't be having any more of this, Morgan," he said. "You gotta keep these pups in line."

Morgan whistled toward the back and tossed the paper towels and the cleaner to Rolly. "Spic-and-span," he ordered, "like it was your own mama's kitchen." Then he leaned his elbows on the counter and ran his fat hands up over his freckled scalp, smoothing down what was left of his hair. "What those boys need is a hitch in the army," he said.

"Amen to that," Tump agreed. "Worst thing ever happened to this country was they got rid of the draft."

"Don't know if I can agree with that," I said, thinking, I suppose, how people like Jerry Rathburn might have turned out differently if they hadn't been put through a war.

"'Course you don't agree with it," said Morgan, pressing the heels of his hands to his eyes. "You never been in the service." Morgan was an infantryman who'd been on Iwo Jima and Guadalcanal.

"The service is good training for anybody," Tump said. He pointed to a framed piece of paper on the wall above the grill, but it was so blotted with grease I couldn't tell what it was. "The Marines is where I first learned to cook," he went on. "And after that they even taught me judo."

"Well, that makes sense," said Morgan. "The way you cook, self-defense was the next logical step." He started to laugh, but it turned into a deep, wheezing cough that took him nearly a minute to bring under control. When the fit finally passed, he wiped the water from his eyes with a napkin and took a few slow, rattling breaths. "But Tump's right, Junior," he said at last. "The service can help anybody along." His voice was hoarse now, but more urgent, as if the emphysema had reminded him he was running out of words. He turned to my father. "Jimmy, you need to take this boy in hand," he chided. "Let him know what's what. Explain the virtues of the military life."

"Too late now," my father said. "He's old and he's slow."

"Nothing wrong with slow," said Tump. "Slow means officer material. 'Course he's not fat or stupid enough to make general." His grin stretched wide, and his gold teeth flashed in the sun.

Morgan shook his head. "These punks today—they think the army's just some kind of hard-ass summer camp where you have to get up early and clean the toilets. They ain't got a goddamn clue." He turned to me. "Junior, your daddy was a bombardier in the Army Air Corps, in case you didn't know it."

"Yeah, I know it," I said. "He was on a B-24." I said this like I was some kind of expert on my father's military career. In fact, I knew almost nothing about it. I'd heard a little bit from relatives who didn't know much themselves, and that was about it. The war was something my father didn't normally talk about, at least not around me. In my thirty-three years I'd heard him bring it up only once, one time when I was about twelve. We were in a dime store together and I was looking at all the plastic model kits of World War II planes. He pointed to the green picture on the B-24 box and said it was the kind of plane he had flown. I even remember thinking that that was a good thing for me to know. But I bought the B-29 instead, because it had more guns.

"He flew thirty-five missions over Germany," Morgan went on, "and believe me, he *got* something out of all that."

"All I got out of the service was a sweet tooth," my father said. "Never cared much for sweets before I went in. I guess because my mother used to mix in honey with the cod-liver oil she gave me when I was little." He shook his head and smiled. "She thought the honey would make the medicine taste better. But all it did was ruin the honey."

"So," I said, "how'd you get a sweet tooth in the Air Corps?" It was the first question I'd ever asked him about the war. He looked over at me in surprise.

"Well," he said, "they always gave us each a box of candy to take with us on a mission. English hard candy. For sustenance. Because we were gone eight or ten hours at a stretch. So you'd take off your oxygen mask and stick a piece of hard candy in there, and then put your mask back on. That way you could suck on the candy and still have your oxygen."

"But tell him about the *war*," Morgan said, obviously disappointed in my father's sense of drama. "Tell him what happened. Tell him some of the things you saw."

"I didn't see much of anything," my father said. "I was up in an airplane most of the time. When you're six miles off the ground, everything looks pretty much the same. It all just flattens out, like a big map. It was you boys"—he nodded to both Tump and Morgan—"it was you boys on the ground who saw the war."

There was a pause while Morgan turned this over in his mind. He looked disturbed, as if it had never before occurred to him that someone could fight in the same war he did and not know what it looked like.

"You must have seen *something,*" he insisted. "Jimmy, they gave you the D.S.C., for Christsakes. They don't hand those out for milk runs."

"What's the D.S.C.?" I asked. Both Tump and Morgan looked at me in disbelief, as if I'd asked what lungs were for, or why the sun moved across the sky. My father focused his eyes on his coffee cup, which he began to rotate between his palms, like a potter working in slow motion. He seemed embarrassed, but I couldn't tell if it were for himself or for me.

"The D.S.C. is the Distinguished Service Cross," said Morgan, a seriousness in his voice now I'd never heard before. "They give it for exceptional heroism in combat. Not just heroism, you understand, but *exceptional* heroism. The D.S.C. is just a notch down from the Medal of Honor."

Tump picked up the coffeepot and freshened my father's cup. "Didn't you get shot down?" he asked.

My father didn't answer right away, but then he looked up and smiled. It was his hollow, insurance-salesman smile, the one I'd always seen in him as a sign of retreat. "Yeah. Yeah, we did," he said brightly. "But in most ways it turned out all right."

"Jimmy, that's not the point," said Morgan. "We know it turned out all right—you're *here,* for godsakes. The point is the *impression* it made on you. The *good* it did you. How it *affected* you."

My father looked genuinely puzzled. "I don't think it affected me much at all. I mean, I didn't get hurt or anything. It was just sort of—well—a bad day."

Tump snorted. "A bad day," he repeated. "The guy gets shot down and calls it a bad day."

"Does this go here?" Rolly called out, positioning the poker table near the rear corner.

"Yeah, that's fine," Tump told him. "Now just straighten up those chairs around it and clear away those empties."

Ricky Malone came up holding the tin of poker chips and set it on the stool beside Morgan. "Me and Rolly both cashed in already," he said. "Count yours if you like, but keep in mind we ain't giving anything back."

Morgan smiled and plucked a handful of bills from the tin. "This looks fine," he said, though he barely glanced at the wadded cash. Even I knew Ricky Malone wouldn't dare shortchange Morgan.

"Here, sign this before you go," Tump said, handing his petition back across the counter.

Ricky took the clipboard. "That Frank James thing?" He studied the sheet and then nodded. "Yeah, all right. Gimme a pen. I'd like to see a plaque up here about that." I gave him my pen and he scribbled his name in broad strokes across two signature lines. "You know," he said, sliding the clipboard across the counter, "those were wide-open times. If I'd lived back then, I coulda made a real name for myself, I guarantee it."

"Yeah, you woulda been famous, all right," said Morgan. "You woulda been the guy Frank James shot."

Ricky gave Morgan a last cold look and sauntered toward the rear door. Tump followed after him to inspect the cleanup work.

"Good enough," Tump said as Ricky disappeared into the alley. "I'll mop up later." He slapped a dish towel across his shoulder and walked back to the sink. Rolly snatched up his baggy yellow sport coat from the back of a chair and followed Ricky outside. The rest of us sat there for a minute in the calm.

"It was our twenty-first bombing run," my father said suddenly. "I remember because it was also Danny Durbin's twenty-first birthday. Danny was our pilot. Great guy, I still get Christmas cards from him. But imagine—just twenty-one years old. And Danny was the old man on the crew, two years older than anybody else. Three years older than me."

"What was your target?" Morgan wanted to know.

The question seemed to startle him, as if he'd forgotten for a moment we were there. He took a sip of coffee and dabbed his napkin at the corners of his mouth. "Well, it's funny," he said, "but when I think about those missions, the numbers seem to stay with me more than the names. I guess that's because the numbers were my countdown for going home." He tilted his head back and thought for a moment. "But I think this one might have been the rail yards at Dresden."

Tump stopped washing the dishes. "You bombed Dresden?"

"I bombed just about everything," my father said. "Morgan had it right—thirty-five missions." He sounded almost cheerful about it, but there was a distance in his voice, too, like he wasn't really talking to us at all.

We got quiet again. I knew about the Dresden raid—not that my father had been part of it, that was news, but that it had been one of the truly terrible chapters of the war. Not even Morgan could cheerlead for the firestorm at Dresden.

"Dresden was tough luck," Tump said solemnly.

"It was a disaster, all right," my father said, though still more to himself, it seemed, than to any of us. "I've never seen such a total snafu in my life." He sat up straight on his stool and swiveled slightly toward us, smoothing his hands along the tired creases in his trousers. He looked nervous, artificially alert, like someone on the witness stand, and I could see that, for whatever reason, he had determined to speak the whole thing out, once and for all. And then, I suppose, be done with it. "There were bomber groups there from every base in England," he went on, "—way too many for the size of the target zone. There wasn't space enough to hold us. But we all went in, all at once, because that's what they'd told us to do.

"And in all the confusion, one of the other bomber groups flew right across the top of us, and we could see the bombs falling from their planes. Hundreds and hundreds of bombs, strung out all across the sky, and us right in the middle of it. That might have been the end, right there, but Danny tipped the plane up on its side so the bombs wouldn't be as likely to hit our wings. And that saved us, we passed on through. But when he tipped us up like that—see, we couldn't get all our own bombs to release, and we had one stuck halfway out the bomb-bay door. Well, we straightened up after we made our run, and started back for England. But we still had that one bomb caught in the bomb bay. It just wouldn't release.

"In the meantime, from flak we had one engine shot out and another was throwing oil, so we only had two good engines. And Danny said, 'I think maybe I can land this thing, but I don't know.' He said, 'I'm gonna give you guys your choice—you can either bail out, or you can stick with it, stick with the plane.' And we all said, 'Well, it's pretty cold out there, we'll stick with the plane.' So Danny told the planes ahead of us what the trouble was, and that we were gonna try to land somewhere behind the lines. Then they flew on back to England, and we started down.

"Well, we were lucky again, because about three miles behind the lines there was this airport—I keep thinking it was at Reims, but I'm not certain, I've forgotten the town. And we notified the little airport there about our problem, said we had a bomb that might be armed, that might go off when we landed. So of course just about everybody cleared the area right away. Usually, you know, there'd be crowds of people coming out to welcome you down, but this was a different situation. Only two people came out on the runway to greet us. I saw them both through the bomb-bay doors, waving up at us while we circled the field. I found out later that one was a prostitute. The other was a little kid who thought he might get some of our candy." My father stopped and took a swallow of coffee.

"What do you mean about not knowing if the bomb was armed?" I asked.

He shrugged. "Well, just that: we didn't know. See, the fuses on the bombs had these little propellers, and once that propeller had spun 250 revolutions, the bomb was armed. Normally there'd be a little wire stuck in the propeller blades to keep it from turning. The wire had a little snap on one end, and that's what you attached to the side of the bomb bays. When the bomb dropped, naturally that pulled the wire out and the propeller would start revolving. And that would arm it on its way down.

"Well, what had happened in this case was the front bomb shackles had released like they were supposed to, so the front part of the bomb had dropped down into the slipstream. But the rear shackles hadn't released, either because they were bent or because they were frozen. So that was the problem. The bomb wasn't all the way out of the plane, but it had dropped just far enough to pull that wire out, and I could see the propeller down there, going *ching, ching, ching,* making little slow circles at the edge of the slipstream. So we just didn't know."

"That's when I woulda jumped," said Tump.

"I thought about it," my father said. "But then Danny told me I should climb down into the lower bay and try to kick the thing loose somehow. Well, I was the bombardier, after all, so it made sense that I'd be the one to try, if anybody did. But I never imagined for a minute that it might work. Bombs are heavier than you think. It was like trying to kick a Chevy off the side of the road. But anyway, I climbed on down, and Danny said to hurry because he couldn't keep us in the air much longer, so I started kicking at the shackles over and over. Kicked until my feet went numb. But even then I couldn't stop because I was afraid that if I did we might all blow up. So I just kept at it and kept at it and then Danny said, 'Ready or not,' and my stomach got light as the plane dropped down—we weren't positioned for the landing yet, but still the plane was dropping down—and I figured this was it, this was it for sure. The plane began to buck and shake, and the two good engines started to sputter. But I kept on kicking at those shackles. I shut everything else out of my mind and just kept kicking and kicking, while Danny banked us across the runway to come around for the final approach. And then I sort of heard the explosion beneath us and the cheering in the plane. But even then I didn't stop kicking. It was like nothing had registered—the bomb was gone and I didn't even know it.

"But then, of course, I did know it, and for a second I was glad, because I'd done my job. But we weren't home free, not yet, we were still going down. And now we had a different problem, because the bomb—it was the damnedest thing, but somehow I had kicked loose the bomb at the worst possible moment, and now we'd

blown a hole in our own runway and set half the landing strip on
fire—because these were more than just bombs, these were incendi-
aries. But there was no choice now. So down we went, and in we
came, and the tires hit the hard-packed dirt and the ground blurred
beneath me. Then Danny steered us hard to the right, out toward a
field, away from the crater and the wall of fire, and I felt us tip again
as I climbed up out of the bay, and the left wing scraped and banged
along the ground and for a second I thought the plane might cart-
wheel and kill us anyway, for all our trouble. But it didn't, it just
spun sideways off the runway and plowed into a field of matted
weeds and frozen black dirt. Then everything was still—not quiet
yet, but still, and we all knew it was over. We knew that we had—
survived." As he told us this last, my father's face seemed burdened
with wonder, as if survival were the one thing he would never
understand.

"You see?" said Morgan, turning from my father to me. "That's
what I'm talking about. Putting your lives on the goddamn line together and pulling each other through—that's what the military's all
about. And I don't give a good goddamn if you go on to win the lottery or get elected president, you'll never find anything that good
again." His face grew red as he spoke, and for the first time I realized what a truly indelible mark the army had left on Morgan. Two
teenage years in the South Pacific had made him a sergeant for life.

My father took off his glasses and polished them with his dirty
napkin. "So that was it," he said. "We stayed there eight days fixing
the plane. Then we flew back to England, to our home base. They
gave us all medals for not being dead."

Morgan slapped the counter and laughed. "Dead? You boys
were in heaven!" he said. "Eight days in a liberated town—what in
hell could be sweeter than that!" He winked at me and Tump. "I
think I'd like to hear a little more about that prostitute who came
out to meet you."

My father looked at him strangely, then cleared his throat.
"Well, that's what I've been telling you," he said. His voice was patient and apologetic, as if he were explaining some misunderstood

clause in a homeowner's policy. "The woman and the little boy were killed. It turned out I had killed them both." He waited, as if he expected some kind of reply, but Morgan didn't seem to know what to say. None of us did. Finally, when it was clear we had nothing to contribute, my father checked his watch, frowned at the time, and pushed himself up from his stool. He drew a handful of change from his pants pocket and portioned out a few coins onto the counter by his coffee cup. "Well, I'll see you boys later," he said, and walked out the door into the sunshine. He stood there for a minute on the sidewalk, watching, I guess, the farmers arranging their tomato and peach baskets on the benches across the square. He seemed, right then, to be a truly harmless man, and for the first time in a very long while, I didn't hate the sight of him.

Cheap Imitations

A T FIRST THE LIZARD WAS JUST one more source of tension between us. Laney bought it secondhand from some woman down
in Huntsville who said it kept her cockroach problem under control. She told Laney it was a fine lizard, whatever that means, and
she flat hated to sell it but she was just about to get married and
didn't think she'd need a lizard anymore. I guess we all start out
with high expectations.

I have to admit, this wasn't just a spur-of-the-moment purchase
on Laney's part. We'd seen a TV news show about how people in
New York kept geckos in their apartments to eat the insects, and
right then Laney said she wanted one. Then when the carpenter
ants showed up in the pantry, she brought the idea up again. I still
didn't take her seriously. Big lizards weren't exactly the pet of
choice in our part of the country. It never occurred to me that she
might actually go out and find one of the damned things.

And, strictly speaking, she didn't. This particular lizard was no
gecko. The previous owner said it was something *like* a gecko, but
not a gecko exactly. I tried to look it up in a couple of reptile books,
but I never could find a picture of it. So I don't know what the hell it
was. Just some big lizard. Laney paid 200 dollars for it.

That bothered me—200 bucks for some off-brand lizard. It was
ugly, too. Fat and brown and bumpy, like a small fire log with legs.
And slow. Real slow. The poor bastard couldn't catch a cockroach
if its life depended on it.

Its name was Randall.

Well, right from the start Laney acted like Randall was the best thing that had come into her life in the last ten years. He was all she talked about. Randall was so cute. Randall was so friendly. Randall was so clever. Turn the air conditioner down, Randall might catch a chill. Keep those cupboard and closet doors open, Randall needs to explore his space. Don't use the insect spray, Randall might swallow a contaminated bug. Watch where you step, watch where you sit, watch when you flush. She bought him little lizard treats at the pet store—reconstituted fly pellets, or some such abomination. She bought him little sticks and bells to play with, little ladders to climb on, and little padded boxes to sleep in. She spent vast stretches of time scratching his head, stroking his tail, and talking baby talk to him. She even made him a goddamned sweater.

To Randall's credit, he never went for any of it. Laney was just one more piece of odd weather as far as he was concerned. That was one of the things I liked about him.

And I did like him. He wasn't cute, or friendly, or clever, or affectionate, or any of the other things Laney imagined him to be. But he was stoic. I had to give him that.

So I guess Randall turned out to be a pretty versatile pet. Laney liked him because he had the sort of personality she could relate to. I liked him because he had no personality at all.

Anyway. The week after we found Jerry Rathburn's body, Dell and I worked a string of twelve-hour shifts. Not because of Jerry— we didn't officially involve ourselves in that headache—but because of the time of year. Early summer is the prime season for repo work. For one thing, there's more afternoon light to work by, and believe me, only a fool tries to do our kind of labor after dark. But the main reason is contractual: summer is when all the Christmas credit runs out. That means we have to take back all those expensive holiday presents guilty husbands have given their wives. If some divorce lawyer followed us door-to-door after Memorial Day, he could pick up enough work to retire on.

I don't know why people spend their money like they do. Why

does a man who makes ten bucks an hour heaving feed sacks off a loading dock try to give his wife a full-carat diamond ring? What the hell is he thinking? I guess it's a way to buy time, if the marriage is shaky. But that's a fool's bet. The benefits only last until the payments come due. If anybody asked my opinion, I'd say cubic zirconia made more sense. Gaudy as a diamond but only fifty bucks. No repo men at the door.

Our family room was a different matter altogether. No shortcuts there, no cheap materials, no shoddy workmanship. But there was a reason to go first-class on a job like that. This wasn't just a cosmetic fix-up, it was a legitimate investment, one that would have raised our property values, one that would have paid us back if we ever sold.

Would have.

When I got home Monday evening, it was already half-twilight and I felt drained—and not just from hauling refrigerators. For the past week I hadn't been able to stop thinking about Jerry Rathburn. One thing that weighed on me was that I couldn't talk about any of it to Laney, not unless I was ready to explain what I was doing in Jerry's house to begin with, and I sure as hell wasn't ready to throw that log on the fire. I know all the magazines say to be open and honest with your spouse, but that's not the universe I live in.

I stood there in the front yard for a while looking at the strange glimmering outline of my house—the right side all trim and proper, the left side a splintered pile of bones. Perfect opposites. Like before and after. Like his and hers.

Laney's car was gone, so at least I didn't have to worry about excuses. I walked up to the demolished addition and climbed through where the picture window used to be. There really wasn't much left of the project but a partial outline and a few jagged piles of debris. And shadows, because the sun was almost down. It was like stepping into a combat zone, like I was suddenly in one of those TV news pieces about bombed-out villages in Eastern Europe somewhere, or even one of my father's cities from the war.

This was the room where Jerry Rathburn should have died.

I maneuvered around the wreckage to the battered kitchen doorway. The frame was so off-level now the door dragged on the linoleum, but I was able to wedge it open enough to squeeze inside. The place was nearly dark—we've got a row of old hackberry trees along the west side of the yard so dusk falls heavy throughout the house—and for just a second I felt like I was still on the job, creeping into some deadbeat's boarded-up home. But this particular half-darkness was all mine, and I felt comfortable enough to move around in it without turning on any lights.

The eyes do adjust, after all. People tend to forget that. My mother used to start turning on lights in the middle of the afternoon, like she was afraid the darkness might sneak up on her. But I like the way nightfall drifts into a room like smoke. I like the way it gathers unevenly around the furniture and along the walls, going dark, darker, darkest. I bet the pioneers used to watch the night come down like that. We don't do that anymore—not many of us, anyway. Edison weakened our talent for living in the dark. We've lost patience, or at least that's the way it's gone for Laney and me. The dark used to be an interesting place. Now we just sleep there.

Here's something I wonder: is there such a thing as the speed of darkness? I had a physics class in high school, and all Mr. Tucker ever seemed to talk about was Einstein and relativity and the speed of light. I was never too bright a bulb in the sciences, but I could pretty much follow what he was telling us. I mean, I couldn't do the math or anything, but I could still get the gist of the ideas. And one of the things he kept on about was how Einstein thought the speed of light was the only constant in the universe. That sounded okay to me at first, but then I started thinking—how could you say the speed of light was constant unless you had some other constant to measure it by? I mean, if you're zipping along in an airplane looking out at the clear blue sky, you can't tell how fast you're going. For all you know, you might be stopped dead-still in a head wind. Hell, you might be going backwards. Landscape's the key—you can't fig- ure speed without it. Let a few trees and houses go by, then you can start to calculate things. So wouldn't the same rules have to apply to light? I mean, if Einstein, or whoever, says light goes by at 186,000 miles per second, doesn't that mean there has to be something else in the neighborhood stuck on zero? And wouldn't that zero always have to be darkness? And wouldn't that mean darkness was a universal constant, same as light?

I tried to have a conversation with Laney about that one night. I told her I thought the speed of darkness had to be zero, or else the speed of light would just be a made-up number. She said she thought it wouldn't be too long before somebody invented a time machine, like in the movies. She said she looked forward to that. She wanted to try out the future.

I know what both my grandmothers would have said if I told them darkness was a universal constant. They'd have said I ought to go to church more. In our county Jesus was the only universal constant that mattered.

Jesus, Jesus Christ, Jesus Christ our Lord, Jesus Christ our Lord and Savior. Jesus H. Christ.

When I was four years old I thought Jesus was one of the stock boys at the A & P. It was an easy mistake to make. For one thing, he wore a plastic name tag that said *Jesus,* and that was the one word my Grandmother Vann had already taught me to read. He had a beard like Jesus. He even had a job like Jesus—always helping people out with the right directions so they could find the things they needed. Plus there was this big curved mirror in the back of the store so he could see down every aisle at once, and, from what I understood, that was just like Jesus, too. I remember running up to my Grandmother Vann in the fruit and vegetable section and telling her I'd found Jesus. At first she got this serious-happy look and hugged me tight as if I'd just been snatched from the fires of Hell. "Praise the Lord!" she said, and things might have been fine if she could have let it go at that. But my grandmother was a woman who always needed to know the details, so she pressed me for the full account. I told her what I knew—that Jesus was unpacking canned peaches back by the meat counter—and then watched her face turn dark and unfamiliar. She jerked me across her knee so fast it made my bones rattle, and then she beat the backs of my bare legs with a handful of celery stalks.

That's when I first started to catch on that Jesus was not exactly a one-size-fits-all proposition.

I pulled open the pan drawer in the bottom of the stove and fished around in the darkness for a pot to boil water in. Laney had probably found dinner somewhere else, but I still figured I'd cook up some macaroni and cheese, just to make the gesture. Our good pot, the one we normally made macaroni in, was still down at the Elks Lodge where we'd left it after the Jefferson Davis birthday pic-nic—so I had to settle for the crummy one I'd bought Laney on our third anniversary. The whole set was crummy, not just the pot. All the pieces had that nonstick coating that's supposed to be so easy to clean, but this was the cheap version and the coating flecked off just about every time you touched it. Macaroni always came out look-ing like it had been rolled in pepper. I guess we should have thrown the set out, but instead we kept it for things like baked beans, or turnip greens, or black-eyed peas—dark foods, where the flecks wouldn't show. God knows how much nonstick coating we've both got in our systems by now.

I ran some water into the pot, letting the sound and the feel of it tell me how much was enough, and then I carefully set it on the front burner of the stove top. The house was totally dark now, but my eyes had adjusted, so when I turned on the heat, the red glow of the element gave me enough light to find the box of macaroni in the cupboard. But then while I waited for the water to boil, a burning smell began to fill the kitchen.

Laney and I aren't tidy cooks. We both tend to spill a lot of food around the stove top, and hardly a day goes by that one of us doesn't let something bubble over onto a hot burner. Our drip pans are always crusty with mistakes. That's a fire hazard, I realize, and we probably ought to pay higher insurance rates because of it. But the only insurance man I know who'd actually nail us for it is my father, so what the hell. I sure don't plan on having him to dinner anytime soon.

Anyway, there must have been a little too much buildup around this particular burner, and now there was an acrid stink coming from whatever leftovers were being cooked away. Nothing flamed up, but I could feel the smoke clouding into my eyes. Since the exhaust fan was broken, I leaned across the sink and lifted the window to air things out a little. Then I turned off the burner and circled through to the third bedroom to raise the window in there to get some cross ventilation going.

That room was where we stored the furniture Laney inherited from her maternal grandmother. Well, inherited might not be the right word. What I mean to say is that when Miss Bessie finally moved into the nursing home, Laney was one of the first family members to show up at her house with a pickup truck. Sometimes Laney wrote letters in here at Miss Bessie's old rolltop desk, but other than that we didn't really use the space.

I guessed this would be the baby's room.

A breeze got drawn in right away and I stood there holding the window up and letting that cool night air bathe some of the smoke from my eyes. I had to hold the window in place because it would've dropped shut otherwise. All the windows had gone crazy on us after the oak tree hit—I guess the frames got jarred out of plumb. Now the ones that used to slide easily got stuck all the time, and the ones that used to wedge in place came down like guillotines. We had to keep paint sticks on the sills so we could prop the loose ones open.

But this time there was no stick there. I held the lower sash up with one hand and with the other I groped along the narrow top of Miss Bessie's desk, figuring that was the next most likely place Laney would have left it. I was right, but the dark made me too clumsy and I bumped the stick off the back edge. It clattered down behind the rolltop.

That desk was massive, and I had no interest in moving it just to retrieve a fifteen-cent paint stick. Instead I took the easier option—while I held the left side of the sash in place, I shoved up hard on the right side, forcing the window out of alignment with the frame. It worked: the lower sash wedged in place.

As I stepped back from the window, a car passed by the front of the house and the headlights swept through the room. That's when I noticed the rolltop desk was closed.

I'd never seen it closed before. The thing was more than 150 years old—Miss Bessie's grandfather had had it shipped over from England in the early 1800s, and then he carted it from New York to Tennessee in the back of a wagon. That's a lot of rough mileage for such a heavy piece of furniture. None of the joints were square anymore, and over the years a lot of the wood had warped. The desk was in sad shape overall, but the rolltop itself was in particular need of repair. It just wouldn't ride the tracks anymore, not unless you forced it every inch of the way. Years ago I'd suggested to Miss Bessie that she might want to get it fixed, but she was afraid to let anybody tamper with it. Some fellow had told her once that if you did anything to improve the condition of an antique, it wasn't a true antique anymore. And that meant it wasn't worth as much money.

The whole notion sounded wrong to me. How could a thing be worth more if you left it broken?

Anyway, the desk never got worked on and the top stayed open all the time, first in Miss Bessie's front parlor, and then here in the room where Laney would probably put the mystery child. So unless that fallen oak tree had miraculously fixed the rolltop the way it had fixed some of our window frames—which was doubtful—Laney had gone to an awful lot of trouble to shut something up inside.

The fact that she'd even bother with it was surprising. Laney knew I wasn't the kind of person to snoop around in someone else's affairs—even hers. Invasion of privacy was a moral violation, in my book—although a lot of folks I knew would have put it in the gray area because it wasn't listed in the Commandments. But for me it fit under the umbrella of the Golden Rule. If you looked at the New

Testament as a sort of insurance policy with God, the *Do unto others* passage was the most comprehensive subclause in the entire contract. And Miss Bessie's closed desktop was one more case where the rule clearly applied. I didn't want to know Laney's secrets, anymore than I wanted her to know mine.

However.

I pressed my palms against the wooden slats and carefully pushed upward. The top slid a few inches, then snagged, then slid a few inches more. When I'd worked it about halfway up, I stopped and peered inside. I couldn't see anything, of course, in that deeper darkness, but then I remembered that my wristwatch was the kind that lights up when you press a little button on the side. Laney had given me the watch last Christmas, before the whole Steve Pitts business got started. So I stuck my wrist into the cave of the desktop and flooded the space with a pale, green light.

There wasn't much there—a handful of ballpoint pens with insurance logos on the side, a box of rubber bands, a stapler, an unopened box of thank-you cards that I recognized as left over from Laney's last birthday, a dog-eared stack of letterhead stationery from my father's office, and a straight-edged ruler with the agency's slogan printed in bold: *We Measure The Future.* Except for the thank-you cards, it was all stuff I'd stolen from work the day I got fired.

The top sheet of letterhead had writing on it, so I aimed my watch face down at the page and leaned in close to see what I could make out. *Darling Steve,* it started, and I turned off the light.

Not that I hadn't expected to find such a thing, but still the sight of it hollowed me out like a paper bag. A love letter from my wife to her boyfriend, discovered by me through an act of personal depravity, stashed among office supplies I'd pilfered from my father: that was a pretty complete summary of my life to the present moment, and I felt sick to know it. If I'd dropped dead on the spot, the newspaper could have skipped the obituary and just run a snapshot of me with my head stuck in this goddamned desk. The Nolan Vann Memorial Portrait.

But after a few slow breaths, once the sound of my own heart had stopped echoing in my ears and my arm had stopped shaking, a spiteful recklessness set in, and I decided to descend a few rungs farther. I shined the watch back onto the page and continued reading.

I don't know what to do, the letter began.

Below that, starting a new paragraph, was a second *I don't know what to do,* and below that, in nearly identical script, a third. Scanning down the page, I saw that Laney had filled the whole sheet with this one phrase, copying it out over and over, like a classroom punishment etched on a chalkboard: *I don't know what to do, I don't know what to do, I don't know what to do.*

Even taking into account that Steve Pitts was her audience, it was a pretty simple letter. I liked it, though. It had some good things to say, if you read between the lines.

But the feeling of recovery that had begun to rise up in me was interrupted now by a second sweep of headlights through the room—a partial sweep this time, freezing all the shadows into place as Laney's car pulled up in front of the house.

I'm not sure why I was slow to react. Maybe I was annoyed by the fact that she'd parked on the street again instead of in our driveway. I'd told her twenty times not to do that—a car by the curb was an open invitation to vandals, all the studies from the Underwriters Association had proven that. But Laney wouldn't listen. She hated to back out of the driveway because of some bushes in our neighbor's yard that blocked her view. She *said* they blocked her view, anyway. I never had any problem with them.

I watched her get out of the car and start up the sidewalk toward the house, then suddenly realized where I was and what I was doing. I gripped the bottom slats of the rolltop and tried to draw the cover back into place, but it wouldn't budge. There wasn't time to coax it down properly, so, in a slight panic, I rattled the top to loosen the jam, then yanked the whole thing toward me. Hard.

The bottom two slats came away in my hands, and a few more clattered to the floor in a god-awful racket.

I looked immediately to the yard and saw Laney stop dead-still halfway up the sidewalk. She stared at the window between us, her head cocked slightly to the side, listening. A dog in the next block began to bark, while the crickets and tree frogs went quiet. I knew she couldn't see me—the moon and the streetlights made the yard a relatively brighter place—so I kept still myself to see what she would do.

At first she didn't do anything but stand there, a vague outline in the early night. Vague, but still striking, still unmistakably Laney, and I felt a slight grief as I tried to separate her face from the darkness.

Her face. In junior high we used to have pep rallies—with the girls in the bleachers on one side of the gym and the boys on the other—and I could pick her out right away, every time, without even trying. My eyes just automatically moved to wherever she was, even if she was sitting behind someone else or had her head turned away.

That much hadn't changed. I could still recognize Laney anywhere, under any circumstance, in any degree of darkness. If there were such a thing as a group photo of the whole world, I swear I could spot Laney's face in the crowd a full year before I could ever find my own.

If I saw two people's shadows mingled on a motel window shade, I'd know which half was hers.

And maybe there really had been some kind of hokey, half-baked true love behind it all, at least on my part; some natural flutter in the chest that gave me this unasked-for ability to see through all the clutter and the dark to wherever Laney might be.

Or maybe I was wrong. Maybe this talent I had was nothing but an instinct for survival, some animal sense that instantly locked my attention on the thing that held the greatest threat.

Either way, it had always been scary to take my eyes off her.

"Hello?" she called out. "Nolan?" She left the sidewalk and edged slowly toward the window. "Nolan, are you home?"

I don't know why I couldn't answer. Something about the word *home* seemed to trip me up.

"I know somebody's in there," she said as she moved her face up close to the screen. "And I don't mind calling the sheriff."

I barely breathed. Soon her eyes would adjust and she'd see me standing there in the darkened baby's bedroom. She'd ask what the hell was going on, and I wouldn't have an answer, not an easy one, anyway, because I wasn't sure myself what the hell was going on. Then she'd come storming inside and discover what I had done to her grandmother's desk. I didn't know what to do.

I didn't know what to do.

Then a remarkable thing happened. Just at the moment when I thought there was no way around it, when I thought there was no choice left but to speak up and let Laney know that I was there, that she had caught me, that I had broken Miss Bessie's antique rolltop, that I had read the letter, that I knew about Steve Pitts, that I'd always known about Steve Pitts, in fact, ever since I'd spotted Laney's car at the Stone Bridge Motel last Valentine's Day when she was supposed to be visiting her sister—and, what the hell, why stop there—that I'd never insured our new family room and had no money to pay for the damage, that I was barely on speaking terms with my father, that I'd lost my job at the agency and was now a part-time repo man, that I'd found a dead body at work, that I knew Laney's baby probably wasn't mine, but—sure, why not say it—that Laney still looked good, damned good, even after all these years, even in the goddamned dark—just as I was on the verge of saying all that and more, maybe a whole lot more, about junior high and the speed of light and how I didn't believe a thing could be worth more if you left it broken, just at that very moment Randall the second-hand lizard waddled out onto the windowsill between us.

Apparently, he'd been lounging along the back of the over-stuffed chair next to the window, and the sound of Laney's voice had drawn him forward. So as she cupped her hands around her eyes and peered into the room, it wasn't me she focused on but Randall, perched calmly behind the screen, inches from her face, waiting for Laney to give him a cricket.

Laney's tone changed at once. "Randall," she cooed. "What have you been up to in Mommy's room?"

So that's what this place was.

"You just wait right there," she said. "I'll bring you some goodies."

As Laney moved from the window toward the front porch, I tried to map out a plan. My first idea—which was all I had time for—was to get to one of the other bedrooms and flop down on a bed as if I were asleep. That would explain why the lights were out and why I didn't answer Laney's calls. I'd just have to claim ignorance about the rolltop.

As Laney opened the front door and turned on the living-room lights, I set the two broken slats gently into the cavity of the desk and hurried toward the hallway. But just as I turned the corner to make my escape, Laney swung the front door solidly shut behind her and a shiver of vibration passed through the house.

A second slam came from the room behind me, from the baby's room, from the room where Bessie's antique desk had just grown a few decades older.

I knew what it was, of course, but still I had to turn back and look. And sure enough, there was Randall, his chunky body sticking up from the sill at an odd angle, and his head wedged beneath the heavy fallen sash. I crossed quickly to the window and lifted the weight from his neck, but it was too late. After a couple of spasms jolted through his legs, he went limp. I held him up and looked into his eyes for some flicker of life, but there was nothing there. His mouth was opened wide, and for the first time since I'd known him he seemed to have an actual expression on his face. He looked surprised.

I probably did, too, when Laney walked into the room and turned on the light.

Stone Bridge

ABOUT NINE O'CLOCK THE FIRST explosion of the morning echoed up from the Elk River, rattling a few of the old tin storefront awnings around the square. I was sitting on a concrete bench in the shade of the Confederate monument figuring my day's options, and I felt it pass—an odd rumble in the ground, rolling by like boxcars on broken track. The wave of it moved through me like I wasn't even there.

None of the truck farmers seemed to notice. My maternal grandmother, Miss Rosebud Winston Hart, did glance up like she thought she heard thunder, but with no cloud in the sky she turned her attention back to the peach baskets set up on the tailgate of Ed Clifford's old mud-spattered Ford. McDonald Construction was already into its second week of dynamiting the riverbed, so I guess most folks had already stopped paying attention to the blasts.

I couldn't do that—explosions bother me too much. Once when I was about ten I saw Dell hold onto a cherry bomb a little too long. His father drove him to the hospital while his mother Eileen and I stayed behind to hunt for Dell's little finger. We looked all through the grass and the bushes, even in the rain gutter on the porch roof, but we couldn't find it. After a while Miss Eileen got the idea to bring their old bloodhound, Kyle, up from the barn, so we tried that. But not even Kyle could get a clear fix on things. He sniffed and howled and trotted back and forth in the center of the yard, but he never seemed able to settle on a spot or even on a direction.

That's what really got me. I mean, Kyle didn't act like the finger was *gone*, he acted more like it was *everywhere*.

So. Twenty years later I was still nervous around gunpowder. Pretty chickenshit. I mean, right now there were probably a thousand war veterans in this town who'd had worse experiences than that—with bombs or land mines or mortar shells or hand grenades—and they didn't seem affected at all. Most of them still crowded right up front for the Fourth of July fireworks displays. Most of them could still light a bottle rocket with a dry, steady hand. If I'd been through the kind of stuff they had I'd probably dive for cover every time a car backfired. But they seemed to know something I didn't.

It was good to see my grandmother out doing ordinary things, letting the morning sun bring a healthy glow to her face. After my mother died, Gram seemed to pull back a little from me and my father, and I hardly ever saw her anymore. I still called her up from time to time to see if she'd let me take her out to eat, but she always said she was tied up with her bridge club. Gram hadn't played bridge in years, but I never challenged her on it. Sometimes you just had to give people room.

She paid for her small basket of peaches and, with some effort and a heavy breath, stepped up onto the sidewalk in front of my bench. Up close, her healthy glow turned out to be just a careful smear of rouge across her sharp cheeks. Her eyes were still bright, but more sunken than I remembered.

"Why, it's Nolan Vann," she said. She touched the back of her sleeve lightly to her forehead, then pressed her hand against the side of her blue-white, beauty-parlor hair as if she were adjusting a hat. A pair of yellow jackets followed her from the produce truck and buzzed in confusion around her bright orange pantsuit, but she didn't notice.

"Yes, ma'am, it's me."

She took a step closer and squinted down at me. "Boy, somebody told me a tree fell on your house."

"Yes, ma'am, it did. A few weeks back, when we had that bad string of thunderstorms."

She set her peaches on the end of the bench and leaned in close. A worried frown ran fresh cracks through her morning makeup. "Hon, I hope you know that's the wrathful hand of the Lord," she said. Gram was pretty much an expert on the wrathful hand of the Lord. My grandfather, John Bunyan Hart, got snatched off their front porch by a tornado the year I was born. It carried him up over their house, over the post office, over the Union Bank, and then dropped him on his head in Rosehill Cemetery. Gram called it providence and buried him where he landed.

"I mean it, Nolan," she said, widening her eyes for emphasis. "It's the hand of the Lord."

"I sure hope you're wrong about that," I said. "I've got trouble enough with local folks. I'd hate to think the Lord had it in for me, too."

She laughed and patted my arm. "Oh, hon, the Lord's got it in for all of us. We step on His toes every day we draw breath. But He'll still scour us clean in the end, don't you worry."

"Well, I'll look forward to that, then," I told her.

"Don't just look forward to it," she said, hooking the basket handle back into the crook of her elbow. "If you want to be bound for glory, you've got to make an effort. You've got to climb onboard the train." She readjusted the basket further up her hip and tottered slightly on the steep heels of her sling-back sandals.

"Let me help you with that," I said, getting up from the bench. "Those peaches look pretty heavy."

"They're ripe, except for a couple of young ones on top," she said, handing over the basket. "Fruit's always heaviest when it's ripe. I've always thought that, anyway. Don't know if it's true."

I took the basket in one hand and Gram's elbow in the other and escorted her down the sidewalk to her Cadillac. I put the peaches on the backseat and we stood there for a moment with the doors open to let the heat pour out.

"These things are like ovens sometimes," she said. The leftover smell of cooked perfume radiated from the car's dark interior, thickening the air with hot lavender and lilac.

"You might leave your windows down a crack," I suggested.

"But then it would rain," she said, "and I'd have to sit in a puddle." She eased herself stiffly into the driver's seat and closed the door. She held up a finger to tell me not to leave yet, then dug through her pocketbook for her keys. Once she got the car started, she pressed the button to lower her window. "I miss the old crank windows," she said, leaning her head out into the sunlight. "Nowadays you've got to have a key just to let the window down. That's way too fancy."

"Some cars still have crank windows," I offered.

She frowned and shook her head. "None that I'd want to drive."

I patted the roof as if it were the flank of a skittish horse. "Well, you take care now, Gram. Keep it under ninety."

"You know," she said, "if you were still little, I'd give you a nickel for carrying my peaches."

"That's about what my rates are now," I told her. "I must not be making much headway."

She barked a short laugh. "Why, boy, that's no secret in this town." She reached back to the basket behind her. "How about a young peach?" she said. "That ought to keep you alive until lunchtime." She picked out a smallish yellow one and pressed it firmly into my palm. It felt like a golf ball.

"Thanks," I said. "But why not a ripe one?"

She looked amused. "Hon, no one eats a ripe peach in public. Didn't anybody ever teach you that?"

I shook my head. "No, ma'am. I guess I must've been absent that day."

"Well," she said, smiling, "now you know." The tinted window whined smoothly back up into place.

She tapped her horn twice—partly, I think, to say good-bye, but also to warn anyone who may have been passing behind her—and then gunned her Cadillac backward onto the quiet street. A number of the truck farmers looked up apprehensively to watch her maneuver the big car around the square. My grandmother was a highly regarded churchwoman around town, well known for her charity work in the community; but along with her strong belief in the Lord was an equally strong belief in automobile bumpers, and anyone who knew her knew she was a hazard behind the wheel. When I worked at my father's agency, we used to process two or three claims a year from people whose cars she'd rammed in parking spaces.

But for the most part Gram's automotive shortcomings were considered a pretty harmless idiosyncrasy. She'd never killed any-body after all—and that was more than a lot of people in this town could claim.

She also had the VFW behind her, because her only son—my Uncle Bobby, whom I never met—had died in Korea.

Today, though, she found her way out of the square without a mishap, and as I watched her Cadillac disappear around the corner onto North Lincoln, the second blast of the morning thundered up from the bridge construction site. I took a too-tart bite of my peach and began walking toward the river.

I angled my way across to the southwest corner of the square where there was a trash barrel outside Dawes Hardware Store. As I dropped the remainder of my sour peach into the barrel, old Mr. Dawes came out onto the sidewalk, dragging his ladder-backed rocker behind him. Normally, he wore a green stock apron with a deep pocket across the front where he kept hard candy for kids who came into the store, but today he'd traded in his apron for a light blue seersucker sport coat. He didn't look dressed for work at all.

"That rocker's a smart move," I said. "Too nice a day to be inside."

"Hey, there, Nolan," he said as he struggled to position his chair next to the cluttered doorway. One rocker rail got caught in a loose bundle of bamboo fishing poles, and I stepped up to help him pull it clear. Mr. Dawes was only a few years older than my father, but he had a slight palsy that made him seem almost completely spent. The skin on his gaunt face looked paper-thin, with broken blood vessels mapping both cheeks. His nose was bulbous and battered as a drunk's, though as far as I knew, Mr. Dawes didn't drink.

Of course, that was my mother's public image, too—a strict

teetotaler, politely turning down drinks whenever they were offered. But the truth was she hardly had a single sober day after she lost my little brother.

"Any day's too nice to be cooped up in this place," Mr. Dawes said.

"That's not a healthy attitude for business. Maybe you ought to hire me to run things for you."

He eased himself into the rocker and pretended to regard me seriously. "You know anything about hardware?" he asked.

"I know which is the hammer and which is the nail," I told him.

"Why, hell, boy, that's practically a master's degree. But you're too late. I've already made a deal to close out my whole inventory. After forty-five years I'm finally cutting myself loose."

"Don't tell me you're fixing to retire," I said.

He leaned back in the rocker until the shade of the awning covered his face and propped his right leg against the casing of a clearance-priced lawn mower. "Only from the hardware part. I'm not the type to sit home and count chickens. Already got a new project lined up." He waved his thumb toward the picture window of his store, where "Dawes Hardware" was spelled out in bold red-and-white letters. "A month from now," he said, "that sign'll say 'Dawes Marble Emporium.'"

"What do you mean?" I asked. "Like marble headstones or statues or something?"

"Nope," he said, raising his hands like a magician with no tricks up his sleeve. "I just mean marbles."

I had no idea what to say to that, so I just nodded politely and then focused my attention back on his broad front window. The inside of the glass was covered by an even coating of dust, and dead wasps littered the sill. Finally, Mr. Dawes creaked forward in his rocker and told me again. *"Marbles,"* he repeated, squinting in the sunlight. "You know what marbles are, don't you? Those little round glass things. Come in all colors."

"Yessir, I know what marbles are. I just never heard of a store like that."

"It's a little offbeat," he admitted. "I think maybe that's what I like about it. Maybe I just want to sell something useless for a change. And, hell, who knows? It might catch on."

"Mr. Dawes, I don't think there's enough kids in this town to keep a marble store in business."

"Kids ain't the market I'm after," he said. "Look here." He stuck a thin hand into the side pocket of his sport coat and pulled out a small handful of clear red marbles. They sparkled in the light like miniature crystal balls. "What I'm talking about is *gourmet* marbles—the kind you heap up in a bowl and set out on your coffee table for people to look at."

"Nobody I know puts marbles on their coffee tables," I said.

"Not around here, no," he conceded. "But they do it in places like New York and California. I've seen it in home-decorator magazines." He held the marbles out to me. "Here's your free starter set," he said, and poured the half dozen of them into my hand.

"Thanks," I said, rolling them around in my palm. "I hope this pans out for you."

"It just might," he said as I carefully funneled the marbles into my shirt pocket. "I'll run a few ads in the right places, try to get a mail-order business going. But boom or bust, I'm happy either way. The main thing is I won't ever have to sort machine screws again for as long as I live."

"I never knew you took such a dislike to your business."

"Never was *my* business," he said, shaking open the front of his coat to circulate the air. "It was my father's. He was the hardware man."

"I don't guess I ever met him," I said.

"Oh, you knew him when you was little. Him and your grand-daddy John Bunyan was good friends. Back in the Second World War, they was co-commanders of the county's scrap-metal drive. Did a lot for the war effort. Then later on they started up a committee to get the government to make the old Stone Bridge a national Civil War memorial. Never got too far with that one, though."

I'd heard stories all my life about the old Stone Bridge. I knew it had been built by an Italian stonemason before the Civil War, and I knew it was regarded as an engineering marvel because there were no keystones in the spans. I knew General William Tecumseh Sherman had been so impressed by the architecture that he had chosen to spare this particular bridge in his devastating march through the region after the Battle of Shiloh. I even knew it was where Philo Buchannan got Edna Winslow pregnant in tenth grade. But I'd never heard about my grandfather's attempt to turn the place into a war memorial.

"I guess they'd have had a better case," Mr. Dawes went on, "if Sherman had gone ahead and blown the damned thing up. When it comes to military history, it's hard to commemorate something that didn't happen. You cain't put a date on the plaque."

"Well, maybe there's enough war memorials in the world already," I said.

"You got that right," he agreed. "But they both took it as a real disappointment. They'd already bought up the flood plain between the Stone Bridge and the Andrew Jackson monument."

"What Andrew Jackson monument?" I asked.

"Oh, you know—that big rock sticking up in the field next to the Wal-Mart parking lot. The DAR had it put in when I was a boy. Nobody really tends to it anymore—I guess most folks have forgotten it's there. But that was where Jackson set up camp at the start of the Creek Indian campaign." He shook his head and sighed. "A military theme park, that's what your granddaddy had in mind. Like Gettysburg, or Shiloh—only this one would have the War of 1812 thrown in, so you'd get two wars for the price of one. My daddy thought sure it'd be a tourist bonanza."

"Too bad it didn't work out. We'd both be sitting pretty."

"Oh, I doubt that," he said. "I imagine we'd both be stuck at some souvenir stand selling made-in-Taiwan war trinkets to a bunch of strangers in straw hats."

"There's worse ways to make a living," I said, thinking of every job I'd ever had. "And worse places to do it in. I might've liked hanging around that old bridge. It's a pretty spot. All those white stone arches. No gas stations or minimarts around."

"Well, it's *scenic,* all right," he agreed. "But anything that calls itself a bridge ought to do more than just look good on a postcard. These days I wouldn't even trust it to foot traffic." He rocked forward into the sunlight and shook his head. "'Course, that's not how my daddy looked at it—nor your granddaddy, neither—so for them it was a tough break when the government turned down their idea.

"Then right after that my daddy got glaucoma, so he couldn't even stay with the hardware business. Had to turn it all over to me—and he sure by-God hated that. He'd been in hardware all his life. Hell, we used to sell buggy whips and wagon tongues, that's how old this place is." He took a long breath and closed his eyes. "But I'm done with it now, thank the Lord."

"What made you finally give it up?"

He opened his eyes and laughed. "The fact is Daddy finally died. Heart quit on him last month out at the nursing home. He was in that new one—the one they built out on the east bypass next to the fire station. Healthy Acres. Stupid name, but it's a nice place compared to most—still has a clean smell to it. Anyway, they tell me he just keeled right over on his supper plate."

"I'm sorry, Mr. Dawes, I hadn't heard."

"It's not the biggest news. Somebody dies in that place just about every day. Besides, he made it to ninety-eight. I guess that's a long enough hitch for anybody."

Another explosion rumbled up from the work site, and the store's tin awning vibrated noisily above us. Mr. Dawes scowled toward the river. "I sure wish they'd finish up with that dynamite," he said. "There's fault lines around here, you know. Those morons are liable to set off a goddamn earthquake."

"I'll tell Bill McDonald you said that. Maybe he'll have the crew switch over to pickaxes."

"Bill McDonald don't know what a pickax is. That shit-for-brains never hefted a tool in his life." He took a handkerchief from his coat pocket and blew his nose. His shopkeeper's hands looked

frail and yellow—old, but still oddly unweathered, without a gnarl
or a wrinkle—and I wondered if it had bothered him to spend a life-
time handling tools without really learning to use them. "You going
down to watch the blasting?"

"Not really," I told him. "Thought maybe I could hire on for
some day labor."

"So you really are looking for work," he said. "I thought you
was just throwing the bull."

"No sir, no bull about it. I'm out of the insurance business. Now
I do whatever pickup work I can find. So far it's been mostly debt
collection for Hometown Finance. But Dell's playing golf up at
Horton today with Morgan Motlow's bunch, so I'm on my own."

Mr. Dawes rapped his knuckles lightly against the arm of his
rocker. "Good for you, Nolan. Take my word for it, when a boy
works for his father, even unemployment is a big step up."

"I'm not sure my wife would see it like that," I said.

"Wives do complicate a picture," he said, nodding. "You'll
never be more than half right, whatever you do."

"I'd settle for half," I told him. Then I wished him luck again
and resumed my walk toward the river.

Instead of keeping to Market Steet, which would have brought
me right to where they were blasting holes for the new bridge pylons, I took the longer route, veering west down Firehall Hill and
cutting through the mostly black neighborhood behind the old condemned high school. I had spent a lot of time here when I was a
boy—my mother would drop me off with various families we knew
while she spent the day in Nashville or played bridge with one of
her groups. There had been plenty of kids around in those days, and
we spent whole summers throwing rocks at rusty cans and playing
night Wiffle ball under whichever streetlight hadn't been shot out.
Now most of the guys I had played with were gone—some into the
army, some off to other towns or states where they could look for
decent work. There was nothing for them here. Lincoln was still basically the same backwater farming community it had always been,
so good jobs were scarce, and all the real career chances were

passed around among the older, well-established families. The poor in Lincoln either stayed poor or left the county.

I took Mr. Dawes's bright marbles out of my pocket and tossed them into one of the yards, a treasure for some little kid to find.

Over the past month I'd come to feel at home again on these streets, even though I knew my job made me unwelcome. It was an odd thing, but I felt most comfortable among the worst of the run-down houses—the two-room shacks with tar-paper shingles peeling in the heat, and yards piled with truck tires and cinder blocks, and cats laying low in the weeds. I'd see people—older couples, mostly, or widows with wild gray hair—rocking smoothly on yellow front-porch gliders, watching me nervously, wishing me to pass them by, maybe even wishing me dead.

And who could blame them? Maybe I felt comfortable here for the worst of reasons. Maybe I liked seeing hardship that wasn't my own. In this part of town I could look straight into the misery that dogged these people's lives, and call my own life good by comparison.

On that side of town the last real landmark before the river was the massive jail, which stood alone on a rocky bluff. Except for the Stone Bridge itself, which spanned the Elk just 200 yards to the south, the jail was the oldest standing structure in the county—and at four stories it was also the highest. The brick was reddish brown, like dried blood, and the tiny windows of the cells along the two top floors gave the place the look of a fortress.

There had actually been a real fortress there once, about four centuries back. When I was in eleventh grade my American History class took a field trip out here to climb around on the rocks and look for artifacts that might have been left by the early Spanish explorers. Hernando de Soto himself, later famous for discovering the Mississippi, had stopped off here first to discover the Elk River. He told the local tribes that he was a warrior god, and then proceeded to piss them off in all kinds of violent ways. Things got so nasty that he had to build himself a granite stronghold here on the north bank of the river. When spring came, he decided the future might be brighter for him if he headed farther west, so he pushed on to the Mississippi, where he got sick and died. His men dumped his body in the river—along with about eighty pounds of body armor so he wouldn't come bobbing back up to embarrass them. Warrior gods weren't supposed to be so puny.

It was a good field trip, but I never did find any artifacts. Laney was there, too, with her World Cultures class, and we sneaked off together, down by the Stone Bridge, and started making out there on the riverbank. The slope of the ground kept us hidden from our classmates, but not from the prisoners on the top two floors of the jailhouse. A few of them started yelling things down at us, dirty stuff mostly. I felt pretty uncomfortable, but Laney didn't seem to mind. She just laughed and waved back.

At the time, I took it as a sign of her good nature.

Another blast shook the ground as I passed below the jailhouse, only this time I could see the narrow spray of water and dirt shooting up into the sky. It arced above the river cut like the spume of a whale, then rained harmlessly back into the water and disappeared. Five seconds, that was all, and it was over. Everything looked normal again.

The crew was working just 300 yards upriver, and their dump trucks and backhoes were scattered like bright yellow toys along the opposite bank. After the debris settled, ten or twelve crewmen stepped out from behind the larger pieces of machinery to see what good the blast had done. I was too far away to recognize anybody, though I knew Steve Pitts would be in charge of the dynamite.

I couldn't even begin to guess whether Steve and Laney might live happily ever after. My power to predict a rosy future was about as faulty as Hernando de Soto's.

As I reached the Stone Bridge's broad, grassy approach, I stopped for a moment to imagine what my grandfather's plans might have been for the place. There wasn't much potential, from what I could see. From this angle it didn't even look like a bridge—more just a narrow, grassy field stretching oddly between the riverbanks, a gentle bulge blanketed with sawgrass and dandelions and flanked on each side by a pair of low white-granite walls. This was the view that never made it onto postcards, and with good reason. There was nothing interesting about it. Nothing dramatic.

As I started up the hump, I turned my attention to the construction crew upriver, trying to gauge my chances of getting hired on for shit work. There was usually plenty of that at a construction site—jobs too dirty or dangerous for the regular crew to mess with. Most of it went to high-schoolers or half-wits—guys ignorant enough to crawl headfirst through a sewage pipe, or check dynamite connections, or wade along the riverbank testing for caves and sinkholes. I knew what it was like. I'd worked some heavy construction the summer after high school to pay for Laney's engagement ring, and I could still handle a backhoe without rolling it over. That's how most construction workers got hurt—not falling off buildings, but getting crushed by one of their own machines. The escarpment where they were stringing the pylons was pretty steep, so any heavy equipment that approached it on the slightest angle would either flip over or slide sideways into the river. That kind of work called for somebody who was either extremely careful or desperately stupid. Either way, I felt qualified.

As I reached the weed-covered crest of the bridge, still focused on the men upriver, a woman's high voice called out from the far bank.

"I see you there! Don't you think for one minute I don't!"

It was Grace Elder, stout and straight-backed as ever, sitting on a red-and-white cooler at the edge of the drop-off. A thick brown rope, staked to the ground beside her, dangled down the bank to the water fifteen feet below, where her teenaged boys, Louis and Sammy, were wading waist-deep in the current. Each boy carried what looked like a garden rake rigged up with a burlap bag laced into the tines.

"Morning, Grace," I called back. "I see you, too."

She steadied her glasses on her nose and squinted through the lenses. "Who is it knows my name?" she demanded. Sammy kept his eye on the water, but Louis looked up at me and waved.

"It's okay, Mama," he said. "It's just Mr. Vann."

"Mr. Jim Vann or Nolan?" she asked, still skeptical.

"The one you used to put diapers on," I answered.

"Nolan? Is that you?" She dropped her hand to her lap and shook her head. "I got to go see the eye doctor. These dime-store glasses ain't worth spit."

I rounded the end of the low bridge wall and joined her at the edge of the drop-off. I hadn't seen Grace since last fall's homecoming game—both her boys were starting defensive linemen—but she seemed lively as ever. Her coffee-colored face had the same plump and owl-eyed look I'd known since childhood. "Didn't mean to sneak up on you," I said.

"Cain't nobody sneak up on me," she huffed. "I got the vigilance of the righteous." She smoothed the wrinkles from her long flowered skirt, and glanced away upriver. "But I best not get too cocky," she said, touching a thick hand to the gold cross at her throat. "When it comes to sneaking around, even Satan takes a backseat to the repo man."

"So you've heard about my career change."

She looked up at me and frowned. "Heard about it? How am I not gonna hear about it? That kind of news travels fast in my neighborhood. I just thank the Lord I ain't ever been so bad off I had to ask the finance company to pull me out."

"Grace, you know I'd never take anything of yours," I told her.

She smiled, but kept her hand closed around her cross, and I could see a sort of formal dignity welling up around her, the genuine kind, like what you'd expect from preachers or washroom attendants. "Boy, them's easy words when my name ain't ever been on your list," she said. "But you carted off Sadie Moore's 'frigerator, and she's my daddy's cousin. So don't act all innocent with me."

I stepped closer to the edge of the drop and watched Sammy wade slowly toward the riverbank. "It's just a temporary job, Grace. If I didn't do it, somebody else would."

"Child, that's what all the Devil's minions tell theirselves when they props their feet up after work." She stared upriver for a moment, then leaned forward and called down to the water. "Boys, you be awake down there. I think they about to blow up another rock."

"You the lifeguard here today?" I asked. I'd heard that some of the more reckless kids around town had tried swimming in the Elk River this summer, dangerous as it was. Back in April a state safety inspector had condemned the county pool, and then the parks commission paved over it to put up some tennis courts. There was still the country-club pool, but that wasn't open to the general public.

"Well, lifeguard might not be the word," she said. "I'm ready to holler for help if somebody needs it, but I wouldn't jump down this riverbank to fetch Gabriel's trumpet." She squirmed a little on the cooler, and gripped the edges with both hands as if she were worried about tipping over. "Anyways, they both big boys now." She craned her neck forward to peer down the embankment. "'Specially Louis," she said, raising her voice for his benefit. "He thinks he's big enough to quit high school, big enough to go into the army. Any boy that big don't need my help, whatever might come along."

"Sounds like y'all are on your own down there," I called.

"Yes, sir," said Louis, poking the free end of his rake handle gently into a mossy overhang. "That's exactly what I been telling her. She thinks we're down here with the Lord."

"Hush," Sammy told him as he eased toward a small, still pool in a recess of the bank. "You gonna get us both bit."

I turned back to Grace. "What are they after?" I asked, though I thought I knew. Grace was a member of the Mount Zion Divine Brethren, which at one time was connected with the Church of Christ but which had recently branched onto a more irregular path.

"Cottonmouths," she announced, her voice cheerful and defiant, as if she were naming some prodigal friend. I scanned the shallows for water trails, but saw no movement outside the current. "Sammy got one already." She patted the side of the cooler. "You want to see?"

"No, ma'am, I surely don't. If you've got a cottonmouth in there, you can just keep that lid on tight."

"We put ice in with him, so he's pretty slowed down," she said. "He's just a little one. Probably couldn't kill a jackrabbit."

"I don't care," I told her. "Water moccasins are too mean to mess with. Did Brother Willis put you up to this?"

"Brother Willis ain't involved. Not directly, anyways. This is just something I got to do for the congregation."

"Why?" I asked.

She shrugged. "We running low on snakes."

I stared at the cooler, imagining the snake coiled and frozen in the darkness, just waiting for a chance to thaw out and strike. "Well, there ought to be a better way than this," I said. "Isn't there some kind of supply store or something?"

She laughed and rocked back on the cooler. "Honey, the Sears and Roebuck don't carry no vipers."

Men's sharp voices came to us on the breeze, and we both looked upriver to see the last few crewmen scramble over the crest of the scarred embankment and take cover behind the earthmovers.

"Well, you sure picked a bad day for it," I said. "With all that blasting going on."

"Dynamite ain't usually one of my favorite things," she admitted. "But today it's all part of the Lord's business."

"What she means," said Louis, jabbing his rake harder into the bank, "is that every time they blow a hole in the riverbed, it drives the snakes farther downstream."

Grace nodded and smiled. "That's the time to catch a cottonmouth," she said. "You got to get him in unfamiliar water, when he don't know where to hide out."

"Grace, cottonmouths don't hide. They come after anything that moves." I crouched at the edge of the bank and watched Sammy and Louis troll their burlap sacks slowly through the river muck. "Nice knowing you boys," I said.

"Don't even joke about it,' Louis groaned. "It's like one of them god-awful slow-motion dreams when you cain't outrun what's coming after you."

"You won't never beat a fear by running away from it," Grace said, though I heard Brother Willis in her words.

"Well, Mama, you cain't beat it by getting killed, neither. And I ain't too pleased about the possibility of being up to my ass in water moccasins."

"Don't you use that language with me, boy," she said, shaking a warning finger down at him. "What you gonna do when the army sits you down in some jungle rice paddy somewhere with Lord-knows-what trying to crawl up your pant leg."

Louis sighed and stretched his T-shirt up to blot the sweat from his forehead. "They don't fight in rice paddies no more, Mama. It's all regular places now."

"Don't you believe that for one minute," she said. "They'll plop you down anywhere they want. They'll have you wrestling gators in the Amazon. They'll have you shooting penguins at the South Pole. Tell him I'm right, Nolan."

"She's right, Louis."

"Well, I don't care," Louis told her. "Even the South Pole sounds better than this."

"You're down in that river for the sake of your souls," she said. "So just get used to it."

Louis let his rakehead rest on the bottom and looked up at his mother. "Twenty-five dollars a snake, Mama. That's what I'm down here for."

"Amen," said Sammy, without looking up from the water.

"Twenty-five dollars is a pretty good price," I said.

Louis lifted his rake upright and leaned on it in the current. "I thought so, too, when I was on dry land," he said. "But from down here Brother Willis is starting to look like one sorry-ass cheapskate sonofabitch."

"Don't be talking that way," said Grace. "Brother Willis is a healer and a cleanser. When he takes up the serpent, it becomes a tool of faith." She lifted a thick black book from a tuft of grass near the cooler. "Besides," she said, hoisting it overhead for both sons to see, "there's barely a lick to worry about—the facts is on our side." She held it above her head like a trophy and started to proclaim something more, but the book proved heavier than she'd thought, and her stout arm wavered under the weight, then tilted suddenly forward. "Oh, my," she said as the book slipped from her fingers. We both fumbled to catch it, but it was too late—the book grazed the edge of the precipice and splayed open, then tumbled end over end down the rocky dirt wall and plunged into the muddy water at Louis's feet.

Louis plucked it out with his free hand and shook it gently, then closed the cover and squeezed out a thin brown stream from the soggy pages. When the dripping slowed, he studied the front cover and laughed. "Well, this is a surprise," he said. "I thought you was throwing a Bible at me."

"What is it?" I asked.

Louis heaved the wet book up to me, and I read the gold-embossed answer on the cover: *Handbook of Actuarial Statistics. Calendar Years 1960 through 1969. Compiled by the Insurance Underwriters of America.*

Strange as it seemed, I knew the book well—or at least later editions of it. It was a collection of national mortality tables. My father's favorite Book of Numbers.

"They threw that out at the library," Grace explained. "But it still tells a straight story. It says that in the whole United States, only six people a year die from snakebite."

"Maybe that's why they threw it out," said Louis. "Maybe it was flat wrong."

I knew the book would not be wrong. In fact, the very idea that the library could discard even an outdated edition was startling to me. In the years I'd worked for my father, I'd been taught to regard it as indispensable, as the sourcebook we made our living by. It was the foundation beneath every policy we issued and every premium we were paid—and we never made a move without checking its charts. We studied it, we analyzed it, we consulted it like an oracle. I don't know what toll it took on anybody else in the office—maybe it was just another book to them—but I finally got to the point where I could hardly look at people without calculating their risk factors, assigning penalties in my mind like some judge passing sentence. Five years for those cigarettes, pal, plus five more for that gut you're carrying—and let's lop off a decade for those empty quarts of Scotch.

Those tables divvied up all the lost bodies of the earth into neat little bloodless piles. Heart attack and stroke, cancer and diabetes. Sudden infant death syndrome. Even the loaded shotgun on the closet shelf, the bald front tire, the puddle by the circuit-breaker box—everything was covered by the book. And the message, from the salesman side, was clear: the world was an infinitely fatal place, but with built-in profit margins for those who knew the odds.

Yet here was a version of my father's book that had lost its power. I could hold it in my hands without fretting over its sad mathematical weight, its cold tally of life's consequences. I could squeeze the river water from its ruined pages, and not worry that the ink might run.

A single warning call echoed along the river, followed a moment later by the fifth explosion of the morning. This time I was near enough to feel its absolute power shuddering through the ground, shifting earth and rock and bone. Again the spray of mud and hard debris flowered high into the air, then showered down into the river, a falling mimicked this time by a small separate shower of pebbles and dirt sifting down from the undersides of the old Stone Bridge.

"Could be any time now, boys," said Grace, shading her eyes with both hands and staring down at the freshly disturbed riverbed. I stared, too, and saw that she was right—there was movement in the water all along the banks, though for the most part it was impossible to tell exactly what was there. Fish, certainly, because the river was full of them. Probably turtles, too, and frogs where bubbles broke the surface in brief underwater trails. Even a few muskrats were probably churning the slight ripples now rolling from beneath the overhangs. But the easiest to spot were the water snakes—and I did see them—whipping broad wakes behind them as they skated the shallows, racing in short bursts downstream.

Cottonmouths

NONE OF US SAW THE SNAKE until after it struck. It came at Louis from downstream, from behind him, and we were all looking the other way—Grace and Sammy at the water, watching for movement in the aftermath of the last blast, and me at the yellow backhoe that was rumbling along the riverbank, heading our way. I heard the yelp and turned in time to see Louis spin sideways in the current, the cottonmouth still hanging from below his left shoulder blade, its fat body whipping a trail through the water as Louis thrashed around. Snakes can be slower to let go in water, maybe because they've got no traction for a recoil, and this one—a four-footer at least—was hooked in deep. Louis wasn't helping things, either. When the tail end of the moccasin slashed in front of him, he grabbed on and tried to yank the snake loose. That was a natural reflex, I suppose, but it was like setting a hook in a fish. I mean, snakes have reflexes, too, and when Louis grabbed this one, it naturally fought to hold on.

Then Louis went under. I don't know if he stumbled on a river rock or just decided on a new strategy, but the second he disappeared, his mother wailed out his name like he was gone for good. Sammy kept still, waist-deep in water not ten feet from his brother while I stayed rooted on the bank above, both of us knowing there was nothing we could do. Not that we had all that long to think about it—a couple of seconds, maybe—but this was a situation that didn't take much thought at all. It was plain to me, and to

Sammy, too, I guess, that as long as Louis had that granddaddy cottonmouth wrapped around his back, he was by-God on his own.

Grace, of course, saw things differently. After her scream she jittered around on the bank for a moment like the ground was electric, revving up her panic until it was strong enough to propel her out over the edge of the drop-off. "Wait—" I said, but she was already on her way, plunging awkwardly down into the shallow water between her sons. Her legs buckled against the rocky bed and she pitched forward, crying out again, more sharply this time, and I knew at once she'd hurt herself. Sammy grabbed her by the white lace collar of her dress and pulled her toward him while I scrambled down the slippery bank to help. As I splashed my way toward them, Louis burst up from underwater, still flailing and writhing, but finally free of the snake. He gasped hoarsely for breath, then steadied himself in the mild current, his arms stretched out like he was balancing on a ledge. "Goddammit!" he croaked, then coughed hard and retched up a thin brown stream of river water. Grace pressed her fists to the side of her head and cried, "Oh, Lord, oh, Lord," as Sammy dragged her toward the bank. I waded out to Louis and grabbed him by the arm.

"Let's get you out of here," I said. He stood there for a few seconds looking puzzled and panting heavily, but then finally he nodded his head, and the two of us trudged back to shore, where Sammy was just propping Grace among a cluster of smooth stones in the shallows. I thought at first she had passed out, but when Sammy tried to shift her legs aside to make way for us, she cried out and slapped his hands away. Louis, already exhausted by the combined rush of panic and poison, slumped against the mud wall of the overhang and took the end of the climbing rope in his hand. His T-shirt was ripped along the back and the side, and a bright red stain pooled outward from the tear.

"Are you all right?" Sammy asked him.

Louis looked at him in disbelief. "Shit, no, I ain't all right!" he said. "Goddammit, boy, what planet you living on? I'm fucking snakebit!" He looked at the rope stretching above him and shook his head. "This is bad, man. This is real bad."

"Lord Jesus," Grace moaned, louder this time, and her body seemed to tighten like a fist. Sammy tugged back the hem of her dress and carefully pressed his fingers against her left shin. She winced and clutched at his arm.

"I think Mama done busted something," he said.

I took the rope from Louis's hand and looped a quick knot over his wrist. "See any blood?" I asked, looking over to where Sammy was still crouched beside his mother.

"They's some in the water," he said, "but I think that's Louis."

Louis lifted his arm and studied the spreading stain on his shirt. "Well, there's some great goddamn news," he said. "I'm bleeding to death, too." He leaned his head back into the mud and closed his eyes.

"Keep her leg in the water," I told Sammy. "The cold might help some. I'll see to Louis."

Louis groaned a little but lay still as I pulled the knot tight around his arm. "Sure, that's it," he said, "tie me up like some wild-ass dog. I probably got rabies, too."

"Just grab onto this," I told him as I fitted his fingers around the rope. "Try to keep on your feet while I pull you up."

He loosed his grip on the rope and nestled his face against the muddy bank. "I feel a nap coming on," he said.

"Bad time for it," I told him.

"That's a *dirt* nap you talking about," said Sammy. "Now get your scrawny butt up that rope." But Louis just sighed, and mumbled something I couldn't make out. "I mean it," Sammy warned him. "Open those eyes, or I swear to God I'll pop you one." When Louis still didn't stir, Sammy fished up a softball-sized rock from the river bottom and chucked it into his brother's face.

Louis reeled awake and looked around in confusion. I think he had it in his mind to say something, but then he realized he was in some brand-new kind of pain, and his words just melted down into a long, low groan. He put his free hand to his nose and felt the fresh trickle of blood. "Great God Almighty," he cried. "What the hell did you do to me?"

"You fell," I told him. "Now grab onto this rope and get ready to climb." I took off my loafers and tossed them up the embankment, then hoisted myself up the soft dirt wall, gouging out toeholds for Louis along the way.

As I heaved myself over the top of the bank, the backhoe I'd been watching earlier pulled up beside Grace's cooler. Steve Pitts was at the controls. He shifted into neutral and gunned the engine twice to keep it idling, but the timing was too rough and the old motor choked out on him.

"Give me a hand here," I yelled. I took hold of the rope near where it was staked to the ground and began to pull Louis up from the river. I couldn't see him yet, but apparently he was still on his feet because it wasn't a hard pull at all, and live weights always lift easier than dead ones.

"I'm on break," Steve said, lifting his ball cap and smoothing back his hair. I scowled over at him, but he just ignored me, like always. He replaced his cap and scratched absently at the sunburned hand grenade on his right bicep. "Got any cold drinks in that cooler?"

Sometimes it was hard for me to like Steve Pitts. Fifteen years ago, when we played Pony League together, I liked him a lot. He was the kind of ballplayer every team loves to have—a flat-out mean sonofabitch, aggressive as all hell and strong as a bull. We always cheered for him when he charged the mound after a brushback pitch. We always laughed when he spiked some poor second-baseman on a slide, or beaned a runner already safe on base. Steve could intimidate like nobody else who played the game, and that was fine with us because he was on our side. We applauded every dirty thing he did. I guess none of us ever really stopped to think what it would be like when we weren't Steve's teammates anymore—how uncomfortable we might someday feel about the kind of guy we'd rooted for.

"Louis Elder got snakebit," I said, still hauling on the rope. "Grace and Sammy are down there, too."

"This ain't the best place for a swim," he said, hopping down from the backhoe. He trotted over to the edge and knelt by the rope. When Louis came within reach, Steve grabbed him by the back of his belt and dragged him up over the top.

"Jesus Christ," he said, looking down at Louis's bloodied back. "Boy, something tore you up good."

Louis took a heavy breath and swallowed. "Wouldn't let go," he said. "Had to rip it off me. Still stings like hell."

Steve stared closely at the wound. "No shit," he said. He glanced over at me and then pressed his palm against the ragged hole in Louis's shirt. Louis flinched and drew another sharp breath. "You hold still for a second," Steve told him, then he carefully reached down and plucked out an inch-long piece of fang. "Good job, Louis," he said, holding the white sliver up for me to see. "You cut that scaly bastard's diet in half." He tossed it into the grass at my feet and wiped his bloody hands on his shirttail. "This boy here's a fighter."

"We've got to get him to the hospital," I said, shoving my foot back into one of my wet loafers.

Steve shaded his eyes and scanned the construction site upriver, where the last couple of pickups were kicking up a trail of dust as they moved south toward the highway. "Well, I just let my whole crew knock off for lunch," he said. "Too late to catch a ride from any of those boys."

"We can take the backhoe," I told him as I retrieved my second loafer from beneath the dredging bucket. "Just cross the bridge and cut straight back over the hill by the jailhouse—that'd be quicker than a car anyway."

Steve looked at the mud-spattered machine ticking in the sun and shrugged. "I guess," he said. "If you think you can find a place to hold on."

He was right, this was strictly a one-man rig, the kind we always used for small-cut excavations or minor trench work. Steve had driven it around town all year, ever since McDonald had put him in charge of prepping the new bridge site. His "company car," he called it. In fact it was his only car, which is why he and Laney always had to take her Chevy when they sneaked off together. Not that they really did much sneaking. Steve usually took her to semi-public places like the Boaz Tavern or the drive-in, and word usually got back to me pretty fast. I even heard about her Chevy being parked right out front at the Stone Bridge Motel two Saturdays ago, another one of those weekends she was supposed to be in Lynchburg with her sister Donna.

But none of that was the problem right now, I realized. The problem now was putting Louis somewhere on the backhoe that wouldn't get him or me killed, and except for the lone saddle seat for the driver, there was no safe place to sit. Like with most earthmoving equipment, the body design was basically skeletal, all rods and joints and axles. No fenders, no flat surfaces. The boom arm was too upright to balance on and the bucket itself was hardly wide enough to carry a cat. It looked like a giant mechanical scorpion, dangerous even to get close to.

"We'll have to straddle the engine casing," I said. I knew the casing would be hot as a fry pan on a day like this, but there was no other stable way to ride.

Steve smiled. "Fine with me," he said. "I'll just drop you boys off at the burn ward when we get there."

I leaned over the drop-off and told Sammy we were leaving.

"What do I do about Mama?" he called up.

"Just stay with her," I told him. "Keep the snakes away until we can send somebody back for you."

"Yessir," he said, "But if you could maybe hurry I'd sure appreciate it." He picked up his rake from the water's edge and stepped out near Grace's feet to stand guard.

"Louis—" Grace called out. Her eyes were still squeezed tight, but I could tell by the way she steadied herself on her elbows that she was coming back to herself again.

"Louis is just fine," I said, though I barely believed it. Like every Boy Scout, I'd learned the proper way to treat a snakebite. But what I realized now was that the Scout handbook dealt only with best-case scenarios—small, clean punctures on the foot or the forearm. You can tie those off with a tourniquet and drain the poison through two parallel cuts above the bite. But there were no guidelines for the messier cases, no instructions for what to do when the snake strikes from behind and leaves a ragged tear across somebody's back. Where do you put the tourniquet then? Which way does the poison go? And how do you keep it out of the heart?

As I turned back to Louis, Steve picked him up by the waist of his jeans and carried him like a suitcase over to the backhoe. He set him down by the front wheel and frowned at me. "Get a move on there, pal. I ain't planning to piss away my whole goddamn lunch hour on this shit."

It was hard to imagine what Laney saw in Steve Pitts. Except of course that he wasn't me.

~

The ride to the hospital wasn't bad. Over Steve's objections I scooped a few quick handfuls of mud from the underside of the bank and caked it over the hood of the backhoe so Louis and I wouldn't get singed. Holding on turned out not to be much of a problem—driving heavy equipment is one of the things Steve does pretty well and he kept the ride smooth, if only from habit. Louis sat in front and I kept my arms locked around him to keep him in place. From time to time he did start to nod off, but then his legs would settle against the side of the casing, and even through his wet jeans the heat coming off the engine block was enough to scorch him back awake.

My only misgiving came as we chugged our way over the crest of the Stone Bridge and I glanced down to check on Grace and Sammy one last time. Sammy pointed to something beneath the bridge and shouted up at us, but the noisy sputter of the backhoe made it impossible to make out anything he said. My guess was that he'd spotted more snakes. The blasting upriver had been enough to spur Louis's snake to attack, so there was no telling what effect our rumbling across the bridge might have on the other cottonmouths that were undoubtedly still down there. Except for the occasional bicycle, there probably hadn't been any vehicle traffic across this span in twenty years, and I knew that the noisy weight of the earthmover would send vibrations racking through every stone support. Most of the mortar around the waterline had crumbled away over the years, and any snake nesting in those cracks between the granite slabs would surely be disturbed enough to come out and defend its territory. Cottonmouths are crazy to begin with, always ready to fight and always too stupid to back down. But they're especially vicious when they feel crowded.

There was no choice, of course, but to leave Grace and Sammy behind. Louis's life was clocking down fast, or at least that's what it looked like to me. Steve didn't seem too concerned about any of it— but I couldn't tell if that was because he somehow knew there was nothing to worry about, or because he plain didn't give a damn.

The hospital was perched on a ridge between the poor section of town and the southern bypass. It was about a mile and a half away as the crow flies, and on a backhoe in open country that's pretty much the line you can follow. It took us about four minutes to make it up the back side of the ridge and roll into the receiving driveway outside the emergency room. There was no horn on the backhoe, but apparently we were noisy enough without one, because an elderly black man in a blue hospital smock came out right away with a wheelchair. I guess when you pull up to an emergency room on a piece of heavy construction machinery, people pretty much assume there's a serious problem.

Steve killed the engine and hopped down to the pavement. "You're home free, boy," he announced. "They got every expensive gadget in the world in this place. They'll fix you up just fine."

"That's a fact," the orderly said cheerfully. "Don't even matter what the problem is." He positioned the chair by the curb and stepped away to let us lift Louis from the backhoe.

"Snakebite," I said as Steve and I eased Louis down from the backhoe to the chair. "Cottonmouth got him right below the shoulder blade about ten minutes ago."

The orderly smoothed his hand over the thin gray fuzz on his scalp and nodded. Then he bent down close to Louis's face and frowned. "Why, I know this boy," he said suddenly. "He used to be in my Sunday School class." He straightened Louis in the chair and patted his cheek a few times to bring him around. "Louis! Wake up, son. We got to get you admitted."

Louis opened his eyes and focused on the orderly's face. "Hey there, Mr. Johnson. How you doing?"

Mr. Johnson smiled. "Oh, I been pretty good, Louis," he said, buckling him in place. "How about yourself?"

Louis took a slow, uneven breath. "Thinking about joining the army," he said. "Or else the Marines."

"Well, that's real good, boy," Mr. Johnson told him. "The Armed Forces is a good place for a young man to start out. They'll teach you a good trade."

"Damn straight," Steve said. "The Marine Corps taught me demolition, and I ain't never been out of work."

Mr. Johnson released the brake on the chair and quickly wheeled Louis away through two sets of automatic doors. As they disappeared into the building, Steve climbed back up to his seat.

"I can stand on my own two feet," he added. "I ain't never had to ask my daddy for a job." He smiled down at me—it was that same lazy, condescending smirk he used to show the opposing team just before some ballplayer got hurt. I smiled, too, but I think that was the moment I decided not to go back to construction work.

"Your daddy's in jail," I pointed out. If Steve had still been close enough, he'd have slugged me—I saw the impulse flash across his face. But he let it go. I guess climbing back down to come after me was more trouble than he thought I was worth. He relaxed into his seat and propped a foot on the gear box. "That ain't my point," he said.

I understood his point well enough, and I could see we were about two sentences away from a very ugly discussion about Laney, which was not something I had time for right then.

"Go eat your lunch, Steve," I told him. "I've got things to do.

Thanks for the ride." I stepped over to a silver light pole anchored in the sidewalk and steadied myself against it while I wrung some of the water from my pant legs.

Steve leaned across his steering wheel and brushed a few chunks of dried mud from the engine casing. "Yeah, sure, no problem, Nolan. Sorry about your dead friend."

"Louis'll be all right," I told him.

He smiled again as he started up the engine. "You don't know this place like I do," he said, raising his voice above the racket of the cylinders. "These sumbitches couldn't cure a ham if you locked 'em in a smokehouse."

He pulled halfway around the drive, then abruptly swung the backhoe up over the curb and sped down across the lawn, leaving heavy tread marks in the manicured grass. When he got near the lower end of the grounds, he veered wide to the left and crushed a small dogwood, then waved his hand back over his head at me. He didn't have to turn around to know I was watching.

~

When I got inside the lobby, I told the teenaged girl at the admitting desk about Grace's broken leg and had her send an ambulance out to the Stone Bridge to pick her up. I thought about riding along and maybe lending a hand, but with Sammy already there I figured they wouldn't need me. Besides, I wanted to find out about Louis. Mr. Johnson had ushered him right through to the treatment area without a lot of red tape, which surprised me, but the receptionist was more of a stickler for protocol and wouldn't let me follow them back, partly because I wasn't a relative but partly, I suspect, because I was still dripping mud and river water. Ordinarily I'd have just barged on through, regardless. But the emergency room wasn't really a room, it was a whole maze of cubicles and temporary partitions, all of which were blocked off from the public by electric doors that wouldn't open unless somebody buzzed you through from the inside. I'd been back there a couple of times before—once when my Grandmother Vann had her first stroke and once when my mother doused herself with lighter fluid and set herself on fire. They kept a pretty tight rein on their procedures, which was reassuring, I suppose, but it meant there was nothing for me to do except stand around shivering in the air-conditioning until somebody came out to tell me the score.

The waiting area was done up in a sort of fake hominess, like it was the living room of some compulsively tidy maiden aunt. New-looking wood-and-fabric chairs lined the walls, and end tables with big pastel crockery lamps filled each corner. The broad oak coffee table in the center of the room held a carefully stacked collection of glossy magazines. The walls were decorated with oversized abstract paintings done in the same blues and browns as the carpet, and mellow violin versions of old rock songs drooled down through speaker vents in the ceiling. The only thing that gave it all away was the smell, which was pure hospital, pungent and antiseptic. And after a while even that distinction faded.

There was nobody else waiting—apparently we were the only emergency in town. I tried to distract myself with a bass-fishing magazine from the stack on the table, but I don't fish much and the issue was two years old. I was about to try my hand at sweet-talking the receptionist, figuring maybe she could at least phone somebody in the back and get a progress report, but as I walked out to her desk in the entry foyer, Mr. Johnson came hurrying back through the electric doors. There was a wide spatter of blood across the front of his blue smock.

"How's it going?" I asked.

"Cain't complain," he answered, nodding and smiling politely as he walked past.

I followed him through the waiting room to the service elevator in the far hall. "No," I said, "I mean how's Louis?"

Mr. Johnson turned and peered at me through his bifocals. "Oh, Louis," he said. "Right. You must be one of the fellows who dropped him off." He pressed the Up button, then took a handkerchief from his back pocket and polished away a finger smudge on the chrome plating. "Sometimes I'm not too good with faces."

"I was there when it happened," I said. "I'd like to know if he's all right."

Mr. Johnson shrugged and carefully refolded his handkerchief. "Well, he's sure got a nosebleed, I can testify to that," he said. "Went to pull him up out of the chair so the nurse could take his pressure, and man oh man—next thing I know, I gotta change my shirt." The door of the elevator opened, and I followed Mr. Johnson inside. "But I wouldn't worry too much," he added. "Louis'll bounce back all right, Lord willing."

"So you don't think he'll die or anything?" I asked.

Mr. Johnson shook his head as the elevator began to grind unevenly toward the second floor. "Well, I ain't the doctor," he said. "But I been here thirty-one years, and I never yet seen a body die of snakebite. Bees and spiders, yeah—they kill folks sometimes. Ticks, too, because they'll give you that disease. But snakes, naw—not in these parts. You'd have to be in pretty sad shape already for a snake to put you over the line, and that ain't the case with Louis. Hell, you couldn't kill that boy with ten hours and a two-by-four."

He stepped off the elevator and I trailed quietly along behind him, though I wasn't sure why. I followed him all the way to the end of the skilled-care wing, where the nursing-home patients lived, and waited outside the supply closet while he changed into a clean smock. When he came back out, he seemed annoyed to find me there.

"Look, friend," he said, "the doctor's who you need to talk to. Just give him about fifteen more minutes and I'm sure he'll be able to fill you in." He patted me on the shoulder and moved back down the hall to the nurse's station, where a woman with bright red lipstick and blue-gray hair stopped her typing to chat with him.

The elevator was down that hall, too, but I didn't want Mr. Johnson to think I was still following him around so I turned the other way like I had somewhere else to go. There was only one other room in that end of the wing—the community day lounge for the nursing-home patients. I'd been here a hundred times or more in just the last two years, although after my Grandmother Vann stopped recognizing me, I kind of fell out of the habit. Up until about three months ago the orderlies would still wheel her in here and park her in front of the television so she could stare at the game shows. That's where I'd usually find her—propped up in front of *Jeopardy* or *The Price Is Right*. She was practically a vegetable by then anyway, well beyond the question-and-answer format, so I thought it was kind of insensitive, really, having her watch those things. I mean, she couldn't even remember how to form words. How was she supposed to remember the capital of Madagascar, or guess the price of a new speedboat? How did they expect her to compete?

I walked into the lounge and looked around, half-expecting her to be there, though I knew they never bothered to take her out of her room anymore. Her body had curled up too much now to fit in the wheelchairs. I tried a couple of months ago to take her out for a ride—she'd spent her whole life in this county, so I thought she might like to have one last excursion around town. But there was just no way to do it.

Everything in the room was pretty much the way I remembered it. Red linoleum tile, metal folding chairs, two Formica tables littered with bingo cards and checkerboards. A couple of plastic potted plants. The same old walnut console television set was still wedged in the corner—though I'd never seen it turned off before. I'd also never seen the room empty before, and I noticed for the first time how bare the place looked. No fabric on any furniture, no cushions, no curtains, no rugs—nothing but hard surfaces for easy cleanup. That was understandable, I guess. I'd been here enough to know that all the furnishings in the nursing-home wing had to withstand daily doses of full-strength disinfectant.

The only softness, if you could call it that, came from the gauzy-looking artwork that lined the yellow cinder-block walls. Seascapes at dusk. Mossy trees leaning out over a green pond. Kids with big eyes. The two largest pictures were hung above the TV set, and both of those were technicolor paintings of a handsome and well-groomed Jesus, one with kids and one without. In the one with kids, he looked typically benevolent, but in the other he was throwing the money changers out of the temple and looking seriously upset. His hair in both scenes was a lot more blond than what you'd expect to find in his part of the world. I don't know why so many painters do that. I mean, it's hard enough to believe in Jesus as it is, without having him look like some Norwegian movie star doing a shampoo commercial.

My grandmother believed in Jesus more than she believed in her own name, but I didn't see where it helped her all that much. Her life still came down to the smallest portion I'd ever seen—twenty-four hours a day of lying completely still on a rubber bedsheet, an occasional sponge bath to clean away the accumulating filth, a feeding tube snaking nutrients into her arm, strangers turning her four times a day like a slow-cooking side of beef and smearing ointment on her bedsores. No relief but sleep, and no future but that short, final gurney ride to the freight elevators.

But what did I know? Maybe she was happier this way than she'd ever been in her life. Maybe she was off with Jesus in some dreamworld too good to come back from. Maybe she hadn't been watching those game shows at all—maybe she'd been watching the two Jesuses on the wall above the set.

Both of Laney's grandmothers had lived their last months in this wing, and both of them had held onto a fierce belief in Jesus that fueled every word they ever spoke. The second Jesus was the one they liked, the one who got angry. Miss Bessie was always quick to remind people that Jesus said he had come not to bring peace, but to bring a sword, and Miss Pearl would regularly croak out a loud tuneless version of "Onward Christian Soldiers." Laney used to visit them a couple of times a week, but she always came home mad—and I couldn't blame her. Miss Bessie and Miss Pearl were different people in a lot of ways, but they both had the same take on religion. For them Jesus was a stick to use on anybody they disapproved of, and they beat up on Laney every time she walked through the door. I used to think that if she hadn't been brought up with so many negative comparisons to Jesus, she wouldn't have had

such a wild streak in her. Then maybe she'd have settled down a little more.

But maybe I was just kidding myself.

Both her grandmothers were pretty frail for their last few
months, of course. That was the case with just about everybody
who wound up here. But they never lost a step mentally. Miss Bessie
broke her hip last October and died about three weeks later, and
Miss Pearl got a flu virus in January that killed her in just two days.
But their minds stayed sharp right to the end, which I thought was
the better way to go.

I walked back into the hallway and headed for the elevator, but
stopped at Room 19. The door was open—I don't know how I'd
passed right by it before and not noticed—and Grandmother Vann
lay on the bed facing me. Her mouth hung open in a tiny, toothless
circle, as if she were amazed. She didn't see me, though, I was sure
of that. Her eyelids fluttered a little, but her stare was empty. Her
knees were tucked up against her chest. The fetal position. Like she
was waiting to be born.

Funny, but before they turned this part of the hospital into the
county nursing home, it used to be the maternity ward. I was born
in a room somewhere along this very hallway. So was Laney, and so
was Steve Pitts. So was my little brother, Thomas Winston Vann,
who died here, as well—one of those sad mishaps people never feel
comfortable talking about. But I was twelve at the time, and the
truth is I didn't much care. I mean, sure, I understood it was a tragic
thing, and I acted the way I was supposed to around the grown-ups,
quiet and respectful. I even tried to make myself feel something, because I knew it meant I was a terrible person if I didn't. I called on
Jesus to help me out, to put pain in my heart so I could grieve like
the rest of them. But it was no use. Thomas Winston Vann was
never anything real to me. Just a name reserved on a place card for
a guest who didn't arrive.

That coldness was a hard thing to learn about myself. Like every
kid in my Sunday School class, I'd been taught that there was only
one right way, and that was to be a Jesus kind of guy. And Jesus

would have wept, that was certain, so I knew what a disappointment I was. Standing there at the front of the church beside my little brother's casket—that was the first time in my life I felt like maybe Jesus and I were playing on different teams—like he was the hotshot pitcher with the best record in the league, and I was some skinny nearsighted batter who couldn't knock the ball out of the infield, afraid to step up to the plate. Maybe that should have inspired me to be a better person. But it didn't. I just felt picked on by those invisible God-pounding forces of righteousness. Maybe that was the moment when I started my fall from grace. Or maybe I'd already fallen years earlier and just never noticed. In any case, part of me lost serious ground that day, and I never quite made up the distance.

I guess that's why I hadn't had much to say about Laney and Steve's upcoming baby. It was no more real to me than my own dead brother.

My mother's death was the only one I ever felt really crippled by. She died in the hospital the day after she'd set herself on fire, although it wasn't the fire that killed her. I'd gone up there to see her and she sent me on an errand to the drugstore for a particular kind of antihistamine. Said she had a head cold and couldn't breathe. She was real specific about what to get. I had no idea she was allergic to the stuff. It was like pumping pure venom straight into her heart.

The doctor said I shouldn't feel guilty. Said she knew exactly what she was doing. But I couldn't tell if that made me feel better or not.

I was in high school at the time, concentrating on Laney. Things were pretty good between us back then, but not even Laney could save me from that one. I remember thinking it was something I'd never get over.

I did get over it, of course. Another disappointment.

One thing I've noticed, though, is that I don't seem inclined to cry over big things anymore. I hear about wars or natural disasters or plane crashes on the news, and it's like I'm listening to baseball scores. Even the sorry state of my grandmother curled up on her rubber sheet doesn't make me feel much one way or another.

Instead, it's little stuff that sets me off, things that don't mean anything to anybody. Like I'll see some old lady pick up a candy wrapper from the sidewalk—something that trivial—and I'll get so choked up I can hardly breathe. Or some slow kid at the gas station will carefully count out the correct change on my five-dollar bill, and suddenly there'll be a lump in my throat so big I can't even say thanks. It's crazy. I don't know what ails me.

As I stood there in the doorway of my grandmother's room trying to invent reasons not to step inside, someone spoke my name from the room directly across the hall. I wasn't surprised—Lincoln was a small place, and most of the residents in the skilled-care wing were people I'd known from other times. Nearly every face there was a more weathered or stricken version of some face I'd always known, and my visits sometimes seemed like trips to an all-too-personal warehouse where the cast-off pieces of my life had come to be stored. My grade-school principal, Mrs. McDermitt, lived here now, as did Joe Riley, who coached me for three summers when I pitched for the American Legion ball team. Mr. Becker, the barber who gave me crew cuts as a kid, and Mrs. Lamb, who ran the refreshment counter at the Capitol Theatre, and Reverend Crabtree, who oversaw my confirmation and gave me my first Bible—all of them had found their way to this terrible last stop. Some, like my grandmother, were bedridden, but some could move around in wheelchairs, and a few could still inch along the hallway with aluminum walkers. Whenever I saw them, if they were awake, I always spoke first out of obligation, and usually they'd recognize me as Jimmy Vann's son and force out my name in hoarse, reedy voices. Sometimes, though, they'd be a little disoriented and mistake me for someone else, someone who had promised to do things for them, someone who had promised to take them away. Those were the times I hated. I couldn't get away without lying, or being rude, or pretending to be deaf.

I turned to see who had called my name and found Colonel Hereford trying to navigate a wheelchair through the door of his room. Colonel Hereford had the sharpest mind in the whole facility, and that included the nurses, but he was past ninety, and his body had finally started to shut down. The last time I'd been here, he had just made the transition from cane to walker, and now, apparently, even that option was gone. He eyes were still lively, but his spotted forearms poked out from the sleeves of his robe like thin, dry branches, and his left leg ended at mid-thigh. The chair's empty left footrest was caught on the door frame, so I tugged the apparatus a few inches to the side and rolled him forward into the hall.

" 'Preciate that, son," he said. "Cain't get this sumbitch to maneuver anymore. Seems like it gets bigger every goddamn day."

"It's the doorways, Colonel," I told him. "Doorways keep getting smaller all the time."

"Ain't that the truth," he said. He tilted his bald head toward the room behind him. "Hey, I saw your buddy run down that dogwood. That boy's got a problem."

I looked past his bed to the tall, light-filled window, where all the clutter of the room was concentrated. The sill was littered with what must have been the staples of the Colonel's life — an asthma inhaler, various medicine bottles, a small vial of pills, a bag of chocolate chip cookies, a half-empty glass of water, an overturned box of crackers, and a large pair of binoculars.

"Gave me chills to see him act that way," he said.

"Yeah, me too," I agreed. "But don't you worry about it. I'm sure the hospital'll put in a new tree before you know it."

He shook his head and tucked his robe neatly under the stump of his leg. "You must figure me for one of those old farts who stares at shrubbery all day. Well, I don't give a skunk's ass about dogwoods. What I'm talking about is a boy out of control. I've seen it too many times. He's got ditch panic."

"What's ditch panic?" I asked.

"What the hell you think it is? It's when you sit in a ditch too long, and you panic." He could see I didn't get it. "It used to happen to some of us in the war," he explained. "The Great War — you know about that one, don't you?"

"Yes, sir," I said. "We came out on top."

"So I've heard," said the Colonel. "But you know what they called it? The 'War to End All Wars.'" He arched a thin, white eyebrow and grinned. "Now tell me again if you think we won."

The paper had recently run a story on Colonel Hereford because he was the last surviving World War I soldier in the county, but he'd been famous long before anybody thought to write an article about him. As the ranking officer among all the local veterans, he was the one who had always headed up the town's holiday parades. In fact, I'd never been to a parade in my life that didn't have him at the front of it, waving to the crowd from a flag-draped white convertible. Always a white convertible. White was supposed to represent purity, as I understood it.

But it was clear that the Colonel was down to his last few parades, and his spot in the convertible would soon be up for grabs. After the Colonel the honor would go to someone from the Second World War. Possibly my father. He lacked the Colonel's rank, but he still had plenty of appeal as a local war hero—which for me was still about as mysterious a phenomenon as anything I'd encountered in the universe.

"What exactly do you know about that war?" the Colonel asked.

"Well, just a few highlights," I admitted. "The Argonne Forest. Dogfights. Mustard gas and the flu epidemic. The trenches."

"The trenches, that's right," he said, leaning forward in his chair, "that's what I'm talking about. We'd sit in those damned wet trenches until our feet turned gray. 'Course I was just a lieutenant back then, so there wasn't much I could do about the situation. But it was sure a lousy way to fight a war, I can tell you that much. You couldn't even peek over the edge because there'd be sharpshooters waiting for you to do just that. So all you had to look at was mud walls, or else the sky. Nothing in between. I don't know how to explain it, but people just aren't made to have their vision cooped up like that. The sky didn't count, because it wasn't anything solid to focus on." He pulled the front of his robe tighter across his chest as if the memory had made him cold. "You try to go a couple of weeks sometime with nothing but up-close mud to look at, you'll understand the strain I'm talking about."

The other thing the Colonel was famous for was his willingness to elaborate on his war experiences. More than a willingness, really. More like a determination. That in itself set him apart from most of the local veterans. Maybe it had something to do with his being a colonel, like that made him some sort of official spokesman for the horde of dead veterans under his command. I'd heard that the library had even sent somebody over with a tape recorder to turn him into one of their oral history projects, which I'm sure was fine with the Colonel. He'd been his own oral history project since before I was born.

With some effort he pushed his right wheel forward, pivoting the chair sideways so he could see back into his room. "Hell," he said, lifting his arm and extending a chalky finger toward the window, "that's why I still get a kick just looking out at the neighborhood. It's a true pleasure to do that and not have to watch for muzzle fire."

His arm began to shake from the weight of the gesture, and his breathing began to rattle in his throat. He shifted sideways in his seat and began to cough. I glanced down the hall, but the other residents were still in the cafeteria so I had no easy rescue from the conversation. I looked again at my grandmother, who held her same expression, and wondered if she knew how cooped up her own vision had become, wondered if the high point of her day was glimpsing shadows passing in the hall.

"Some fellas would get too antsy after a while," the Colonel went on, "and they'd pop their heads up for a quick look around. That always drew fire, like we were ducks in a shooting gallery, but if you were quick you could get away with it.

"Sometimes, though, it all just got to be too much—the cold, and the dysentery, and the skin rot, and the constant shelling—and then some old boy would just snap. Scramble up out of the trench like he was leading a charge. I'll tell you straight, you don't want to be around when that happens. A fella goes that crazy, he'll shoot anybody who's there. And you cain't ever second-guess him—he'll move opposite to whatever you might think. Like some kinda wounded animal."

I thought of the cottonmouth charging Louis in that steep-cut channel of the Elk—how crazy that was, how the way it happened was something none of us could have predicted.

I also thought of Jerry Rathburn.

"So you figure Steve Pitts has been stuck in the ditch too long?" I asked.

"Pitts?" The Colonel lifted his head and looked at me closely, then took a long, labored breath. "Might have known it was a Pitts. I knew that boy's granddaddy. Milo Pitts. Ran a gas station on Elk and Main. Used to cheat at cards. If I were you, I'd steer clear of anybody in that family. They've all been in the ditch too long. Hell, they're going on three generations."

"I appreciate the advice, Colonel," I told him. Then I pushed up my wet sleeve and looked at my watch. "Time for me to get back downstairs," I said, though condensation had clouded the watch face so I couldn't see the hands.

"Downstairs, right! That's what I meant to ask you," he said. "Who was that other boy you brought in?"

"Louis Elder. He got snakebit."

The Colonel frowned slightly and held it, as if he were trying to decide whether this news carried any weight for him or not. "Well," he said at last, "I'm not sure I know any Elders. But you can give him my regards."

"I surely will, Colonel," I said, and headed toward the elevator. As I stepped inside and turned to face the closing doors, I saw that the Colonel had already found a new audience. He had wheeled himself across to my grandmother's doorway and was perched awkwardly on the edge of his chair, telling her something. I guess I thought that was nice, though I couldn't imagine what he wanted to tell her. Bad news about her grandson, maybe. Dark dispatches from the war.

A lot passed through my mind on the short ride down. I wondered, as I always did when I left the skilled-care wing, if I had unknowingly said any last good-byes. Death was a fixture in places like this, as much as light sockets and plumbing. When my grandmother first applied for a room on this hall, she was twentieth on a waiting list. Three months later she moved in.

So I couldn't help but wonder. I wondered about my grandmother, and about Colonel Hereford. I wondered about Louis, and even about Grace.

Most of all, though, I wondered about Steve Pitts.

Colonel Hereford was an insightful man, and he did pinpoint a good portion of that particular problem. It was just like he said: Steve Pitts had ditch panic, and my best bet was to stay the hell out of his way. A reasonable assessment all the way around.

But there was one thing the Colonel hadn't figured into the equation. I don't know how he could have have missed it, what with my standing there all mud-spattered and stinking of river water. But Steve Pitts wasn't the only one who'd seen too many trench walls lately. I had a slight case of ditch panic myself.

There was no telling what either of us might do.

Monsters of the Midway

THE INSTANT WE GOT STUCK at the top of the Ferris wheel, my nephew Darwin began to cry. He'd been afraid to get on in the first place—this was his first county fair, and I guess he wasn't ready for the barrage to his senses. He'd held up pretty well through the livestock shows and the 4-H exhibits, but the carnival part turned out to be more than he could handle. Even the merry-go-round had frightened him.

But Donna had insisted that I take him up. She wanted him to love carnivals the way she used to, and she figured the Ferris wheel was the way to win him over. She thought once he got up there—up above the dazzle of the lights and that bullhorn blare of the calliope music, up where he could feel the cool night breeze on his face and look down at the spinning rides and screaming teenagers and side-show barkers calling everybody in—once he got safely up there above it all, he'd surely see how wonderful it was.

Donna's determination to make Darwin love carnivals was a pure mystery to me. She'd more than likely been raped here six years ago, the night she got runner-up for "Fairest of the Fair." As I understood it from Laney, Donna had been pretty upset about not winning and she got real drunk after the pageant. She woke up the next afternoon in a big cardboard box underneath the Tilt-A-Whirl. By the time she figured out she was pregnant, the fair was over and the carnival was long gone.

This year Donna had agreed to be one of the judges for that

same contest, which was why she and Darwin had come over from
Lynchburg. She'd gotten Darwin all worked up about the trip, too,
telling him what great fun he'd have on the carnival midway. By the
time they got here, the kid must have expected some kind of para-
dise. Now he was finding out what a carnival really was: raw material for about fifteen years' worth of nightmares.

It might have been easier for him if his mother had gone on the
rides with him instead of me. I didn't know how to talk to little kids
anymore—lately, everything I said seemed to come out stupid or
hostile. But Donna had developed some kind of ear infection that
gave her motion sickness—said if she got on any rides, even the slow
ones that barely did anything, she'd probably throw up. That was
why she'd called Laney—she needed somebody else along to help
Darwin cope with the fun parts. I guess it didn't occur to her that
Laney might have motion-sickness problems of her own, now that
she was however-many months pregnant. Anyway, the job finally
fell to me.

And that was fine, I was glad to be included. Until this Darwin
thing came up, Laney hadn't said a word to me all week, not since
the night I'd killed Randall.

That was how she saw it, too—not that Randall had died in a
freak window accident, but that I had killed him. When she saw me
there that night with Randall dead in my hands, she just went
nuts—screamed at me for ten solid minutes, then shut herself up in
our bedroom and cried for half an hour more. When she came out
she acted calm, but she avoided any eye contact, as if we were
strangers on the same late-night bus. She told me to go out into the
backyard and dig a hole for him, which I did even though it had
started to rain. She gave me a department-store Christmas box to
bury him in, which meant I had to make the hole twice as wide—but
I didn't dare complain. When I got down deep enough to frustrate
the neighborhood dogs, Laney came out to oversee the burial. She
stood there in the drizzle with no hat or umbrella while I set the box
into the hole and covered it up.

I was upset myself, but I knew better than to let on about it.

Sometimes there's just not enough grief to go around, and in the case of this dead 200-dollar lizard, Laney had the bigger claim by far. Still, I felt like I was supposed to say something, if only to show Laney that I wasn't a total jerk.

"He was a good lizard," I said, which I think would have been a safe enough observation if I hadn't stopped to think about it. But as I stood there in that dark yard with chilly rainwater running down the back of my neck and a stricken woman rooted in the broken sod across from me, it occurred to me that I had no idea what a good lizard was, that I had just made one of the most thoroughly ridiculous statements of my life. And I started to laugh.

I swear if Laney had had a gun she would have dropped me on the spot. It was too dark to see her face, but I didn't need to—I could feel her rage mushroom through the yard. But she didn't say a word, she just turned from the grave and stalked back to the house. She didn't even knock the wet dirt clods off her shoes before she went inside, that's how mad she was.

And that was the last exchange we'd had. Not another word about Randall, and not another word about my murderous insensitivity. No chitchat about groceries, or bills, or the weather. She never even mentioned the broken desk, which I took to be the worst sign of all.

Then Donna called, and suddenly my usefulness was restored.

Up to a point, anyway. This Ferris wheel had thrown everything back into question. I didn't know what to say to Darwin to calm him down, partly because I wasn't all that calm myself. Heights bother me, for one thing. Also, I happened to be a little bit familiar with the failure rate for carnival equipment, since my father once sold a group accidental-death-and-dismemberment plan to a small family-owned circus that passed through here a couple of years ago. I had to do the research on that policy—which is how I know that, even after you factor out the elephants, the lions, and the high-wire acts, the mortality tables for these traveling amusement parks make working as a crash dummy look like a better career option. Statistically speaking, Darwin and I were perched on top of about seventeen tons of stress-fractured, metal-fatigued steel that had been hastily bolted together by ex-convicts, dropouts, and drifters too stoned to hold down a regular job.

On the other hand, there was an interesting view. Laney and Donna had moved around back of the Ferris wheel, behind the power generator and away from the main traffic of the midway, and they were talking to some guy with an armful of oversized red teddy bears. Flirting, it looked like—they were both laughing and making a lot of gestures and leaning in close when they talked to him. They hadn't even noticed that Darwin and I were stalled at the top of a death trap—which was annoying. But at least they couldn't hear Darwin crying above the racket of the generator.

"It's okay, Darwin," I said. "There's nothing to be upset about. Just look how pretty everything is. This is the best seat in town."

"I want to get down!" he wailed.

"Look, there's your mama," I said, pointing down past his feet. "And your Aunt Laney."

"I want to get down!" he cried again. Then he wiped his nose on the sleeve of his T-shirt and peered over the safety bar. "Mama!" he yelled, "I want to get down!"

"Maybe we'll get you one of those big red bears," I offered. "Would you like that?"

"I don't want a red bear," he said, more sullen now than tearful.

That was a lucky break for me, because I wouldn't have known how to get him one. The big prizes were always just come-ons. I could probably have tossed softballs at milk cans until doomsday and still never won more than a refrigerator magnet. The guy talking with Laney and Donna was just a shill, I knew that—some local lowlife who'd hired himself out to walk the midway and brag about how easy it was to win the big red bears.

Jerry Rathburn used to do that, in fact. Jerry wasn't the kind of guy you'd run into at the hardware store on a Saturday morning, but if there was ever any nighttime action going on, some carnival or ball game or fair with a lot of people milling around with money in their pockets, he'd more than likely turn up. The last time I saw him alive was on this very midway, a couple of years back. He had a giant stuffed panda under each arm, with his elbows crooked tightly around their necks like he wanted them to hand over their lunch money. I was hanging around with a couple of my old ball-team buddies after the tractor pull, and Jerry came walking right up to us with a big scary smile on his face.

"Hey, Jerry," somebody said, "looks like you've had a good night."

"It does look that way," Jerry agreed, then he sort of half-laughed and half-coughed and looked over toward the penny-pitch booth, where a dozen more giant pandas were strung up on a rope beneath the canvas awning. "You boys ought to try your hand at that game right over there. Pick yourself up some nice prizes."

"That shit's all rigged," somebody else said.

Jerry's smile got a little more intense. "Everything's rigged, friend," he said. "But that don't mean you cain't still win a prize."

"Not me," I told him. "I never won anything in my whole damn life."

Jerry stared at me for a few seconds and nodded his head. Then he dug into his jeans pocket and pulled out a small handful of change. "Here you go, bud," he said, flipping a coin my way. "You just won yourself a lucky nickel." Then he laughed loud, and waded with his pandas back into the traffic of the midway.

But this new shill was even more generous than Jerry Rathburn. As Darwin melted down into a steady stream of loud honking sobs, I watched the shill hand over one of the red bears to Laney. She hugged it tight, then stepped forward and kissed the man. When she stepped away from him, he tipped his ball cap to Donna and walked around through the shadows to the front of the ride, giving the wheel operator a friendly slap on the shoulder as he passed by. When he got out to the bright center of the midway, he held his other bear up in front of him and waved a comical good-bye with its stumpy red arm. But he didn't seem to be waving at Laney and

Donna, who had moved around to the exit gate on the far side of the wheel. He seemed to be waving at me. That's when I realized the shill was Steve Pitts.

"Hey, Darwin," I said. "How'd you like to throw things down at the crowd?"

That got his attention, but he couldn't collect himself enough to say anything just yet. His little body shuddered as he heaved out a few more sobs, and his breathing stayed ragged while he rubbed his fists into his eyes to stop the tears. But after a minute he managed to calm himself down.

"What do you mean?" he asked. I could see by his frown that he suspected some kind of trick.

I took a box of cinnamon red hots from my shirt pocket and rattled it between us. Then I opened the flap and carefully shook a few pieces into his hand. "You can eat these if you want to," I said. "Or you can just pick out a target." He didn't hesitate at all, but just flung the entire handful straight ahead over the safety bar, raining candy on two teenage girls in the seat directly below us on the wheel.

"Hey, what the hell you think you're doing?" one of them yelled. She had big, puffy blond hair, teased into a sort of weather-proof hat, and now she prodded into it with her fingers to check for any red hots that might have lodged there. I hadn't seen hair like that in years.

"Sorry," I called down. "Just a little accident." Darwin looked up at me to see if he was in trouble. "Good shot," I told him, and he giggled. Then I poured some more red hots into his hand. "But you need to conserve your ammunition," I said. "Try just—" I was going to tell him to throw just one at a time, and to aim somewhere off to the side so he wouldn't bother the two girls. But apparently Darwin liked the game the way he was playing it, so before I could finish the instructions he'd already let loose with his second handful.

"Well, goddamn!" the girl said as the candy pelted her again. She turned in her seat and glared up at us. Darwin tucked his head against my side, hiding his face. "Mister, I don't appreciate this one bit," she said.

Mister. That was a word that always caught me by surprise, like I'd been mistaken for one of my father's gray-suited friends.

"My fault," I apologized. "It won't happen again."

"It better not," the girl warned, and Darwin squirmed closer.

"It won't," I repeated. "Here, you can have the rest of the box." I closed the flap and tossed the last of the red hots down to her. But apparently she hadn't expected that sort of friendly gesture, because instead of just catching the box she tried to duck out of the way, which wasn't really a possibility in a Ferris-wheel seat. The red hots stuck in her hair like a smokestack.

"Uh-oh," I told Darwin.

"Uh-oh," he agreed.

The girl snatched the box from her hair and whipped it over the side, away from the midway. It sailed out toward the equipment trailers and disappeared into the dark. The girl's companion started to laugh.

"It's not funny," the girl hissed. "I worked all day to get this look."

Her friend shook her head. "Dee Dee, that's not something I'd advertise," she said. She twisted around in her seat and smiled at Darwin and me. "Nice move, Nolan," she said.

I looked at her more closely. She was older than I'd thought, late-twenties maybe, with short red hair and an even spread of freckles across her cheeks and nose. She wore large tortoiseshell glasses that made her eyes look big, which was fine because they were a deep green and real pretty. "Do I know you?" I asked.

She laughed again. "That question kind of answers itself, don't you think? If you knew me, you wouldn't have to ask."

"Don't talk to him, Alma," the younger one said. "The guy's a creep."

Alma. I didn't know anybody named Alma.

"Yeah, I know he's a creep," she said cheerfully. "He's a lousy dancer, too. Moves like he's got snowshoes on his feet." She turned her attention to Darwin. "And what's your name, sugar?"

Darwin squealed and tried to burrow in behind me.

"No, really," I said. "Do I know you from somewhere?"

The Ferris wheel lurched forward a few feet and stopped. Down below, the ride operator lifted the safety bar and let the first group off.

"*Oklahoma!*," she said.

"I've never been to Oklahoma," I told her.

"Not the state, Nolan, the musical. We were in the chorus together. Dance partners. Mrs. Witt paired us up for a couple of the big production numbers."

Darwin emerged from beneath my arm and began to wiggle on the seat with his hands in the air. "I'm Darwin," he announced. "I'm a good dancer."

Oklahoma! had been a real low point for me in high school. Laney had talked me into trying out—I think she figured that because we had this hot romance going, we'd probably get cast as the leads. But neither one of us had any talent, so Mrs. Witt stuck us in the chorus where we couldn't do much damage. Laney almost quit after the first week, but then we started rehearsing with the orchestra and she got interested in Bob Sheffield, who played the trumpet.

"What's your last name?" I asked.

"Polk. But it used to be McGilivray. I was three years behind you."

"Oh, sure," I said, certain that I knew the McGilivray name from high school. But I seemed to know the Polk name from somewhere, too. "I thought you looked familiar, Alma. How've you been doing?"

She shrugged. "You ought to know, Nolan. Last Tuesday you repossessed my car."

"He took your car?" the blond asked.

Alma Polk. A fifteen-year-old Dodge Omni, high mileage, poor condition. Current wholesale of about 200 bucks, and she owed 350. Dell did all the talking while I carried the clipboard and pretended to study the paperwork. I barely looked at the woman on the porch because I felt too embarrassed about what we were doing. I mean, when we took away somebody's old junker, we knew we were hurting them bad. It wasn't like repossessing Corvettes or Camaros or Trans Ams—those were all idiot cars, oversized toys bought by kids too stupid to keep track of the payments. But a beat-up Omni—Jesus, that was about as pathetic as it could get.

"I'm . . . sorry to hear that," I said.

Alma took off her glasses and arched her eyebrows, and for a second I could have sworn I remembered that look from years before, not from Alma McGilivray but from Mrs. Witt herself, who always seemed affronted when I missed a step in her choreography. "Sorry to *hear* it?" Alma said. "Honey, you were *there.*"

The wheel swung forward again, dipping Darwin and me all the way to ground level and moving Alma and her friend up behind us. The operator lifted the bar and Darwin scrambled out of the seat and charged down the exit ramp toward his mother. I looked back at Alma as I stepped off the ride. She brushed a couple of red hots off her lap, then draped her arm over the side of the seat and gazed casually out at the midway. Her friend, meanwhile, continued to glare at me.

"So long," I said, but neither woman answered. I wanted to say something more, but as I stood there trying to figure out what it was, the operator ushered a pair of pimply teenage lovebirds into my former seat, and the wheel rotated Alma a few more spaces away. I turned and walked down the ramp toward Laney.

She and Donna and the big red bear were all huddled over Darwin, who seemed to be giving an animated account of his ride. Donna carried the bear.

"Thanks, Nolan," she said as I joined them at the gate. "He loved it."

"It looks like he's been crying," Laney pointed out. She bent down close to Darwin and rubbed a thumb across his flushed, tear-stained cheek. "Sweetie, is everything okay?" she asked him.

Darwin looked to me for the answer.

"We were a little nervous at first," I said. "But we got over it, didn't we, pal?"

"We sure did!" Darwin said.

"Do you want to go again?" Donna asked. "It's all right if you do." She checked her watch. "Mommy's still got some time before the contest."

Darwin pretended to think about it, then shook his head.

"I think he wants to try out some of the other stuff," I said. "We saw a lot of fun things from the Ferris wheel, didn't we, Darwin?"

"Whose bear is that?" he asked.

Donna seemed suddenly surprised by the bear in her arms, like it was a party guest she'd neglected to introduce around.

"Why, this is yours, sweetheart," she said, presenting Darwin with the bear. She glanced at me, then held the bear steady while Darwin hugged its enormous head. "The carnival people gave him to Mommy for helping them with their beauty pageant," she said.

A gift to Donna from the carny people. That was probably more true of Darwin than it was of the red bear, and I almost said so, I felt that reckless. But Donna wasn't really the one I was mad at, so I just let it pass.

"What would you like to do next, sweetie?" Laney asked.

Darwin peered around the side of his new bear and then pointed to the brightly painted trailer across from the Ferris wheel. "There!" he shouted. "I want to go there!"

The large cutout sign propped along the roof of the trailer read MONSTERS OF THE MIDWAY in tall, wavy black letters. The trailer front itself was decorated with exotic airbrushed paintings of all sorts of human oddities—a wolfman, a skeleton-like ghoul, a massively obese woman, a pinheaded man. One painting showed a wide-eyed penguin-boy with normal-looking hands and feet, but no arms or legs. Another showed a lovely but forlorn giraffe-girl with a tragically elongated neck. There was a voluptuous bikini-clad woman who boasted four oversized breasts, and a sad-sack daddy longlegs man who had no torso at all.

SEE THE MOST HIDEOUS FREAKS OF NATURE! read the come-on above the door. EXPERIENCE THE HORROR OF GROTESQUE SUBHUMAN DEFORMITY! BEAR WITNESS TO THE WORLD'S MOST GRUESOMELY MISSHAPEN CREATURES!

Donna looked seriously concerned. "But that's not a ride, baby," she told him. "That's something else. That's what they call a freak show. You don't want to see that, do you?"

"I think it's just a funhouse," I told Donna. "The real freak shows are usually someplace off to the side. They don't like to put them on the midway." She and Laney both gave me a sharp look.

"I want to see the funhouse!" Darwin yelled.

Donna bit her lip and looked around for a more suitable alternative. "How about those cute little boats?" she suggested, pointing to one of the mildest of the kiddie rides. But I knew she'd never get him to go for anything that lame again, not after sending him up on the Ferris wheel.

"I want to see the funhouse!" he yelled again.

"Fine," Donna snapped. "Then you can take him, Nolan, since you know so much about it."

"I'll hold your new friend, sweetie," Laney said, pulling the bear from his arms. I took Darwin by the hand and the two of us threaded our way through the crowd toward what I earnestly hoped was just a funhouse. The last thing I needed right then was an honest-to-god freak show. I'd already seen more than my share of the grotesque and the subhuman, just on a daily basis.

"Two tickets each," said the shirtless, tattooed man sitting on a stool at the entrance. Separate strands of blue-inked ivy stretched up each of his arms, then spread across his shoulders and twined together around his throat. The vine on his left had thorns.

"Is the Wolfman in there?" Darwin asked as I handed over our tickets.

The man flicked his cigarette toward a tangled mass of electrical cables at the edge of the midway. "Sorry, kid," he said, "It's Wolfman's day off."

"What about the boy with no arms?" Darwin asked.

"Huh? Oh, yeah, yeah, sure," the man said, stifling a yawn. "Got all kinds of shit in there. Scare the crap outta ya."

Darwin gripped my hand tighter and we stepped inside.

The place was pretty much what I'd expected: a maze of mirrored hallways and glass walls. Some of the mirrors were normal, but others had curved surfaces so the reflections they threw back were distorted in all sorts of ways. Darwin had never seen anything like it, and he was delighted. He let go of my hand and danced from mirror to mirror, posing and making faces and hooting at all the different deformities he could conjure up in the glass. By the time we'd moved through to the last mirror, he'd turned himself into nearly every freak we'd seen on the outside trailer wall, even the penguin-boy.

As we came in sight of the exit I spotted Donna and Laney waiting out front. Donna waved when she saw us, and Darwin raced forward to tell his mother all about what he'd seen. But the exit doorway turned out not to be an exit after all—it was a Plexiglas barrier, the final joke of the funhouse, and Darwin hit it at full stride. He bounced backward and fell down, leaving me a clear view of the opposite reactions on the two women's faces: involuntary fear and involuntary laughter.

For a few short moments Darwin was stunned into silence. Then he sat up awkwardly, took a deep breath, and launched into a long, ear-splitting wail. I scooped him up and maneuvered him through the real doorway to the outside, where Donna met us on the exit ramp. I passed him into her arms, and he clutched her around the neck and wailed louder, so loud that even passersby on the midway turned to look. A scraggly teenage couple paused behind Donna and looked from Darwin to the funhouse to each other. "Let's give this place a try," the boy said, and the girl cuddled against his side.

Laney hung back with the crowd, waiting for the tiny drama to pass. Her arms were folded around the red bear, and she'd scoured away all traces of her first response, looking now like the stern and unwavering good aunt, the one who disapproved of Uncle Nolan's failure to take proper care of little Darwin. For his part, Darwin finally eased into a lower, less hysterical cry, and Donna was able to pry him from her neck and check him for damage.

"Baby, are you okay?" she asked. She set him down and wiped the tears from his cheeks with her fingers.

"I hit my head!" he cried.

"I know, baby, I saw you," she said. "But you're all right now." Donna took some toilet paper from her purse and held a wad of it to Darwin's nose. "Blow," she instructed him, then she wiped his face and tossed the tissue aside. "There," she said. "All better."

Darwin sniffled somberly, and nodded his head. "I need a snow cone," he told her.

"Then we'll get you one, baby." She picked him back up and turned to me. "I'll go clean him up a little," she said, "and get him his snow cone. We'll meet y'all down by the grandstand." She shifted Darwin's weight to her hip and checked her watch. "I've just got ten minutes," she said, "so look for me." Then she shouldered her way back into the flow of the crowd, and let it carry her toward the concession stands at the far end of the midway.

Laney still hadn't moved from her spot, so I threaded my way over to her. "Darwin won himself a snow cone," I told her. "We're supposed to meet them down by the grandstand." Laney nodded, and since I couldn't think of anything else safe to say, I just stood there beside her, watching people go by. I wished she weren't still carrying that bear.

"I couldn't help but laugh when he hit that wall," she said. "God, I felt just terrible. Donna didn't say anything, but I know she was pissed."

"Oh, I doubt she even noticed," I said. "Anyway, I don't know why she'd want to bring Darwin out here in the first place."

"To show him his father," Laney said matter-of-factly, and she strolled away toward the grandstand.

"I thought that was a mystery," I said, following along after her. "Who's it supposed to be?"

Laney shrugged. "Anybody who looks like Darwin, I guess." She laughed. "Why do you think Donna's so touchy about those freak shows? She's afraid she'll see a family resemblance in some two-headed goat-man with wings."

"Well, none of these folks look like prizewinners to me," I said, glancing toward the row of gambling booths where so many of the carny workers were on display. "It might be better not to know."

"It's always best to know," Laney said, a slight weariness in her voice. "Anyhow, none of this was Donna's idea. Daddy put her up to it."

My father-in-law, Barnett, was a hog farmer from the south end of the county. He was a pretty solid sort of fellow, low-key and hard-working, but he'd always made me uncomfortable. I first met him when I was a junior and Laney and I had just started to date. I remember I came out to the house to pick her up for a school dance, and while I waited for her in the front room, Barnett walked through three or four times in his underwear. The last time through he had a deer rifle slung over his shoulder. But I had to give him credit, I sure as hell got his daughter home on time.

"What's your daddy have to do with it?" I asked.

Laney shook her head. "He told her he quit having nightmares about D-Day after he went back to Omaha Beach and walked around awhile. Said seeing the place in a different circumstance somehow made him feel more peaceful about everything, even about all his war buddies who got killed there. He figured a trip back to the carnival might do the same thing for Donna."

"I don't know," I said. "Sounds like a stretch to me."

"Yeah, well, Daddy ain't exactly a board-certified psychiatrist, that's for sure. But once he got the idea, he wouldn't let go of it. Hounded Donna all week—even called up the pageant people and got her put on the judges' panel. She finally gave in." Laney sighed. "Daddy means well. We're just lucky he didn't tell her to burn all her clothes and join the Marines."

She stopped and pointed past the Scrambler to one of the small sideshow tents, where a cluster of people stood waving hand-lettered poster-board signs. "Blasphemy!" one of signs proclaimed. "Cruelty to animals!" read another.

"What do you figure that's all about?" she asked.

"Looks like some kind of protest at the geek show," I told her, and right away I had a pretty good idea what was going on. I scanned the crowd for familiar faces, and sure enough, there was Brother Willis on a soapbox off to the side, preaching something through a megaphone to the protesters, who waved their signs in full support of whatever he was saying. I spotted Grace in the crowd, too, propped up on crutches, with Sammy by her side.

"I've never been to a geek show," Laney said. "Let's go take a look."

"Save your money," I told her. "I've seen a few, and they're all pretty much the same—just some guy in a jungle suit pretending he's the Wild Man of Borneo."

"What do you mean?" she asked. "What does he do?"

"Well, basically he just jumps around and makes animal noises—you know, like he was raised by wolves or something. Then at the end he bites the head off a chicken."

"You're kidding," she said. "A chicken?"

"Well, usually it's a chicken," I told her. "But some do snakes instead. I imagine that's what all the fuss is about. This geek's probably a snake-eater."

"I get the cruelty-to-animals part," she said, nodding to the protesters. "But where's the blasphemy come in?"

"With Brother Willis," I said, pointing out the small black-suited man barking at the crowd. "That's him and his congregation out front. I guess he figures the geek stole his act."

"Mama told me we had snake-handlers in the county, but I didn't believe her," Laney said. "I've got to check this out."

"We're supposed to meet your sister," I reminded her, but she was already headed for the sideshow.

I was reluctant to follow her over. Grace and Sammy were a couple of loose wires in my life right then, and if they said the wrong thing to Laney, all the lies I'd been telling her could short-circuit. On the other hand, this was the first time in weeks Laney and I had gotten along, and I didn't want to be the one to break off the conversation. I edged along after her, hoping to go unnoticed among the mob of believers.

But there was no need to tiptoe—everyone's attention was riveted on Brother Willis, and nothing short of a sonic boom could have broken their concentration.

"The serpent is the instrument of the Lord!" he was shouting, "and no man shall defile what the Lord has deemed useful!" A murmur of agreement rippled through the crowd. "Even as Jesus loved Judas who stung him," he went on, "we got to tame that serpent's heart with our courage and our steadfast love. The Almighty God is with us on this point, brothers and sisters, I guarantee it!" Several people applauded, and a few others added amens. Brother Willis pointed an accusatory finger at the carny geek's tent. "This house will be brought down!"

A big man in jeans and a black Harley-Davidson T-shirt stepped out of the tent waving his hands in the air, the same way Mrs. Witt used to when she needed to interrupt a bad rehearsal. "Now hold on there, pardner," he said. "I don't mind you drawing a crowd, but don't go pushing things too far."

Laney turned to me. "This is cool," she said. "Maybe there'll be a fight."

"Not much chance of that," I told her. "The sheriff'll shut them both down if there's any real trouble, and they know it."

"Maybe so," she said. "But nothing puts a brain in neutral like a dose of religious frenzy."

Laney was right, of course—anything might've happened. What did happen, though, still came as a surprise. Brother Willis reached into his inside coat pocket and pulled out a young cottonmouth, probably the same one that had been in Grace's cooler there on the riverbank. It was a neat trick—I don't know how he managed it without getting snakebit. He held the cottonmouth high above his head, and the snake opened its jaws, showing its white inner throat to the crowd.

"This is the sign of the believer!" he shouted into his megaphone, and the congregation roared its approval. "And those who doubt will taste the serpent's venom!"

The man from the geek tent just smiled and ducked back inside. When he came out again he had a serpent of his own, a young hognose, which was an easy snake to handle because it'll always play dead around trouble. "Here you go, folks," the man said. "I'll show you how to taste the serpent's venom!" As all eyes turned his way he savagely bit the head off the hognose and spit it at the crowd. A thin stream of blood squirted from the snake's ragged neck, while the tail end thrashed back and forth from some useless reflex. "Tastes like chicken!" the man laughed, and then disappeared into his tent.

I believe Brother Willis could have touched off a riot right then, if he'd wanted to—and I did see the temptation flicker across his face. Instead, he paused to collect himself, and then sadly shook his head. "This poor man is obviously sick," he told the crowd, gesturing toward the tent with his cottonmouth. "Let's all just stop for a minute and pray for his soul." He dropped the megaphone to the ground, folded his free hand over the poisonous snake, and stared serenely into the night sky. Several people murmured their admiration, then the whole congregation settled into a cattle-like stillness and joined Brother Willis in silent prayer.

Laney looked at me and raised her eyebrows. "They sure put on a better show than the Presbyterians," she whispered. "And that preacher's got the beatific look down pat."

"Time to go," I suggested. Laney took my arm, which surprised me, and we moved back toward the midway.

"I tell you all," shouted Brother Willis, his voice reedy and more distant without the megaphone, "when evil strikes us low in the belly, the Lord don't leave us sucking wind! He comforts us with goodness all around!"

I didn't bother to look back, but Laney did, and she pulled me to a quick stop. "Hang on a second," she said. "He's revving up again."

"Look around you, friends," Brother Willis cried. "We're all angels in each other's paths, no matter who we are! The Lord makes helpers of us all, no matter how we try to hide! Even this brute," he said, nodding toward the geek tent, "this brute who bites the heads off God's creatures is still yoked in service to the Lord, whether he knows it or not! Remember, friends, even the Disciple Matthew was once a tax collector!" While the crowd added a chorus of amens, Brother Willis paused to tuck the cottonmouth back inside his coat. Then someone handed up his megaphone, and he continued in his louder, more artificial voice. "Even the least among us is blessed," he said, carefully eyeing the crowd. Then he raised his arm and pointed. "Just look at that man there!"

The congregation turned to see who else besides the geek had earned Brother Willis's attention. I tried to pull Laney away, but it was too late. Everyone was already staring at me.

"Nolan," Laney said under her breath. "I think he means you."

"That man," shouted Brother Willis, "that very man who invades our homes to repossess our worldly goods,"—he paused for emphasis—"is the selfsame man who leaps into the river to repossess our brethren from the serpent's jaws!" A few people offered hallelujahs, Grace and Sammy the loudest among them. Apparently Grace had made some effort to repair my reputation in her circle of friends. "So don't be telling me the Lord don't work in mysterious ways!" Brother Willis went on. "If that man can do good works, so can we all!"

Then Brother Willis tucked the megaphone under his arm and applauded in my direction, an approving grin filling his face. The rest of the congregation joined in. I forced a weak smile and waved back politely.

"What the hell's he talking about?" Laney asked.

"Must be some kind of parable," I said. "Let's get out of here before they start handing out free snakes." I pulled her into the midway traffic and hustled her along toward the grandstand.

"That didn't sound like any parable I ever heard," she said as I guided us through the crowd.

"Sure it did," I insisted.

"Which one?"

"All of 'em."

"*All* the parables?"

"Well, no, not all. Just, you know, the ones about rivers and snakes."

I didn't think she took that as an acceptable answer, but at least it confused her enough for me to get us all the way down to the corn-dog wagon without any more questions. By that time we could see Donna waiting with Darwin at a side entrance to the grandstand, just across from the American Legion bingo tent.

"You wouldn't believe what we just saw," Laney began, but Donna cut her off.

"Honey, I ain't got time to believe anything. They already started the pageant parade." She passed Darwin over to me since Laney's arms were still taken up by the bear, and then she brushed down some of the wrinkles in her blouse. "Don't let him have any more candy," she instructed. "And for God's sake don't take him to any more of those freak shows. He's all mixed up about the monsters."

"*I'm* the monster!" Darwin chimed in happily. "I'm *all* the monsters! Tell her, Uncle Nolan!"

"All but the Wolfman," I agreed, and Donna gave me a not-too-playful slap across the arm.

"Behave yourself, Nolan," she said. "He don't need any more bad examples."

"It's Wolfman's day off!" Darwin giggled, and Donna frowned at me as if I'd said it.

"I'll keep these two in line," Laney promised.

She gave Laney a quick, tight hug, and I began to see how nervous she was about going off alone. "All right, then, folks," she said. "I'll meet y'all back here soon as we pick a winner. Shouldn't be but about an hour." She pinched Darwin on the cheek. "Bye now, precious," she said. "Be good for your Aunt Laney and your Uncle Nolan." Then she hurried off through the livestock tunnel to the front of the stands.

B-4! blared the loudspeaker from the bingo tent. *That's B-4!*

"Well, what now?" Laney asked.

"I wanna go back to the funhouse!" Darwin said. He made a monster face and growled, wiggling his fingers in the air like claws.

"Let's try this end of the carnival for a while, sweetie," Laney suggested. "There's a lot we haven't seen."

G-41! The number is G-41!

Darwin dropped his monster act and scowled at her. "Like what?" he asked.

"Like that over there," I said, pointing to the bronze pedestal and plaque outside the bingo tent. "You know what that is?" Darwin shook his head. "That's a memorial for a plane crash. Except for the grandstand, that's the only part of the whole carnival that stays here all year."

"What plane crash?" Darwin asked, still wary.

N-32! That's N-32.

"A bad one," I told him. "It happened right here, right where we're standing."

Darwin looked at the ground around our feet for some sign of destruction. "How do you know?" he asked.

"I was here when it happened," I said. "I was just about your age, and my mama and daddy had brought me out here for the county fair. There was this fella giving rides in a biplane for five dollars."

"What's a biplane?" he asked.

"It's an old-timey kind of airplane with two sets of wings," I explained, and Darwin nodded as I carried him over to the memorial. "They used biplanes back in World War I, and this man here—" I pointed to the name at the top of the list of the dead—"Captain Edward W. Wheatley had been what they call a flying ace, which means he shot down a lot of enemy planes in the war."

"Look at this," Laney said, touching the dates by his name. "The guy was seventy years old when he crashed. What the hell was he doing up in a biplane at that age?"

"Maybe that was all he knew how to do," I suggested.

Laney frowned at the plaque. "That's a piss-poor reason to risk people's lives. He probably had a heart attack or something."

"More likely it was just bad eyesight," I said. I pointed into the sky at the far end of the midway. "He came in along there and hit a power line they'd strung up for the new grandstand lights. The plane nose-dived right into the crowd. Right on this spot."

While Darwin scanned the night sky for planes, I shifted his weight to my other arm and watched Laney as she studied the account on the face of the memorial.

B-1! B-1!

"Did people die?" Darwin asked.

"Yeah, they did," I told him. "About half a dozen."

"I can't believe how long it's been," Laney said. "That was when Darlene McAllister got killed. She was my first Sunday School teacher." She traced her finger across a row of raised bronze letters. "That's her name right there," she told Darwin.

"Who put it there?" he wanted to know.

"The American Legion," I said. "The same folks who run this bingo tent."

"Why?" he asked.

I shrugged. "It's just something they do for people sometimes," I told him. That was a lame answer, I knew. Laney knew it, too, and tried to help out.

"Memorials are for people who shouldn't have died," she explained.

Wasted lives—that got pretty close to it, all right. It wasn't the whole answer, of course. Patriotism had to figure in somewhere. I knew that from all the other bronze tablets I'd encountered over the years. And everything the Legion did, it did under the banner of patriotism. But there was no need to confuse Darwin with that carnival pitch just yet.

"We can go in and play bingo if you like," Laney offered.

Darwin looked at the drab, yellow tent, then shook his head. "I wanna go back to the funhouse!" he said.

O-55! The number is O-55!

Laney wandered over to the tent opening and eased the flap aside with the bear head. "Hey, Nolan," she said, "look at who's calling bingo tonight."

I carried Darwin over and ducked beneath the flap. The smoky tent was crowded with row after row of folding tables and gray metal chairs. Every seat was taken, and people lined the tent walls waiting for spots to open up. Down front, decked out in a white straw boater and red arm garters, looking like the turn-of-the-century, barbershop-quartet singer he'd always wanted to be, my father stood smiling before the crowd, spinning a giant red, white, and blue bingo wheel and calling the numbers into a microphone when they came up.

B-17, announced my father, *That's B-17!* Then he stepped away from the wheel and grinned at the crowd.

"Hey, what gives, Jimmy?" someone finally called out. "There ain't no *B-17*."

Well, of course there ain't, Virgil, he said into the microphone. *The B-17s got decommissioned when the B-24s came along!* Some of the older men laughed, and my father gave the wheel another spin.

"Looks like he's having a good time," Laney said, folding her arms more tightly around the bear. "Maybe when he goes on break, you could ask him about getting your job back."

I-19, called my father as the big wheel clicked to a stop. *That's I-19!*

I lowered Darwin to the straw-covered dirt, suddenly dizzy in the stale, humid air of the tent.

I-19, my father called again, more insistently this time, and the whole room held its breath, waiting for someone to bingo.

The Fifty-third Sermon

REVEREND SINCLAIR HAD SHRIVELED UP a lot since the last time I'd seen him preach. That was five years ago at Darwin's baptism—which remains the only time I've ever seen Laney inside a church. Except, of course, for the day we got married. Church services of any kind have always given her the creeps. The only reason she showed up for the baptism was that Donna had picked us to be Darwin's godparents, so she couldn't get out of it.

I'm not sure why she showed up for our wedding.

Anyway, for this one Sunday I'd returned to the fold—not to reconcile with Jesus, but with my father. Laney figured church would be the best place to catch him with his guard down. The idea, I guess, was for me to wait for some opportune moment of holy rapture and then ask for my job back.

Reverend Sinclair was still as loud and red-faced as ever, which was the way people liked him. His sermon was one of my father's favorites: *Most Accidents Happen in the Home.* That was the one about how we all inadvertently hurt the people we love, although I think my father just liked the insurance undertones that went along with it.

I used to enjoy that sermon myself, but after the first eight or nine times it had started to wear thin. Reverend Sinclair only kept fifty-two regular sermons in stock, and they'd been in a permanent rotation since before I was born. We all knew his themes by heart.

But there was also a wild card—a fifty-third sermon that cropped up now and again, whenever a leap year or the natural fall of days put an extra Sunday on the calendar. We never knew what to expect from that floating fifty-third, because it was always something different, some offbeat ecclesiastical experiment. My favorite was the most infamous, the one he'd delivered during the Vietnam War. I don't know if Reverend Sinclair really knew what he was doing or if that particular fifty-third was just a rush job that he bungled, but whatever the case, it was the most original effort of his career. It was called *Don't Blame God, He's Only Human,* and the gist of it was that human beings were God's way of finding out what it was like to make mistakes.

That was a risky premise to spring on a hard-core Bible Belt audience, but he still might have pulled it off if he hadn't brought in politics. It was the week of that year's draft lottery, I remember, and all the boys in town with numbers below 120 had suddenly found themselves likely candidates for the rice paddies. Reverend Sinclair, in a total misreading of community sentiment, used the war as an example of human error on its grandest scale.

The congregation was appalled. The universal feeling at the time—at least around Lincoln—was that if Vietnam fell, all the other dominoes of Southeast Asia would go tumbling after, and anybody who spoke out against current policy was almost certainly a spy for Chairman Mao. The local DAR even went so far as to publish an open letter of protest in the county paper. Those ladies knew how to play hardball, too—the letter was addressed to J. Edgar Hoover, whom they admired as the finest straight-arrow of all living Americans, and it suggested that if the FBI didn't already have a file on Reverend Sinclair, now might be a good time to start one.

But the Reverend had already learned his lesson about the separation of Church and State, and after a great deal of behind-the-scenes backpedaling he was able to repair most of the damage. A few families did switch their membership to Second Presbyterian, but the bulk of the congregation remained intact. That particular fifty-third sermon was never heard from again.

But on this more peaceful Sunday, as I sat listening to Reverend

Sinclair proclaim once more the benefits of harmonious family rela-tionships, it occurred to me that maybe Laney had been right in sending me to church to ambush my father. Surely if there could ever be a time when he might feel inclined toward forgiveness, it would be right here, in this particular sanctuary, in the familiar afterglow of this particular sermon.

I also found myself relieved that Laney hadn't come with me. Religion was a destabilizing topic with her, which probably meant she was a prime candidate for a conversion experience, and that was the last thing we needed. Our marriage may have been blud-geoned into a coma, but it was still breathing. If Laney were to get caught up in Reverend Sinclair's boneheaded enthusiasm for open channels of communication, we might as well unplug the machine. The only thing keeping us together right now was the fact that we weren't prying ugly confessions out of each other. I don't care what the preachers or the advice columnists say—sometimes it takes a good tangle of lies to keep a relationship going, the same way ivy can hold the loose bricks of a crumbling chimney together.

She'd already broken the protocol by letting me know she knew I'd been fired. But I wasn't about to compound the error by men-tioning Steve Pitts. Damage control, that's what this trip to church was all about. If I could get myself rehired, we might all be able to carry on like nothing had ever happened.

Except for Laney's pregnancy. That was still the joker in the game. The fifty-third card in the deck.

What my chances were with my father, I couldn't have said—I was sitting two rows directly behind him, and there wasn't much expression on the back of his head. He was in the same pew our family had always occupied when I was growing up, but in the spot where my mother and I used to sit was the brown-suited bulk of Morgan Motlow.

I was surprised to see Morgan there. This time of year he usually spent his Sunday mornings on the golf course, playing his regular game—ten bucks a hole, double on birdies, with automatic presses and carryovers. I'd filled in with Morgan's bunch one week when

Eddie Parks had pneumonia, and I shot the best round of my life. It still cost me $326.

The last time I'd seen Morgan in church was at my mother's funeral, where he was a pallbearer. Morgan had known both my parents since grade school, and like everybody else, he'd been pretty shocked when she killed herself. We got our share of unnatural deaths in this county—hardly a Saturday night went by without somebody losing his last bar fight—but suicides weren't common at all.

It made for a quiet funeral, too. I mean, when a woman sets herself on fire and then finishes off the job with drugs, there's not that much you can safely say to the family. But everybody there must have wondered: *Had her situation been that terrible? Had she been that weak? Had she been that crazy? Were there secrets in her life she just couldn't bear to know?*

Did she have a lousy husband?

Did she have a lousy son?

In a sudden silence, I realized that Reverend Sinclair had wrapped up his sermon and was coming out from behind the pulpit to lead us in the Gloria Patri. He nodded to the organist, and we began:

> *Glory be to the Father.*
> *And to the Son,*
> *And to the Holy Ghost.*
> *As it was in the beginning,*
> *Is now, and ever shall be,*
> *Word without end. Amen, amen.*

Of course, that version was unique to our Associate Reformed Southern Presbyterian congregation. Everywhere else in the Christian universe that last line was sung *World* without end, not *Word*. But in 1967 our A.R.S.P. Council of Elders voted eleven-to-two to change it, reasoning that "Word" was a more spiritual concept. They also moved the offering to the end of the service, when people's resistance would be more worn down.

But they weren't a totally radical council: they did hold the line on "trespasses" in the Lord's Prayer, even though "debtors" was coming widely into fashion. I remember feeling glad, too, when I heard that decision. I guess in those days I was more concerned with my trespasses than I was with my debts.

After the Gloria Patri, we slid right into the Doxology:

> *Praise God from whom all blessings flow.*
> *Praise Him all creatures here below.*
> *Praise Him above, ye Heavenly Host.*
> *Praise Father, Son, and Holy Ghost.*

Father, Son, and Holy Ghost. I'd grown up with a version of that. But ours was a pretty lopsided trinity. My mother always knew she'd been miscast.

Then the choir launched into a hymn I dimly recognized, while a few deacons got up and passed the offering plate. I put in two bucks, one for me and one for the ghost. Reverend Sinclair stepped back behind the pulpit and gave the benediction, then told us all to go in peace, which officially ended the service.

But before anybody could make a move he announced that the elders had some business matters to bring before the congregation, so we should all just stay put for a few minutes. A dozen or so elders rose and walked to the front of the sanctuary—my father and Morgan among them—and Reverend Sinclair handed his lapel microphone down to Govy Haislip, who ran the Army-Navy Surplus store just off the square.

"As many of you know," Elder Haislip began, "we've been approached again by the National Council to consider merging with the United Church of Christ. Our closest denominational cousin, Presbyterian Church–USA, has already become a U.C.C. affiliate, much the same way we saw the Methodists merge a few years back with United Brethren. There might be some financial advantages in the merger, although we could end up with some unwanted liturgical changes. So think it over, and when you get your ballot in the mail, just check whether you want the Associate Reformed Southern Presbyterian to remain independent or not."

As if there were a question. The A.R.S.P. was a relatively small, renegade denomination that had been fending off takeover bids from bigger churches for the past twenty-five years. The local view was that the United Church of Christ was trying to become the General Motors of Protestant denominations, marketing essentially identical vehicles under a variety of nameplates. But the suspicion was that the U.C.C. would remain the Cadillac division, while its lesser partners became the Pontiacs and Chevys.

After this announcement Elder Haislip adjourned the meeting to the Fellowship Hall for coffee and cookies, and as we all slowly filed out of the sanctuary, shaking Reverend Sinclair's bony, spotted hand at the door, my father finally saw me.

"Hey, Morgan, looky there," he said from a few places in line behind me. "It's that prodigal son I've heard so much about."

"Yeah, well, I'm kind of prodigal myself," Morgan told him, "so let's be nice to the boy." I turned and waved back to them, then shuffled forward with the line to Reverend Sinclair.

"Nice job today, Reverend," I told him.

He pumped my arm enthusiastically. "Thank you very much," he said. But his smile was all teeth: he had no idea who I was. I passed from the sanctuary into the outer hallway and waited for my father in the murky light of the narrow stained-glass windows.

He and Morgan paid their respects to Reverend Sinclair, then they strolled into the hallway and casually circled around on either side of me, like policemen approaching a suspicious character on the street.

"So, welcome back," my father said.

"I'm not really back."

My father turned to Morgan. "You hear that? The boy's not really back. I'm talking to thin air."

"I'll call the Pope," Morgan said. "Tell him we've had a vision."

"The Pope ain't interested in Presbyterians," my father said. "But we better warn the reverend there's a haint on the loose."

"I'm just visiting," I said.

My father sighed. "Boy, that's the story of your life."

A drill sergeant razzing a new recruit—that was the tone my father had always taken with me. It used to bother me, especially when I was a teenager, but lately I'd been able to ignore it. He didn't outrank me anymore. I'd won my dishonorable discharge from his army.

"I saw you calling bingo last night," I said. "How'd it go?"

"Not bad. We made about 600. Enough for some new playground equipment down at Robert E. Lee Park."

"But we've still got a ways to go on the new courthouse cannon," Morgan said. "So we're hoping for a big turnout tonight. Tell your friends, Junior, if you got any." He checked his watch and tapped the crystal with his forefinger, then frowned and slapped it harder. "My second hand keeps sticking. What the hell time you got, Jimmy?"

My father squinted down at his own watch. "Ten o'clock on the dot. I reckon we'd better get a move on, if we want to get back for bingo."

"No cookies and fellowship?" I asked.

"Not today," Morgan said.

"We've got to swing by the café and pick up Tump Wood," my father explained. "We're going on a little road trip to Alabama. Tump's in charge of the sandwiches."

"We're heading down to Horseshoe Bend," Morgan added. "Tump ain't never seen the battleground."

"Neither has Nolan," my father told him. He stepped over to the window and flicked a dried moth from a stained-glass Wise Man's blue donkey. "You're welcome to come along," he offered. "We ought to be back by sundown."

I'd never been there, but I did know some things about Horseshoe Bend because I did a research paper on it for history class my senior year. Tehopiska, the Muscogee called it, on the Tallapoosa River. It was General Andrew Jackson's first major victory, the one that destroyed the Creek Confederacy and gave Jackson permanent War Hero status in the South. The Battle of New Orleans might have been more famous, but Horseshoe Bend was the one that really mattered because it opened up the whole Southwest for white settlement. All Jackson did at New Orleans was kill an obscene number of British soldiers after the war was already over, but at Horseshoe Bend he successfully annihilated a thousand-year-old tribal culture. He could never have won the presidency without that feather in his cap.

"You're a little overdressed for it, aren't you?" I asked, ignoring for the moment my father's invitation.

"Got our change of clothes in the van," Morgan said.

"How'd you talk Tump into such a pain-in-the-ass trip on his day off?"

"Didn't have to talk him into it," said Morgan. "He's got a natural interest. Says a couple of his ancestors fought with Jackson in the war. Wants to see if the Park Service knows anything about it."

"Sounds like a long shot to me," I said, "unless they were colonels or something."

Morgan shrugged. "You know how it is. We all think our ancestors was somebody famous."

I turned to my father. "What about us? We got any famous characters in the family tree?"

"Not that I know of," he said, still studying the stained glass. "Just preachers and horse thieves."

Morgan watched the last few stragglers head down toward the Fellowship Hall, then nodded to my father. "You ready?"

"Guess so," he answered.

"Me, too," I said, and they both looked at me in surprise.

"You sure?" my father asked. "I didn't think you were all that keen on battlefields."

"Well, I've seen all the others. Might as well add this one to the list."

"All right!" said Morgan. "This is shaping up fine. We can play cards on the way down."

"I'll meet you at the café," I said. "I need to stop by the house and tell Laney. Change clothes, too. And I've got a book on Jackson I can bring along."

"This ain't a school trip," said Morgan, laughing. "You want to bring something, bring a hundred-dollar bill and a fifth of Jack Daniel's."

"And don't make us wait," my father added. "We've got a lot of ground to cover today."

~

Explaining the trip to Laney turned out to be easy, because she wasn't home. I figured she was probably out at her parents' farm with Donna, who'd stayed over after the carnival turned ugly on her again. Donna had held up pretty well for most of the night, all the way down through the swimsuit competition, but then she had a screaming disagreement with the other judges about the final rankings. The girl she voted for only got runner-up, and I think that may have struck a little too close to home. Afterwards, she shut herself up in the women's bathroom of the livestock pavilion for half an hour. By the time she came out, Darwin was asleep on my shoulder and the rides were closing down. I don't think she saw any Darwin daddies, either, so the whole night was a bust. If Laney felt as bad for Donna as I did, she'd surely be out at the farm.

Of course, I hadn't guessed right yet on anything Laney ever did. For all I knew, she was down at the Piggly Wiggly getting pork chops for a romantic dinner for the two of us. Or she might have been curled up somewhere with Steve Pitts, thanking him ever so much for the lovely stuffed bear. I just didn't have a clue.

I threw on some old clothes and grabbed my biography of Andrew Jackson from a short shelf in the living room where Laney kept all our hardcover egghead books—the ones we used to fool company about what kind of people we were. It was the only book on the shelf I'd actually read parts of, mainly because it was the same book I'd used for my senior report. At this point it was more than fifteen years overdue at the Robert E. Lee High School library.

I scribbled a note on a paper towel and left it on the kitchen table: *Gone job hunting in Alabama. Be back late.*

Job hunting. I wasn't sure myself how much truth there was to that. Sure, it would be nice if I could iron out a truce with my father, and I definitely hated repo work. But I sort of liked being out of the agency, and I wasn't at all sure I wanted to go back. Laney didn't need to know that part just yet, though. Our own truce was an even stickier proposition, and I didn't want to violate the cease-fire.

I got back in the car and headed down to the square, figuring Tump, Morgan, and my father would all be waiting for me outside the café, full of standard complaints about how slow I'd been. But I was wrong, again.

My father and Morgan had just arrived themselves. They'd already changed into their tourist outfits—short pants with dark knee-high socks and pastel golf shirts—and they now stood by Morgan's minivan with the doors still open, looking at the front of the café. I saw right away what they were staring at. Tump's storefront window had a bucket-sized hole in the middle of it, with foot-long cracks spreading out in several directions. I pulled into the parking space beside them, grabbed the Jackson book from the passenger seat, and got out of my car.

"What do you think that's all about?" I asked.

"Goddamn kids, probably," said Morgan, slamming his door. We all scanned the square for any likely vandals but the place was a ghost town—like it always was on Sundays. Empty sidewalks, empty parking spaces, empty benches on the courthouse lawn. Just the occasional car creeping through on the way to someplace else.

"Tump must be pissed," my father said as we circled around the hitching post and walked toward the café door. The Methodist church chimes sounded in the distance, announcing the 10:30 service.

Morgan pushed open the door and looked inside. "Jesus Christ," he said. My father stepped up beside him and stared for a moment into the café, waiting, I suppose, for his eyes to adjust from the outside glare. Then he squeezed past Morgan, who seemed rooted in the doorway, and disappeared into the deep shade of the café.

"What is it?" I asked, edging Morgan aside.

"Jesus Christ," he said again, more quietly this time. I followed my father inside to see for myself.

The place looked almost normal. The tables were set, the counter was clean, the dishes were all done—everything was ready for the Monday-morning breakfast rush. Maybe it was just Morgan's good influence as the health inspector, but Tump never left a mess over the steamy summer weekends, not a smudge on the griddle nor a fly on the windowsill. But this Sunday morning there was a scattering of broken window glass on the floor, and a trail of bright red spots that meandered through the room and then ended in a puddle beneath the café chair where Tump now sat sideways. His right arm was hooked over the top rail of the chair, holding him steady, and his left hand gripped his side. Between his fingers, extending about eight inches through the front of his white cook's apron, were the double-razor head and steel shaft of a hunting arrow. The feathered end jutted out from his Sunday dress shirt behind him. My father put a hand on Tump's shoulder and leaned down close to his face.

"Tump?" he asked. "Are you okay?"

Tump opened his eyes and drew a deep breath. "Don't crowd me, Jimmy," he said. "You bump into this arrow and I'll flat have to kill you."

My father smiled, relieved, I guess, to hear so much annoyance in his voice. "Never kill your insurance agent, Tump," he said, crouching down to examine the twin wounds. "It'll complicate your claim."

Tump smiled too, though he closed his eyes again. "So you figure I'm covered for a thing like this?" he asked.

"Oh, sure," my father said. "On-the-job accidents are automatic."

"So that's what this was," Tump said, shaking his head. "An on-the-job accident."

"Well, either that or an Act of God," my father told him.

"I'm Baptist," Tump said. "If God wanted me dead, He'd slip something in my liquor."

Morgan moved in from the doorway and stared at the pattern of blood on the floor, part of which included a concentrated spotting below the pay phone on the wall. "You call the hospital yet?" he asked.

Tump squinted toward the phone. "Yeah, I just got off the line when you boys pulled in. Ambulance ought to be here anytime." He shook his head. "Sure wish we had that 911 thing for the county. Sometimes it ain't too convenient to look a number up."

"We can run you up there right now, if you want," my father told him.

Tump looked down at the arrow and gave a short laugh. "Might have trouble getting the seat belts to fit."

"What happened?" I asked.

Tump grimaced as he turned in my direction. "Well, Nolan, I ain't no doctor," he began, "but I think what happened is I just got shot in the goddamn back with a goddamn arrow."

"Get a second opinion," my father told him, and Tump coughed out another small laugh.

"So who's the goddamn Indian?" Morgan asked, stepping carefully across the trail of blood spots to the lunch counter.

"I didn't see," Tump told us. "I'd just bagged up the tuna sandwiches for the trip—they're on the cutting board there, back by the sink, if anybody wants one—and I was coming around the side of the counter to go to the head. I heard the glass break behind me, and the next thing I know, it's Custer's last fuckin' stand. Excuse my language Nolan, but I ain't in the best of moods right now."

"So you got no ideas?" Morgan asked.

"I didn't say that, Morgan," Tump told him. "It was probably one of your crowd—one of those all-night punks you keep dragging in here for poker games."

"Well, if that's the case," Morgan told him, "you can bet the ranch I'll get to the bottom of it."

"Tump, do you want to lie down or anything?" I asked.

"Hell, no," he said. "Sitting up like this is about as near to comfortable as I can get. Just don't let me keel over. I did that once already—caught the shaft on this here table leg going down. Felt like somebody branded me for the rodeo."

"I got bolt cutters in the van," Morgan offered. "We can clip off the head and pull that thing out, if you want."

"Not a good idea," Tump groaned. "Right now this arrow's plugging up all its own holes. I'd just as soon keep it like that."

My father reached behind the counter for a clean bar rag and gave it to Tump, who packed it gently beneath the forward shaft of the arrow. "How's it look in back, Jimmy?" he asked.

My father bent down and studied the wound again. "Not bad at all," he said. "Just a trickle. You want me to staunch it?"

"Naw, just leave it alone." He cleared his throat and coughed. "You going to Horseshoe Bend with us, Nolan?" he asked.

"Thought I might."

He looked down at the hole in his side and shook his head. "I may have to take a rain check."

"We can go next week," Morgan said.

"I don't know if a week'll do it," Tump told him. He raised his head and squinted his eyes in concentration. "What's on the lower left side? Anything vital?"

Morgan shrugged. "Not that I know of."

"Maybe a kidney," I suggested. "But you got two of those."

"What about the spleen?" Tump asked. "Where's that at?"

"It's right around there somewhere," my father conceded. "But I don't know what the hell it does. How about you boys?"

Morgan and I shook our heads.

"Well, that's a good enough sign," Tump said. "If we don't know what it does, it cain't be all that important."

"The liver's important," Morgan volunteered. "But I think it's more up out of the way. Might be on the other side, too."

"Internal bleeding's what you got to be careful about," my father said.

"Well, I don't know what that's supposed to feel like," Tump answered. "But nothing really seems to hurt inside." He shifted slightly on the chair and sucked in a breath between clenched teeth. "It's these cut muscles around my ribs—that's where the fire is."

"The hospital's not but two miles from here," I said. "Shouldn't we be hearing a siren by now?"

We all paused to listen, but there was still no break in the Sunday-morning quiet.

"Morgan," my father said, "get on the phone to County and find out where that ambulance is."

Morgan picked up the phone book and thumbed through to the hospital page. "Tump, who'd you talk to up there? They got about thirty different listings, and none of them say 'Ambulance.'"

"Emergency," Tump said wearily.

Morgan patted his pants pockets. "Nolan, give me some change," he said. I dug a quarter out of one of my own pockets and tossed it over to him. He mouthed the number silently to himself, then continued to repeat it as he pulled a wad of napkins from a dispenser on the counter and wiped Tump's blood from the receiver.

"So what are we supposed to do now?" I asked.

"Well, you might mop up this floor a little bit for me," Tump said. "I don't want to leave it like this. The blood'll draw flies."

"I mean what are we supposed to do about you, Tump. Shouldn't we be doing some kind of first aid or something?"

"Keep him warm, maybe," my father said. "In case he goes into shock."

"Jesus Christ, Jimmy, it's ninety degrees in here now," Tump objected. "If I was any warmer I'd have heatstroke. Anyway, I ain't about to go into shock. I'm sixty-nine years old—nothing shocks me anymore." He looked down at the arrow and gently repositioned his fingers around the shaft. "Hell, I bet we've all seen worse than this—even Nolan."

I thought of Jerry Rathburn in his easy chair, but didn't say anything.

"A lot worse," Morgan agreed.

"This is nothing," Tump went on. "One time when I was with the Shore Patrol back on Guam, I tried to arrest an AWOL Marine and the drunk bastard shot off my middle toe."

"Which foot?" Morgan asked, as he carefully punched in the hospital emergency number.

Tump looked annoyed. "The right one."

Morgan shook his head. "I never knew that," he said.

"No reason you would," Tump told him, breathing a little heavier. "I don't lay around the swimming pools with my shoes off like some rich lowlife gamblers I know."

"I ain't rich," Morgan corrected him.

"This ain't the same as losing a toe, Tump," my father objected. "There's different consequences."

"I saw a guy lose his whole foot once," Morgan said. "Stepped on a land mine first day on Guadalcanal. Me and this other fellow had to carry him back down to the beachhead. Fat guy, too—he was plenty heavy even without that foot. Took us four hours."

"And the guy pulled through," I said, finishing Morgan's story for him.

But Morgan just shrugged. "I guess he might have made it. I never heard that he died, anyway. He was a brand-new captain with some other unit." He suddenly shifted his attention back to the phone. "Yeah, hello," he said. "I'm trying to find out what happened to the ambulance you people were supposed to send down here to pick up Tump Wood." He listened for a moment, then frowned. "Well, you're one sorry-ass bunch of morons, ain't you," he said. "Who am I talking to? . . . Okay, Mr. Creedmore, this here's Morgan Motlow. You know who I am? . . . That's exactly right. Now, if that ambulance ain't here in under three minutes, I swear to God your hospital cafeteria's gonna have health violations right up until the day you die! Do you understand me?" He slammed the receiver back onto the hook and threw the wad of napkins into the trash can by the door.

"Don't let him break my phone," Tump said quietly.

"What's the problem?" my father asked.

Morgan's jaw was set so tight I wasn't sure at first he would even answer. Finally, he blew out a short puff of breath and stalked over to the broken front window.

"They couldn't find the keys to the goddamn ambulance," he said.

"You're kidding," I said. "Why the hell didn't they call back and tell somebody?"

"Pay phone," he said. "They didn't have the number."

Tump groaned and put his right hand to his forehead. "This just ain't my day."

"But it's okay now—they found 'em," Morgan went on, as he stared out across the empty town square. "They was under a couch cushion in the TV lounge. So everything's back on track, there's nothing to worry about. You just sit tight, Tump. They'll be here directly."

Tump looked up and nodded. "Thanks, Morgan," he said.

"Meantime, I'll take care of this floor for you." Morgan lifted Tump's mop bucket into the sink and turned on a rush of hot water. Then he looked over at us. "Well, don't let the conversation dry up," he said.

"Just what is it you want to talk about?" Tump groaned.

"Nothing," Morgan answered. "I'm too mad to talk about anything right now. But I don't want you to get bored with the company and go dozing off."

"Nolan brought a book on Andrew Jackson," my father said suddenly. Morgan nodded his approval.

"Greatest president we ever had," Tump said, rousing himself slightly. "A self-made man all the way. The first real Democrat, too—never turned his nose up at people with shit on their shoes." He looked over at me. "I had ancestors fight with Andy Jackson in the War of 1812."

"I heard that somewhere," I told him. Morgan shut off the water and lowered the bucket to the floor.

"See if there's anything in that book about it," Tump said.

"I believe there's a whole chapter on it."

"Not the war," Tump corrected me. "I mean my ancestors. See if you can find my family name."

"I wouldn't count on that," I said, but I opened the back of the book and checked the index. To my surprise, there were two entries under the name Wood. "There's something here," I said, turning to page 36. "Rachel and Molly Wood. Is that anybody you know?"

Tump stared down at the floor for a moment, then slowly shook his head. "Naw, I don't think so," he said. "But see what it says anyway."

"Jackson knew them when he was a lawyer in North Carolina," I told him. "Molly was the mother and Rachel was the daughter. Says here they were the only white prostitutes in Salisbury."

Morgan laughed. "There you go, Tump," he said. "Your family made it into the history books." He opened a plastic bottle of disinfectant and poured a long yellow stream into the mop bucket.

"I never had no kin in North Carolina," Tump said defensively. "Anyway, I thought you was too mad to talk."

Morgan smiled as he pulled the floor mop from underneath the counter. "Hearing about whores in your family tree cheered me right up," he said.

"I ain't kin to no North Carolina prostitutes," Tump said. "All my people come out of Georgia." He turned to me again. "Look up the Creek Indian wars, Nolan."

I leafed ahead in the biography, scanning through the same details on Jackson's war record I'd once pirated for my research paper. Some of it was still familiar.

"My great-grandfather was on that campaign," Tump went on. "And so was his brother. See if there's anything in there about William and John Wood. The family records was real sketchy, but I know they was there."

I was about to tell Tump how unrealistic it was to expect a Jackson biography to tell him things his own family couldn't keep track of, when the name John Wood suddenly caught my eye. "Son of a gun," I said. "It's actually here."

"What is it?" Tump asked as I quickly read through the paragraph.

"It says here that seventeen-year-old John Wood joined the camp as a substitute for his conscripted brother, who had to go home to see his family."

"Yes!" Tump said. "That's them! I told you, Morgan."

"*Conscripted,*" Morgan pointed out. "That means they had to *draft* his ass into service."

"That don't matter," Tump said. "He was still there to do his part for his country. Go on, Nolan. What else does it say?"

As I looked at the rest of the paragraph, I was stunned to realize that I remembered it—all of it, nearly word for word. John Wood— how could that name have escaped me? This very passage had been the core of my report. My anti-war, anti-Jackson, anti-American report.

"It gets pretty complicated, Tump," I said, though it wasn't really complicated at all. John Wood had been a boy my own age, and his story had seemed somehow relevant to my own dead-end, teenaged life. What happened to John Wood had made me form a new opinion about certain things, and that was a rare experience for me in high school. Rare as Reverend Sinclair's fifty-third sermon. "Why don't you wait until you're feeling a little better," I suggested.

Tump made a noise that sounded almost like a growl. "Nolan, I'm an old man with an arrow sticking out of me in two places. I might not ever feel better. So just get on with it."

I looked at my father, who shrugged and sat down on the other side of the table from Tump.

"Well," I said, "according to this, John Wood, aged seventeen, was court-martialed for refusing to clean up his camp site. General Jackson had him executed to restore discipline in the ranks."

A silence fell over the room.

"Executed?" Tump said weakly.

"Sorry. But that's what it says here." I placed the open book on the table where he could read it for himself. He looked at the page for a minute, then sighed.

"This really ain't my day," he said.

The siren sounded, finally, in the distance.

"There's other battlefields," said Morgan. "Shiloh ain't but two hours west."

"I could see Shiloh again," my father agreed.

"It's settled then," said Morgan, and he began to mop the floor.

Buried Treasure

WHEN DELL PICKED ME UP for the Monday-morning repo run, his new metal detector was cradled in the rack where he usually kept his twelve-gauge. That was more than fine with me. I don't like it when guns are so handy you can grab one without thinking. I knew a boy in high school—Jeff Lewter—who got his head blown off by Eddie Dupree when Eddie was cruising around the drive-in one night and mistook Jeff for somebody else. I don't know what Eddie's problem was, or who he thought he needed to shoot, but that part hardly matters. The point is, people make mistakes.

Friendly fire—that's what they call it in the army when the wrong guy gets killed.

Voluntary manslaughter is what they call it around here. Eddie got seven years, but he was out in four. Then he went back to technical college and learned how to fix diesel engines. Now he owns his own garage, and he's got a wife and three kids.

Last September Eddie ran unopposed for the school board. Jeff made a good showing against him with write-in votes, but it was really no contest. In the long run, people know not to expect much from the dead.

Dell had won the metal detector in the big VFW raffle at the carnival on Sunday night while I was up at the hospital checking on Tump. Not that Tump needed checking on. He'd lost a lot of blood, but he'd been right about the wound—it wasn't as bad as it looked. The arrow had missed his spleen, it turned out, and Dr. Ashby was able to sew up the holes and the torn muscles. Tump might go around sore for a while, but there was no real permanent damage. If the hospital didn't kill him while he recuperated, he'd probably be back at the café inside of a week.

But I still hung around that night—which was pointless, I guess, since Tump stayed knocked out after the surgery. Even Morgan and my father had left after the sheriff got through taking our useless statements. I guess I just didn't want to go home and face Laney now that I'd decided not to ask for my old job back. So I spent the evening wandering around the hospital and thumbing through educational pamphlets on rheumatoid arthritis, clogged arteries, and prostate cancer—all the things I could look forward to if I managed to live long enough. I read a *Reader's Digest* article on the heroic Dr. Costenbator, pioneer in children's eye surgery, whose brilliant career was cut short by a stroke. I even read half an article on vasectomies.

Here's what I learned: there's no place more dismal than a hospital at night, with its chilled air and soft lighting, and the sound of dank, dark breath seeping out into the halls, and the odor of antiseptic mingling with older, more pungent smells. It felt like the wrong universe—unnatural, artificial, as if incorrect parts had somehow got stitched and stapled together, so the whole world walked with a limp.

Toward the end of the evening, I stopped off at my Grandmother Vann's room in the skilled-care wing—which was probably more than my father had done. As far as he was concerned, she was already gone. I didn't judge him on that point, though. We're all bunglers when it comes to dealing with loss.

I couldn't see much in the little cloud of darkness where she slept—if sleeping is the right thing to call it—but it looked like she hadn't moved an inch in the two days since I'd seen her.

I hadn't moved all that much myself.

Anyway, Dell had told me about the metal detector when I called him this morning to tell him he could pick me up at my house from now on, that Laney knew about the repo job so I didn't have to sneak down to Tump's place anymore to get picked up. He seemed a little disappointed that the game was over. Dell loved being involved in other people's secrets—that's what made him a natural for repo work. That's also what got him so excited about this metal detector. He figured the dirt had secrets, too.

"Do you know what I can do with this thing?" he asked as I climbed into the pickup beside him. No questions about Tump's accident, or about how things stood with me and Laney. Dell was a wide-eyed kid again, totally caught up in his new toy and happy as I'd seen him since his old ten-fingered days. "Do you have any idea?" he asked again.

"Clear the bottle caps out of your yard?" I suggested.

"I can start me a whole new sideline," he said, running his hand along the black fiberglass shaft. "This baby's gonna make me rich."

"And how's it gonna do that?"

"By helping me find stuff," he said, measuring the words like he was talking to a half-wit. "Nolan, this whole countryside's littered with Civil War relics, you know that. Old coins, too, and maybe some Indian metalwork. I might even find some of DeSoto's lost treasure. They say he camped around here someplace."

"Yeah, he did," I said, brushing doughnut crumbs from the seat. "But I never heard anything about any treasure."

"Oh, hell, all them explorers had treasure." He ground the truck into gear and wheeled away from the curb, slinging a spray of gravel into my yard. "And armor, too. I bet museums would pay plenty for 500-year-old armor."

"Well, if you find DeSoto's armor, you'll find him, too, because they buried him in it."

"That's even better. And then there's land mines. I heard some fella on the radio say there was over a hundred million live land mines still in the ground from old wars. Every two hours somebody steps on one somewhere in the world. I could hire myself out for mine sweeps."

"There's not much call for that around here," I pointed out.

He glanced over at me and arched his eyebrows. "That's what

you think. There was a POW camp at Tullahoma in World War II, and the army mined all the fields around it. There's still a shitload of leftover ordnance out there—that's why the government cain't sell the land."

"And you believe that?"

"It was on the radio. There was a testing range over there some-where, too, before they closed down the military base. No telling what's still buried on that land."

"Dell, I imagine the army's got a couple of metal detectors of its own," I told him. "If they wanted the land cleaned up, they'd do it themselves."

Dell smiled. "This is the Armed Forces we're talking about. They *make* the messes, they don't clean 'em up. Besides, from what I hear it's just too big a job. They're gonna need outside contractors."

"And you figure the U.S. Government is gonna hire you to dig up live shells on a testing range?"

"Maybe. I mean, if they're gonna farm the work out to some-body, it might as well be me. I'm telling you, Nolan, it's a worldwide problem. The guy on the radio said every government was gonna need all the help it could get. Said the cleanup was gonna be a billion-dollar industry."

I didn't feel like arguing the point. Dell had already lost a finger, and now here he was, ready to blow himself up entirely. That didn't leave much room for rational conversation.

"Your insurance rates'll go up," I said, and we rode for a while in silence.

When we pulled up in front of the first house on the list, Dell propped his clipboard on the steering wheel and began organizing the paperwork. I leaned back in my seat and stared at the neighbor-hood through Dell's bug-spattered windshield. The houses here were white-frame bungalows, small but well-maintained. Most of the yards were neatly trimmed, and nearly all the dandelions had been weeded. Just ahead of us, an overturned tricycle lay in the lush grass beside a fire hydrant, and two doors away, in the spreading shade of an old cottonwood, a couple of grade-school kids played mumblety-peg. This was a family neighborhood—a full step up from our usual haunts. There were no boarded-up or broken windows, no rusty cars on cinder blocks, no drugged-out transients napping on termite-ravaged porches. But even the tidiest family neighborhoods could still have deadbeats—that was one thing the repo business had taught me—and in fact I knew we'd worked this street before.

"I guess you heard about Tump," I said as Dell clipped a yellow form to the top of his stack of papers. Yellow meant large appliances. We used pink for cars, blue for jewelry, and green for electronics. Beige was for everything else, from sofas to hay balers.

"Yeah, Morgan called me," Dell said, nodding. He checked his watch and wrote the time at the top of the yellow sheet so Ray would know we'd started on schedule.

"Who the hell would do a thing like that?" I asked.

Dell shrugged. "Somebody with shit for brains, I guess—which narrows it down to about half the county. But I imagine we'll find out soon enough." He got out of the pickup and glanced casually around the neighborhood. The two boys up the block stopped playing with their knives and began to watch us, so Dell waved hello. They waved, too, then went back to their game. I stepped out into the street and leaned across the hood of the pickup.

"What makes you think we'll find out?" I asked.

He tucked the clipboard under his arm and carefully smoothed back his hair, which probably meant our first client was a woman. "Simple," he said. "Anybody dumb enough to shoot an arrow through a storefront window on the town square is probably dumb enough to talk about it. Word'll get around. And Morgan's offered five hundred for the name." He started up the sidewalk toward the house, and I followed after him.

"Five hundred dollars? Why didn't he tell me that?" I asked. "I spent the whole damned day with him."

Dell stopped at the top of the porch and laughed. "Maybe he knows you don't move in the right circles."

I wondered if that could be true. I'd moved in circles my whole life. Surely, some of them must have been right.

Dell walked across the porch and banged on the screen door.

"What about the back?" I asked.

"No need," he said, patting down his hair. "Alma won't run."

"Alma?" I looked more carefully at the house and understood why this street looked so familiar. "Oh, man, Dell, we already took her car."

"And now we're back for the washer and dryer," he said cheerfully.

He rapped on the wooden frame again just as Alma opened the front door. The first time we'd come here, I'd been too embarrassed to look her in the face, but this time I was too embarrassed not to. She seemed even prettier now than she had on the Ferris wheel.

Some women were made for colored lights and a dark sky. Laney was one of those—a smoky, sleepy-eyed beauty with her face perfectly painted on and her forever-teenaged body sheathed in bright elastics. But Alma was the other kind of lovely, a woman with a well-scrubbed morning look, rosy-cheeked and bright-eyed, offhandedly appealing in loose jeans and an untucked cotton shirt. Her red hair was still damp from her morning shower, and it dangled across her forehead in short, scraggly spikes. There were wet spots on her shirt, too, so I figured she must have still been drying herself off when Dell knocked on the door. But she didn't seem put out at all. In fact, she was smiling—and it wasn't one of those "I-give-up" smiles like we got sometimes from our more sheepish clients. She looked genuinely pleased to see us, which was about as rare as a thank-you note in our line of work.

"Morning, Alma," Dell said, holding up the clipboard to indicate our business there.

"Hey, Dell," she answered, holding the screen open for him. "You boys are out early today."

"We're hard workers," Dell said as he stepped past her into the front room.

"I doubt that," she said. "I bet you just didn't know what else to do with yourselves now that Tump Wood can't fix your breakfast."

"So you heard about that," Dell said.

"It was the main topic on the midway," she said. She continued holding the screen and looked at me expectantly. "Well, come on, Nolan. Don't make Dell do all the lifting."

"Good to see you, Alma," I said as I edged past her. She smelled of talcum powder. "I'm really sorry about this."

"Oh, don't sweat it," she said. "Why would I need a washer and dryer? I've got no use for clean clothes. It's not like I had a car to go anywhere." She let the screen door bang shut behind me. The room was empty—not a stick of furniture, not a picture on the wall, not a carpet on the floor.

"Don't give the boy a hard time," Dell said. "He's real sensitive."

"Then he ought to find some other line of work."

"That's not so easy to do," I told her.

"It is if you're not too picky," she said.

"Alma, I'm already doing repo work. What's less picky than that?"

"Field hand," she said. "Chopping out stumps for seven bucks an hour. Let me know if you're interested." She patted me on the cheek and turned to Dell. "So have you tried that metal detector yet?" she asked.

"Sort of," he told her. "When I got home last night I put some quarters under my living-room rug and then hunted for 'em. But I'm not sure that was a good test."

"So you went back to the fair," I said to Alma.

"I go every night. It's my favorite thing all year."

"Tonight's the harness races," Dell said. "I might go back again to see that."

"How about you, Nolan?" Alma asked.

"I don't know. I think I've had enough carnival fun to last me for a while."

"Too bad," she said. "There's more than just the harness races. There's that guy they shoot out of the cannon."

"Yeah, that cannon guy's great," Dell said. "Our Lions Club sponsored him last year, so I got to meet him. He was real nice—you could talk to him just like he was a regular person. But you could still tell there was something special about him."

"It's a different fellow this year," Alma told him.

Dell frowned. "How do you know that?"

"I keep up," she said simply. "The guy you're talking about missed the net once and wouldn't do it anymore. I heard he had a weight problem, but I don't know if that figured in or not."

"That's a shame," Dell said. "But I bet the new guy'll be just as good."

"You know Elmore Parsons' son, don't you?" Alma asked.

"You mean Emmett? Yeah, I know him. Dumber than dirt."

"Well, that's who it is."

Dell looked at her closely. "You're kidding. Emmett Parsons couldn't pour piss out of a boot if the instructions was written on the heel."

Alma folded her arms and leaned against the edge of the opened door. "Well, apparently he's found his calling," she said. "Now he's 'The Great Emmettini, Daredevil Extraordinaire.'"

Dell shook his head. "Emmett Parsons. That sure takes the mystique right out of it." He sighed and looked at me. "I guess we'd better load up the truck, Nolan. Go get the dolly and bring it around back."

"You didn't ask her if she's got the money," I objected, still hoping Alma might be able to fend us off. But Alma was the one who laughed.

"Nolan, I've got money," she said. "I'm just not giving it to Hometown Finance."

"She's gonna build a zoo," Dell said, as if that explained everything.

I went back to the truck and got the dolly.

It's the subtleties of a business, I guess, that separate the amateurs from the pros. Whatever the job—selling insurance or chasing bad debts or crouching in the barrel of a giant circus cannon—success means knowing the angles. Dell was a pro because he understood the business from the inside out, as if it were his own invention. He felt comfortable in it. But I was still just an amateur—and a pretty feeble one, at that—clueless about the fine points and uneasy all the way. I was the wrong guy in the cannon. I kept missing the net.

I dragged the dolly around back and swung it up on the cement stoop just as Dell opened the door.

"We might as well take 'em out through the front," he said as I guided the dolly past him into the kitchen. This room was empty, too, except for the washer and dryer, which sat ready in the middle of the bright linoleum floor, the electrical cords duct-taped to the sides. I was beginning to doubt that anyone really lived here.

"You get 'em belted," I told Dell. "I need to speak to Alma."

"Go ahead," he said. "I can handle the dryer myself. But I'll need you back for the washer, so don't go wandering off."

I walked into the bare front room, but Alma wasn't there. "Where'd she go?" I called back to Dell, but Alma answered from one of the side bedrooms.

"I'm in here, Nolan," she yelled. "The room on the left."

I stepped into the hallway and saw that both the bathroom and the second bedroom were as empty as the rest of the house. The door to the other bedroom was slightly ajar, and through the opening I could see overpacked boxes bunched in the far corner and a bare mattress propped against the wall beside them. The floor was strewn with piles of clothes and bed linens, and a tall stack of books teetered above the disarray. I eased the door open and walked into the room, taking care not to step on any stray dishes or picture frames.

The floor, it turned out, was the wrong thing to be careful of.

When I looked up, there was Alma, standing at an ironing board, ironing out the wet spots from the white cotton shirt she had worn to the front door.

She was naked from the waist up.

"Oh, my," she said in a small voice. She kept her grip on the iron, but moved her free hand to cover herself. I guess I should have looked away, but I didn't, I couldn't, she was just so perfect to see.

"I guess what I meant to say," she said softly, "was that I'd be right out." But still I couldn't look away, in spite of all propriety and the growing embarrassment between us. I knew there was every possibility she might hit me with the hot iron, but I was still helpless.

She didn't hit me, though. As I watched the color flush through her cheeks and across her breasts, she slowly lowered her hand to the ironing board and let out a slightly shuddering breath—not a sigh, exactly, but more a gathering of spirit to stem the awkwardness that was sweeping us both away. She breathed again, more smoothly this time, and I watched the tension fall away from her shoulders and her neck. And while I still struggled to regain some level portion of myself, she stood suddenly at ease, amazingly unselfconscious about the heart-swallowing beauty that had stopped me stone-dead. A brightness flickered in her green, green eyes, and I hoped against all reason that it was some kind of smile, some sign of forgiveness for my inexcusable failure to turn away.

"Well, I guess we're both adults," she said simply. She turned off the iron and carefully shook the shirt out in front of her, then draped it across the ironing board, making no further effort to cover herself up. She looked at me again, patient and noncommittal, as if she were trying to make up her mind about something. I felt dizzy with risk.

"Long as you've seen the show," she said, "I might as well ask what you think."

"I think I missed a lot of good things in high school."

She crossed around the ironing board and moved up close in front of me, so close I could both see and smell the fresh dusting of powder across the faint freckles of her breasts. "Then it seems silly not to do this," she said, and before I could think, or run, or breathe, or even say yes, she leaned up and kissed me.

If I had been sixteen, it might have been the perfect teenage kiss, the one never to back away from, the one to make me scrap all plans, quit the ball team, comb my hair, drive endlessly around the block where her parents lived.

But I wasn't sixteen anymore. That was the part I had to remember.

From behind me came the squeak and rattle of the dryer being carted through the house, and I pulled away from Alma in surprise. More than surprise, really. Alma just smiled, then retrieved her shirt from the ironing board, still calm as the moon. I listened as Dell wheeled the dryer outside and eased it down the wooden porch steps in a series of muffled thumps.

"What was it you wanted?" she asked as she slipped her arms into the sleeves and tugged the top up over her shoulders.

I hated even to speak, because speaking would take us further from the moment, and the moment was disappearing already, dwindling down toward its last clear pinprick of light. There was no way to stop it from going. My real life was resuming its path.

"What's all this about a zoo?" I asked.

"Like Dell said, I'm building one." She turned away to rebutton her blouse, and as she did, the world slumped back into place, nearly normal again, with all its beige forms to fill out, and all its beige possessions.

"How can you build a zoo? I mean, I never heard of anybody doing that before."

"Especially somebody who can't even pay off the finance company." She yanked the cord of the iron from the wall socket. "That's what you mean." She set the iron on the windowsill, then folded up the ironing board and propped it against the boxes in the corner. "Look, I'm not a poverty case," she said stuffing her shirttail inside her jeans. "I've already got the land and enough money to get started. I've also got a degree in animal husbandry from over at Tech. This is not some harebrained spur-of-the-moment idea."

"I never said it was," I pointed out, surprised by her tone.

She frowned and started to say something more, some part of the argument she obviously knew by heart. But then she stopped herself and let out a small, whistling sigh. Her look softened again.

"Sorry, Nolan," she said, shaking her head and smiling. "I think I just mistook you for my ex-husband."

"I didn't mean to pry," I told her. "I'm just trying to find out if what you said earlier about field-hand work was an actual job offer."

She turned away again and lifted a half-dozen large hardcover books from the crooked stack beside her. She set them carefully into a shallow empty box near the closet, then returned to the stack for a second armful, going about her packing as if I weren't even there. I took the silence as a clear-enough answer, but instead of leaving her alone I stepped over to help her with the few remaining books. They were encyclopedias, and I had to strain to get the last dozen volumes up from the floor. But the box was already full from Alma's two loads, so I had to set the books back down where I got them. I must have looked like a moron. Alma folded her arms and studied me for a moment, her face full of misgivings, like I was a discontinued model with no backlog of spare parts.

"Yeah, it was a job offer," she said finally. "But it's real grunt work, just clearing out brush and small trees."

"For part-time, I might be interested," I said.

"It's my daddy's old farm," she went on. "A big rocky patch up at the north end of the county. He never could get the right things to grow on it, and then after my mother died, he quit putting in crops altogether. Scrub oak and sweet gum just took the place over." She bit her lower lip and considered me carefully. "You do know how to use an ax?" she asked.

"If I get confused, I can ask somebody."

"What I mean is, you look more like an office-work kind of guy. I just want to make sure you know what you're getting into."

I almost never knew what I was getting into.

"When I was a kid," I told her, "my dad used to make me work every summer for Dell's father, down past Skinem. I had to shovel feed corn twelve hours a day from an old tin-roofed crib in hundred-degree heat. I think I can handle a few sweet gum trees."

"It's more than a few," she said. "It's probably about two thousand, scattered out over seventy-five acres."

"My God, Alma, that's practically a forest preserve," I said. "Just tell your dad to call it a tree farm, and let it go at that."

"Daddy died in April," Alma said. "The zoo's my project." She grabbed a pillowcase from a pile of linens and began to stuff stray pieces of clothing and dishware inside it.

"I'm sorry about your father," I said. "But you'll sure need more than just me to clear that much land."

She shrugged. "I ran an ad in the paper," she said, "and I stuck fliers up at the high school. But nobody called. You can't even get kids to do this kind of work anymore."

"Well, I know a couple of fellows who've been catching cotton-mouths for money," I told her. "This might be a real step up for them."

She set the bag next to the ironing board and picked out another pillowcase, which she began to fill with leftover encyclopedias. "If they don't mind working for credit, I could sure use the help."

"Credit? What's that supposed to mean?"

She tried to shove the last volume into the pillowcase, but the fit was too tight and a corner of the book poked through the worn cotton. She pulled it out and frowned at the cover.

"*Vavassor to Zygote,*" she read from the spine. "This used to be my favorite. The end of the alphabet always seemed to have the most interesting words."

Zoo, I thought.

She set the book gently aside. "Everything's tied up in probate," she said, tracing her fingers across the rich, dark cover. "I'm broke until October."

"So that seven-dollars-an-hour you mentioned was just hypo-thetical."

"Well, no," she said, finally looking up. "I mean, I'm good for it."

I couldn't help laughing. "That might sound better if I weren't here to repossess your appliances. No wonder nobody answered your ads."

Alma didn't think it was funny. The color flushed again through her face and neck, and she pressed her lips tight like some vile word was about to burst out in my direction. But it didn't. She just stared at me hard, and I felt myself slipping into the quagmire again, sinking down to where my old life made no future sense, and where I might do something crazy.

"The money doesn't matter," I said.

Then Dell clomped up the porch steps into the front room, dragging the dolly noisily behind him.

"Dryer's on the truck, Nolan," he called.

"Be right there," I answered, but I made no move to go.

Dell stepped around the corner of the hall and stood in the bedroom doorway. "Soon as we get the washer out, we'll start on these boxes."

"That's great," Alma said, forcing a thin smile. "I'll get the rest of this stuff ready to go."

"Just what all are we here to collect?" I asked, turning to look at Dell.

"I made a deal with Alma," he said, stepping into the cluttered room and clapping a hand on my shoulder. "We're gonna help her move the last of her things out to her dad's farm."

"In exchange for what?"

Dell beamed. "Metal-detector privileges."

"Won't that mess up Ray's repo schedule?" I asked, but Dell waved off the notion like a trail of blue smoke.

"Ray's a paper-pushing idiot. I'll tell him a client had us pinned down with gunfire. He'll probably give us a raise."

"You don't have to come along if you don't want to, Nolan," Alma said stiffly. "I'm sure Dell can drop you off somewhere on his way through town."

"The hell I can," Dell said. "This boy's all that stands between me and a premature heart attack. I ain't going anywhere without him."

I was glad Dell took the decision out of my hands, because it meant I didn't have to tell Alma what I really thought: that there was something right for me about all this. And that I truly wanted to see where her zoo would be built. And that I might want to help her build it.

Maybe it was just the idea of doing straightforward work again that appealed to me, swinging an ax in the hot sun, measuring clear progress one fallen tree at a time.

Or maybe what appealed to me was Alma.

But either way I knew I'd take on any chore she asked me to, even if I never got paid a single dime. If she wanted me to chop out two thousand tree stumps from her father's rocky ground, I'd do it. Simple as that. Even if it took from now until doomsday.

Even if Laney might one day shoot me dead.

Some Assembly Required

THE AX BLADE STARTED ME THINKING: the more things fell apart, the more things fell into place.

Then I fell onto a brush pile and passed out. Heatstroke.

I guess I should have paced myself better, but after a while the rhythm of the work lulled me into a sort of stupor and I lost track of the dangers. The trees were small—eight to ten feet high, for the most part, with trunks like the handle on a baseball bat—so it wasn't too tough to bring them down. A few good swings was all it took, and if the job had been just that, I might have kept on my feet, even in that blistering summer sun.

But there was more to it than hacking down those scrawny trees—chopping out the roots was the real killer. For one thing, since I couldn't see the root lines until I'd already broken through most of the tangle around the stump, I was always chopping blind, and that meant a lot of wasted energy. Then, too, the dirt dulled the blade, so every next cut took a little more effort than the last. And even after the main roots were severed, I still had to pull up the runners, which was the hardest thing of all. A few of the shallow ones came up easy, like ropes covered with snow, but those were the exceptions. Most runners eventually dove deep for groundwater, and straining to break that grip could have laid anybody out.

Along about the third hour, I felt myself go clammy. But I didn't want to stop in mid-tree, so instead of cooling off with the lemonade Alma had left for us, I just kept pounding that ax into the dirt, thinking surely the stump would break loose any second if I could just get in one or two more solid whacks. But it was a stubborn stump, and I kept missing the roots. And the more frustrated I got the harder I swung.

Then a cold wind climbed up my spine, and I suspected I was in trouble. I looked toward the highway where Louis and Sammy were clearing briars from along Alma's side of the road, but they had their backs to me and I was too short of breath to call their names. Besides, I didn't want to interrupt. They were talking to Jesus.

I remember thinking how odd it was to see Jesus on a weekday, especially way up at this end of the county. But there He was, shuffling by in the southbound lane, heading toward town. He looked pretty overheated Himself in His long robes, and with that heavy Cross hooked over His shoulder. It was a big Cross, too—maybe seventy pounds—though not quite as rugged as I'd always imagined it to be. There were little wheels on the back end of it that carried a good part of the weight.

Jesus saw me staring at Him and tipped His Crown of Thorns like it was a hat. That's when I knew I'd pushed myself too far, that I was about to collapse, and the only option I had left was to pick a soft spot to land.

A brush pile, I now know, looks a lot softer than it is.

I began to come around as Sammy turned me over, maybe because he rolled me onto a knot of dry nettles and prickly pears I'd dug up a few minutes earlier, and the whole brambly mess spiked into my back like a box of carpet tacks. But even with that kind of discomfort, my head seemed clear—or at least partly so—and when I opened my eyes and saw Sammy leaning over me, I thought I was nearly back to normal. Then I noticed Louis and Jesus standing a few steps off to the side. With His right hand, Jesus steadied the Cross on His shoulder the way a soldier steadies a rifle when he's standing at attention. In His left hand, He held Alma's pitcher of lemonade.

"You've got wheels on your Cross," I said, and Jesus nodded.

Sammy fanned my face with one of his work gloves. "How you feeling, Nolan?"

"What kind of mileage do you get on that thing?" I asked.

Jesus looked confused, like he didn't know the answer, and I thought, *Great, that'll probably get me about ten thousand bonus years in Hell*. But then Jesus cleared His throat and spoke up.

"It ain't got a motor," He told me. "It only goes where I carry it."

That seemed like a good answer to me, and I closed my eyes again. Then Sammy pressed a cold, wet handkerchief to my forehead—which felt nice at first, but then the lemonade he'd soaked it in ran down into my eyes. That stung enough to bring me around for good.

My head felt fat with pressure, like a tire just short of a blowout, but I knew I'd be all right once I got some liquids in me. I sat up and took a few long, careful breaths while I dabbed at my eyes with the front of my T-shirt. Then, when I'd blotted away as much sugary citric acid as I could, I reached around to check my back for nettles or prickers.

"You ought to wear a hat," Sammy said, wringing out the cloth and stuffing it back in his jeans pocket. "That sun's wicked."

"I was stupid," I admitted. "I let the heat sneak up on me."

"You was lucky, more'n anything else," Sammy said. "Somebody fair-skinned like you—you'd have fried like a potato chip if we hadn't been out here with you."

"Thanks," I said. "I appreciate the help."

He brushed some twigs from the front of my shirt. "Baptism by fire, that's what Mama'd call it."

"That's what Mama calls everything," Louis pointed out.

"Well, maybe she's right," Sammy replied. He gave my shoulder a friendly shake. "How 'bout it, Nolan—you feeling like you been bathed in the fires of the Lord?"

"Well, I've got these damned nettles burning the hell out of my back," I told him. "That ought to count for something."

"Amen to that," Jesus agreed. I squinted over to where I'd last seen Him. My vision was a little blurry from the lemonade, but He was still there, big as life, with stringy, tangled hair and a broad yellow-toothed grin. He stepped forward, dragging the Cross with some difficulty over the broken ground, and offered me Alma's pitcher. I was a little hesitant, but I took it and drank down the better portion of a quart.

"Nettles and briars cain't hurt no worse than a snakebite," Louis said.

Jesus looked over at him and tilted His head a little to the side, like He was thinking. "I guess that's true, for the short haul," He told Louis. "But I'll tell you one thing: if somebody was to give me a choice between giving up the Cross or the Crown of Thorns, I'd do without the thorns. The Cross gets all the publicity, but day in and day out, it's these thorns that just about drive me nuts. Always poking into my head." Jesus sighed. "But what can you do? People expect it."

I handed the lemonade to Sammy and slowly got to my feet. Scratches bled through my shirt in a couple of places, but I knew I was all right. Except for seeing Jesus.

"You'd best find a shady spot," Sammy suggested. "You still look a mite peaked."

Louis pointed to the low end of the field. "There's a crik down past that big cottonwood," he said.

I nodded and took a few careful steps. My arms and legs felt heavier than I remembered, and I plodded like a drunk mule over the uneven ground.

"I'm kindly wore out myself," Jesus said as I moved past Him. He shifted the Cross to His left shoulder, staggering a little under the weight. "Mind if I join you boys on your break?"

"I guess that'd be all right," I said, "long as I don't have to hear anything about my eternal damnation. I'm too stove up right now to argue back."

Jesus laughed and combed His beard with His fingers. "That's okay by me," He said, and He began to trudge slowly down toward the creek.

Louis was already halfway to the cottonwood, so I turned to Sammy, who was swigging down the last of Alma's lemonade.

"Maybe you could give Jesus here a hand with His cross," I suggested. "I'll carry that pitcher."

"Oh, he don't have to do that," Jesus said. "I can manage. And by the way," he added, sticking out his free hand, "you can just call me Chet."

"Chet?" I asked.

He saw my disappointment and shrugged. "Nobody can be Jesus all the time. It's too big a load."

"Well, I'm Nolan Vann all the time," I told him, "and that's no picnic either."

I shook Chet's hand and we continued across the field. When we got to the cottonwood, he eased his cross down in the brown grass and sat on the overhang of the creek bank, letting his rubber sandals slap into the shallow current. Louis sat in a more distant patch of shade with his legs drawn up against his chest, more cautious around creekbeds now than he used to be. I leaned down over the embankment and scooped a few handfuls of cold water to rinse the stickiness off my face, then sat next to Sammy at the base of the old tree. The rough bark felt good against the nettle stings in my back, and a light breeze swept along the channel of the bottomland, cooling us all.

"Nice part of the country," Chet said, tucking his robe tighter around his legs to keep the hem out of the water. "How far is it to town?"

"Maybe three miles to the north edge," I said.

"Chet's on his way to the fair," Louis explained. "He's on a mission from God."

"I sort of figured that," I said.

"I wanted to get there yesterday," Chet told us. "But it's hard to make good time with that cross. And I don't have no luck at all hitching rides."

"What are you doing lugging that cross around anyway?" Sammy asked. "Why don't you just get you one of them little ones and hang it around your neck?"

Chet shook his head. "Wish I could, friend," he said, "but I'm a weak man. A weak man needs a big reminder."

"How do you do your shopping?" Louis asked.

Sammy threw a clump of bark at his brother. "What the hell's the matter with you, boy? Holy men like him don't go shopping."

"He's got to eat, don't he?" Louis said. "I just wondered did he carry it inside the grocery store."

"I pretty much stick to fast food," Chet told him. "The cross ain't no problem at a drive-through."

"That must get expensive," I said.

"Yeah, but I'm on disability," he explained. "They say I cracked up in the Marine Corps. So now the government pays for my hamburgers."

"I aim to be a Marine," Louis reminded us.

I expected Chet to speak up against the idea, since religion seemed to be such a power in his life. But he just leaned back on his elbows in the brittle grass and said, "That ain't a bad way for a fellow to get started."

"I'm surprised you'd say that," I told him. "Most of what I know about Jesus would put him pretty much at odds with the military."

"It's all how you look at things, I guess," Chet said. "I figure I'm a better Christian soldier for what I learned in the Corps."

"What was it you learned?" Louis asked, obviously happy to find somebody who disagreed with his mother.

Chet turned his head toward us, and I noticed for the first time what a calm and open look he had. "Well, discipline and endurance were part of it," he said. "But mostly what I learned was not to think for myself."

None of us knew quite what to say to that, not even Louis, but Chet seemed comfortable with the silence. He plucked a long weed and stuck it in his teeth.

"I'm not sure I see the advantage in that," I said finally.

"It's a complicated world," Chet said. "Too complicated for anybody to sort out on his own. But we all still need some kind of handle on it, or else we'd just feel confused all the time. And that's where Jesus comes in—or the Marine Corps, either one. What they both do is take away the guesswork. You ain't got to figure nothing out for yourself, you just got to do what you're told and act like you're supposed to."

"So Jesus is your superior officer," I said.

"He's the Supreme Allied Commander," Chet proclaimed, "and we're all just buck privates. Until Judgment Day, anyhow."

"Then what?" Sammy asked.

"Then we gotta hope for a promotion." He looked over at Louis and raised up a finger of warning. "But don't misunderstand me, son," he said. "If it's a choice between Jesus and the Marines, I'll take Jesus every time. There's some real assholes in the military. The food's flat terrible, too. 'Course, you're still living at home, so you probably take good meals for granted. But I'm telling you, brother, you join the Service and you'll learn to appreciate anything your mama ever put on the table." He looked over at Louis and me and winked. "That's one thing I like about fairs," he said. "I can get corn dogs and cotton candy."

"Well, it's about four miles to the fairgrounds," I told him. "But you shouldn't have much trouble getting there. The road's pretty smooth, and it's mostly downhill."

"It's all downhill, friend," Chet said. "That's why I'm here: to build God's Bridge at the bottom of the Valley."

"We got two bridges down there already," Louis said. "Or one and a half, anyway. The new one ain't finished yet."

"That ain't what he means," Sammy said. "But you're wrong, anyway, Louis. That Stone Bridge ain't hardly a bridge no more. Half the underside dropped out when you and Nolan rode that backhoe across it the other day. Whole thing's just waiting to fall in the river."

"Is that what you were yelling up at us about?" I asked, remembering the panic I'd seen on his face that day.

"That was it," said Sammy. "I thought Mr. Pitts done delivered you boys straight to the Almighty. Scared me half to death."

"It's the Eternal Bridge I'm talking about," Chet said, revving up into a more evangelical tone. "The one that helps poor sinners through the Valley of the Shadow."

"Well, you'll have your pick of sinners on that carnival midway," I told him. "That's for damned sure."

"I expect you'll do real well there," Sammy agreed.

"Like a pig in slop," added Louis.

Chet reached inside the front of his robe and pulled out a bright red Bible. "I'm ready for the worst of 'em," he said, smiling.

But this was Lincoln, after all, and I couldn't help but wonder if Chet understood just how bad the worst of us could be.

∾

Except for being a Jesus-loving lunatic, Chet really wasn't too bad a guy. His favorite Old Testament prophet was Jeremiah, the Doomsayer, so in that way he was a pretty typical religious fanatic, but he also liked Elvis, and Jerry Lee Lewis, and even Buddy Holly, so he wasn't entirely out of touch. He said he'd gone through some bad stuff in the war, so that hooked our attention for a while, but then it turned out he was talking about Grenada and being seasick on one of the ships. Still, he had a pretty good attitude for a guy on a mission from God. We gave him advice on which food stands were the best, and which rides were a waste of money, and he seemed genuinely interested, like he planned on a good time, whether he saved any souls or not. I guess that's the frame of mind you need in a job like his, since everybody knows right off that you're crazy.

I sort of wished Laney had been there to meet him, if only so she could see there were still a few people in the world who were worse off in the job market than I was. She hadn't been too pleased when I told her there was no place for me at my father's office anymore. I stopped short of telling her I hadn't even bothered to ask. No point rocking the boat when it was sinking already.

I didn't quite give her the full picture about working for Alma, either. I just told her I'd picked up a part-time construction job. If she'd pressed me for details, I don't know what else I would have said. I probably would have told her what the project was and who I was working for. I doubt I'd have mentioned how breathtaking Alma looked with her shirt off. But Laney didn't seem curious about any of it. I guess after dating Steve Pitts for five months, she'd used up all her questions about construction work.

Or maybe she'd just used up all her interest in anything I did.

If that was the case, I could hardly blame her. So far every job I'd tried had turned out to be part-time, temporary, or just plain unsavory. I had no identifiable career, and my options seemed to grow fewer by the hour. I was too old for the army, and too unskilled for a life of crime. If things got much worse, I might wind up as one of Chet's disciples.

No, on second thought, I'd have had a hard time even with that. I could carry a torch all right, but a cross was a different matter entirely—even if it did have wheels. I helped Chet haul his cross over to the highway when he set off again for town, and I came away with more splinters than I'd picked up in a whole afternoon of dragging sassafras and sweet gum across the field.

Zookeeper seemed like a possibility, though. I'd had some bad luck with reptiles lately, but overall I got along with animals pretty well. Maybe Alma might want me to stick around.

After Chet left, I felt too drained to pick up the ax again, so I told Sammy and Louis we could quit for the day. Sammy didn't seem to care one way or the other, but Louis looked relieved. It hadn't yet been a week since his snakebite, and I could tell he didn't have his stamina back yet. The three of us walked up the long field together and sat on the porch steps of the old farmhouse that stood at the crest of the ridge.

I wondered what Alma's plans were for the house. Maybe she'd make it part of the zoo. Sloths in the living room, bears in the den, rabbits in the bedrooms—or monkeys, or peacocks. That's what I'd do if it was my dead father's place.

But my dead father wasn't that open to new ideas. His house was more museum than zoo—old photos and slipcovered furniture and the ghost of my mother as a pale young girl, painted softly in religious blues and whites, hanging quietly in a dark wooden frame in the hall. It was a house with no history of animal noises.

Alma had left for town on her bicycle just after lunch, but when Dell drove into the yard to pick us up, there she was on the seat beside him. Her bike was in the back of the truck, along with a big chicken-wire cage. In the cage was a tawny half-grown cougar, sprawled like a big kitten in one well-chewed corner, patiently gnawing on the wire.

Alma jumped out of the pickup and slammed the door, then stormed past us into the house like we weren't even there. Dell climbed down more leisurely and drew his metal detector out after him.

"I see you boys are working hard," he said.

"We got hot," I told him. "What's wrong with Alma?"

Dell glanced up at the house, then walked over to join us in the shade of the porch. "Bad piece of luck," he said in a low voice.

"What kind of bad luck?" Sammy asked.

"Fellow at the carnival was selling off some of his animals," Dell said. He switched on the detector and swept it back and forth over the ground at the foot of the steps. "You know, getting rid of some of the offspring before they got too expensive to feed. Alma took out a $2800 bank loan so she could make a deal before the carnival leaves town tomorrow."

"How come she can get money for wild animals but she cain't get money to pay us for clearing her field?" Sammy asked.

"You ain't a capital asset," Dell told him.

"That still sounds like a lot of money for a cougar," I said.

"Oh, the cougar was just eighteen hundred," Dell said. "The other thousand was for a ostrich."

"I ain't never seen a live ostrich," Louis said.

"You ain't about to, neither," Dell told him, stiffling a laugh.

"What happened?" I asked.

Dell shook his head. "It was the damnedest thing. They put the ostrich in this big old wooden crate with wide slats—not a permanent pen, you understand, but just something we could use to cart it off in. The bird couldn't walk around, but it could stick its head out through the gaps in the boards to look around. So we loaded it into the pickup next to the cougar. We knew the cougar couldn't get at it through that chicken-wire mesh, so we figured everything would be okay for the ride out here. But I guess we should have made two trips."

"What'd you do, lose it on a sharp turn?" I asked.

"Hell, no," Dell said, "I drove like I was hauling Grandma's ashes. You could've played marbles on the hood, I was so careful."

"So what happened?" Louis asked.

"That bird turned out to be dumber than I'd have thought possible," Dell said. "You know how they say a ostrich'll stick its head in the sand when it gets scared?"

"I think that's just an old story, Dell," I told him.

"Well, I don't know if it is or not," he said. "But this particular bird was definitely scared of that big cat. Maybe he was trying to hide his head, or maybe he was just looking for a way out of that crate, I don't know."

"What'd it do?" Louis asked.

Dell glanced again at the front door of the house for some sign of Alma, then leaned in closer to finish his story. "Stuck its head through the food slot in the cougar cage." He paused to let that sink in, then widened his eyes. "Nothing left now but a nub."

"Oh, man," said Louis.

"It was a pretty bird, too," Dell said. "Long black feathers, like they used to put on ladies' hats."

"Where is it now?" Sammy asked, rising from the step and walking over to look into the truck bed.

"The head's still in there with the cougar—he's been batting it around like a cat toy. We dropped the rest of the mess off at the dump, cage and all," Dell said. "Personally, I thought Alma should've kept it. That cougar's still got to eat, and the way I look at it, any bird that don't know how to fly is destined to be a food source anyway. But she said she couldn't bear to do that. So she just made a thousand-dollar contribution to the county landfill."

"You gotta see this, Louis," Sammy called to his brother. "This here's what you gonna look like after the first day of boot camp."

But Louis didn't move from his spot. "I got no interest in bird heads," he said. "You couldn't pay me to look at a thing like that."

"How about I pay you to clean it up?" Dell said. He took a ten-dollar bill out of his wallet and offered it to Louis.

Louis eyed the money carefully. "What you want done, exactly?" he asked.

"I want you and Sammy to carry that cougar cage around back and hose it down," Dell told him. "Spray the cougar, too, while you're at it—but try not to get him riled up. Then come back and wash out the bed of my truck. And I mean scrub it out good—I don't want that ostrich blood to get too ripe."

"No problem," Louis said, snatching the money from Dell's hand.

"What about this head?" Sammy asked. "I ain't about to reach in after it."

"Just leave it for now, I guess," Dell said. "Maybe you can fish it out sometime when the cat's asleep."

"Not for no ten dollars," Louis muttered as he got up from the steps. He joined Sammy at the tailgate and the two of them studied the cougar cage, trying to figure the safest way to pick it up.

"Get a couple of two-by-fours from the barn," Dell finally told them. "Slide 'em underneath the cage and lift it out that way. Then you won't risk any fingers."

"That'll work," Sammy agreed, and the two of them headed across the yard toward the ramshackle barn.

Dell squinted out toward the highway. "Maybe I'll do a little prospecting before we go. Why don't you come on along? I'll let you do the digging."

"Thanks, but I'll stay here in the shade," I said. "Besides, one of us ought to supervise getting that cage out of the truck."

"Louis and Sammy can handle it," Dell said as he tinkered with the dials on the metal detector. "Both those boys are stout as pit bulls." He glanced up at me and grinned. "Like you used to be, before you got all soft and lazy."

For once I didn't feel like returning the insult. As Dell stood there beside his truck, breathing heavily, drenched in sweat, with his thinning hair slicked flat against his head, and his arms blotchy from too many years of sunburn, I realized for the first time how old and out-of-shape he was starting to look. In high school, Dell had been thick with muscle, but now he was just thick. He still had the same old strength in his upper arms—I bore witness to that on a daily basis—but he sagged at the shoulders and his face drooped under a puffy, worn-out look, like he was half asleep.

I wondered if I looked just as bad off to him. Maybe I did. Or maybe that was one thing married life had saved me from. Dell had never settled down—and he still had a lot of good nights, I was sure of that. But it looked like they were killing him.

"Oh, I know they're both strong," I said. "It's the cage I'm worried about. That frame looks a little flimsy to me. One bad step and we'll all be cat toys."

"If you're that worried about it, I'll stick around, too."

"No, that's okay," I told him. "You go ahead with your treasure hunt. Find that pot of gold."

He sighed. "To tell you the truth, this metal detector ain't working out like I hoped. I'm starting to think I put it together wrong."

"I thought gadgets like that came preassembled."

"Oh, most of it was," he said. "I just had to connect up a few of the parts. That's the way companies ship things nowadays—if it's in pieces they can save money on a smaller box. Only now I cain't get the damned thing tuned to the right frequency. Must be too much iron in the soil around here or something. I keep getting false alarms."

"Well, don't give up on it. You're bound to find something good sometime."

"I don't know," he said. "There's room for an awful lot of empty holes out there. But what the hell. At least it's cheaper than playing cards with Morgan." He started down the hillside with the detector, scanning the ground for signals along the way.

I stepped over to the truck to look at the cougar. His coat had a healthy enough sheen to it, but he seemed a little on the lean side; still solid, though, and sinewy—a mass of steel cables wrapped in fur. I guess he was used to being around people, because he took no notice of me when I climbed up into the back of the truck. Even as I picked up Alma's bike and lowered it from the tailgate, he just kept working on that wire mesh. He had a sweet kitten-like preoccupation with what he was doing. The ostrich head lay at his side, but that episode was already gone from his mind. I admired that about cats: they never looked guilty, no matter what they'd done. Unlike dogs. Dogs understood the difference between good and evil. Or at least they understood what it meant to break a commandment—and they'd hang their heads in shame when they got caught.

Here's how it seemed to me: I figured we all started out like cats, but then the world put us on a leash and a collar and turned us into dogs.

I wondered if there was still any cat left in me.

Alma came out onto the porch and stood there with her arms crossed. Her shirttail flapped a little in the dry afternoon breeze. With her stance wide and her sleeves rolled to the elbows, she looked like some sweet but hard-luck kid comically daring anyone to give her a shove. She also looked stronger than any of us—in attitude, anyway—and I wondered how she'd managed to keep the world from leaving its marks on her the way it had on Dell, and the way it probably had on me. I wondered what her marriage had been like, and when it had ended, and why. I wondered whose fault the breakup had been. I wondered if they'd fought like cats and dogs.

"Where's your crew?" she asked.

"In the barn. They need a couple of good two-by-fours to lift this cage out."

"I'm not sure what all Daddy kept out there," she said as she ambled down the steps to the yard. "But I think there's a lumber pile in one of the horse stalls."

"They'll find what they need," I told her. I hopped down from the truck and rolled her bike over to the porch. "That's quite a beast you've got there," I said. "I don't think he knows it yet, but he's about to gnaw his way right through that wire."

Alma stepped over to the truck to see the damage for herself.

"The bottom half needs to be shored up," I went on. "If you like, I can nail on a few extra boards."

"I'd appreciate that. I've had enough animal disasters for one day." She turned from the cage and sat on the lowered tailgate, bouncing her weight so the sheet metal creaked and groaned through several years of rust. When she'd settled into place, she scuffed her shoes back and forth through the dirt, raising a cloud of dust around her feet. The cougar looked up, momentarily interested in this new commotion.

"I wouldn't turn my back on that cat if I were you," I said. "Not until his pen's been reinforced. There's no telling what he's liable to do."

Alma just smiled. "That's what makes it fun." She patted a spot beside her. "Come have a seat, Nolan. See what it feels like to let a little danger into your life."

I knew well enough what danger felt like. I used to feel it in baseball when I crowded the plate on a brush-back pitch. I used to feel it riding double on Dell's motorcycle when we'd lean into a curve doing ninety. I used to feel it all the time around Laney.

Nowadays I felt it at the river, and the hospital, and the carnival, and the old Stone Bridge, and Tump's Café, and Jerry Rathburn's house, and my house. And I felt it all the time around Alma.

The cat yawned and began to lick his paws, so I figured a sudden lunge was unlikely. I walked over and eased myself onto the sagging tailgate. Alma laced her fingers with mine, the same way she used to in *Oklahoma!* before the start of each big dance.

"Scary, isn't it?" she said. She closed her eyes and leaned her head back toward the cage. "Just like a carnival ride."

"Scary hardly covers it," I said, stealing a glance at the cougar. I had to be careful here—no sudden moves, no lapses in judgment.

"I love dangerous animals," Alma said, her eyes still closed. "I plan to get as many as I can afford."

"Most animals are dangerous."

She smiled. "I don't mean rabid chipmunks, Nolan. I'm talking about *dramatically* dangerous animals—ones that can tear you to pieces. That's the kind of zoo I want."

"You're off to a good start, then."

She opened her eyes and looked at me. "Sorry I didn't speak when we drove up," she apologized. "But I knew Dell was bound to tell y'all about the ostrich, and I just couldn't stand to hear it."

I sat there for a moment and watched Dell work his way along the ditch by the highway, waving his wand methodically through the tall weeds.

"We got about three hours of work in today," I said, nodding toward the brush piles we'd left behind. "But to look at it from up here, you'd think we barely got started."

"I can tell you made progress," she said, giving my hand a slight squeeze. "Did you see the old stumps?"

"I saw a lot of stumps, but no old ones."

She pointed back toward the western end of the property, where the sun now hovered orange above a dark wall of trees. "Down there in that low pasture there's about thirty oak stumps. Big ones, two or three feet across. Daddy made a deal with the sawmill in Skinem—two hundred dollars for every tree they cut down. That's how he kept things going after he quit putting in crops."

"No, I didn't see those," I told her. "I never went down that far."

"Well, they're too big to chop out."

"You might could pull them up with a tractor," I suggested.

She shook her head. "Daddy tried that once and broke an axle."

I shrugged. "So leave the stumps in. Work around them. There's still plenty of room out there. You've got enough land here to zone a small city."

"A zoo *is* a small city, if you build it right," she said. "I want to set up real habitats, not just cages. It'll take every inch of land I've got."

"Unless you want to set up a habitat for stump dwellers, I don't know what else to tell you."

"I was thinking dynamite."

I let go of her hand and stood up from the tailgate. "I don't know if that's such a good idea. Dynamite's hard to come by. You don't just walk into a store and buy it. I think you've got to have some kind of permit."

"Can you take care of that for me?" she asked.

"Alma, I get skittish around champagne corks. Dynamite's way out of my league."

She laughed and brushed her fingers along my arm. "I'm not asking you to blow anything up, Nolan. I'm just asking you to find out what the paperwork is. If it takes a permit, I need to know how to get one. And the way they've been blasting that riverbed all summer—well, there must be somebody around town you can talk to about it."

Life's not all cats and dogs, of course. Sometimes it's an oversized flightless bird with its head in the wrong place and its neck stuck too far out.

"Yeah," I told her. "I guess I know somebody."

Demolition Derby

IN THE BEGINNING WAS THE WORD, and the Word that night was about Buddy Pilot.

Buddy had joined up with Ricky Malone for a short bow-hunting trip the previous Sunday morning. Nothing was in season, of course, but that didn't matter. What they'd figured to do was head down to Coldwater Woods, which was pretty remote, and just take shots at whatever Ricky's dogs could flush from cover. Ricky drove his old pickup, and Buddy rode in back to make sure none of the dogs jumped over the side. His bow was in back with him, and when they drove past Tump's Café on their way out of town, Buddy saw his chance to get even for the way Tump had treated him at the last poker game.

He told Ricky later he hadn't meant to hit anybody—said he hadn't even realized Tump was in the café. All he'd wanted to do was break some glass and cost somebody a little time and money. Hitting Tump was just an accident, he said, a lucky shot, so screw anybody who blamed him for it.

Well. I could believe it was an accident. Buddy Pilot was mean enough to put an arrow in anybody's back, but he'd always been lousy with a bow. I was in Boy Scouts with him, and one time on a camping trip I saw him shoot a hole in his own knapsack when he tried to kill a possum outside his tent.

I learned about Buddy's guilt from Dell on the last night of the fair, the night scheduled for the demolition derby and the fireworks display, the night Chet came to preach his warnings to the midway crowds, the night I had a reason to look for Steve Pitts.

Laney was out of town, which, for once, was fine with me. My day had been complicated enough, what with working two jobs, seeing Jesus, and growing more stupid over Alma. The last thing I needed was to get quizzed by my wife on why I had to speak to her boyfriend about dynamite. But circumstances let me off the hook: according to the note on the kitchen table, Laney had driven her sister and Darwin back to Lynchburg, and she planned to stay there overnight. Donna was *still in crisis,* the note explained, and *needed a stabilizing presence*—two phrases she must have picked up from television, because that sure as hell wasn't the way Laney talked. I felt a little insulted by the phoniness of it. Were we so far apart we couldn't even use ordinary language?

Her note was unsigned, too, which also made me wonder. I mean, did that make it more personal, or less?

Or was I nuts even to worry about things like that?

Since Laney had taken the car, I called Dell for a ride to the fairgrounds—I knew he'd be going out there to see the demolition derby—and by the time we'd found a place to park behind the live-stock barn, he'd filled me in on Buddy.

"That boy's about to find out what trouble is," Dell concluded as we climbed out of his truck. "He's got the sword of Diogenes hanging over his head."

"Damocles," I corrected him. "Diogenes was the guy with the lantern."

"Lantern?" He squinted into a slight frown. "You sure?"

"Yeah, I think so. He's the one who said he was looking for an honest man."

Dell shrugged. "Damocles, Diogenes—same difference. They're both shit-out-of-luck. And Buddy's prospects ain't much brighter. I bet he couldn't even get a loan from Hometown Finance right now, with all the risk factors he's got going. There's a stink on him worse than Jerry Rathburn."

Dell was probably right. Except for other lowlifes like Ricky

Malone and maybe a couple of Buddy's little bastard kids around town, nobody was likely to give him any benefit of the doubt. There was no church group behind him, and he'd never joined any civic organizations like the Kiwanis or the Lions Club or the Elks. Worst of all, he'd never served in the Armed Forces, so not even the VFW or the American Legion would be there to stick up for him. It was one thing to be a misfit, but Buddy Pilot was an *unaffiliated* misfit— and that made him fair game for anybody.

We wove our way across the field toward the grandstand, moving in and out of the makeshift parking rows, with Dell pausing now and again to misadjust the side mirrors on all the imports he passed.

"Maybe he'll skip town," I said as Dell twisted the mirror on a late-model Volvo.

He shook his head. "I doubt it. Buddy probably figures it'll all blow over in a week or two. He knows he'll never get arrested."

"Why not?"

"This ain't some FBI show on television, Nolan. The county's not about to waste any time or money taking a case like this to court. There's no proof without Ricky, and Ricky won't never testify. Him and Buddy's been best friends since kindergarten."

"Well, somebody ought to do something."

"I expect somebody will. It just might not be by the letter of the law." Dell looked at his watch. "Tell you what—soon as this derby's over, let's you and me take a walk over to Buddy's booth, see how things are going. Maybe you can tell him how frustrated you are over the legal issues."

"You mean he's here?"

"I imagine so. He's been working the carny all week, running that stall where you throw darts at balloons. Maybe you can even bust a few balloons while you're there. Win a prize for Laney—or for Alma, depending on how things stand."

"Things stand like they always do," I said.

"That bad, huh?"

"Yeah," I admitted. "Just about that bad."

The roar of two dozen rough, unmufflered engines rose above the general din of the midway crowd, and a cheer went up from the grandstand.

"Oh, hell, they're starting already," Dell said, moving more quickly through the fringes of the carnival crowd. "I hate coming in late. The first few crashes are always the best." He scanned the disorganized assortment of food wagons, carnival rides, and game tents ahead of us, then veered left into the 4-H pavilion. "This way's quicker," he said.

"You go ahead," I told him. "I've got to find Steve Pitts."

Dell stopped by a row of rooster pens. The livestock show was over, and now the farmers were quietly loading all their prize animals into trailers and flatbeds. Swarms of small giggling children— excited, I guess, to be up so late—climbed along the top rails of the empty judging stalls, keeping well clear of the remaining livestock and their fathers. Some of the kids had blue ribbons pinned to their shirt pockets or their overalls. The stink of manure mingled with the smell of the spray paint the 4-H-ers used to touch up the markings on their show cows.

"What the hell do you need with Steve Pitts?" Dell asked.

"Zoo business."

Dell seemed to consider that for a moment, then poked a finger through the wire mesh to stroke the feathers of a sleeping rooster. The rooster stirred slightly, but like most show animals, it had a high tolerance for human prodding and didn't bother waking up. A fighting cock would have leapt up screeching, a flurry of beak and claws.

"Well, Steve'll be easy enough to find after the derby," Dell said. "He's running the fireworks show tonight. You can catch up with him then."

That sounded reasonable. The truth was, I felt uneasy about roaming the carnival alone—not because I was worried about getting into something ugly with Steve, but because I might run into Alma. I knew she'd be there tonight, and with Laney out of town I'd be prone to making more than my usual share of mistakes. Better to lay low.

"All right," I agreed. Dell smiled and smacked the top of the rooster cage, causing a flutter inside.

"Hey, bud, don't spook them birds," a man called from the back of a beat-up flatbed. Dell offered a wave of apology, and then launched himself again toward the grandstand.

"This'll be like old home week," Dell said as we hurried through the pavilion.

"What do you mean by that?" I called after him.

"I bet every junker on that track's one of our repos," he said happily.

"I thought they went back to car lots or something."

"Not the crummy ones," Dell explained. "Ray holds onto those and then rents the whole fleet out to the Jaycees for the derby."

I didn't know quite how to digest this new information. The crummier cars tended to be the ones our clients needed the most. I guess I'd always imagined that when we repossessed something, it went on to some better future, becoming a best-buy for some thrifty hard-luck shopper. I thought we were somehow involved in redistributing property in a positive way—or, if not positive, at least not wantonly wasteful. It never occurred to me that we might be just rounding up fodder for a demolition derby. "Ray rents them out?"

"Cheaper that way," Dell said. "No titles to transfer. Besides, the Jaycees don't want to mess with the cleanup. And this way Ray gets to sell off all the scrap metal when it's over."

"What do the Jaycees get out of it?"

"Plenty," he answered. "Tonight'll be their biggest fund-raiser of the year." He turned to me and clapped a hand on my shoulder. "That's something we can feel good about," he added. "None of it could've happened without you and me."

The main entryway of the grandstand stretched out ahead of us. Dell stood there, gazing down the tunnel to the lighted field, which was already disappearing under a massive swirl of dust. He took in a long breath, apparently savoring this first hazy glimpse of the spectacle. Sounds of grinding gears and shattering collisions reverberated along the corridor.

"That's why this is my favorite night of the fair," he said. "There's probably two thousand people in those stands, and not one of 'em can say my job don't contribute to the community."

"Except the people who had to walk to get here," I said, but he ignored me and moved on toward the track.

The derby was impressive, I had to grant that, with each paint-splashed car plowing heedlessly into wreck after wreck after wreck—rebel flags flying from the aerials, business logos pasted to the doors—and the crowd roaring its approval above the constant, clattering whine of damaged engines and the relentless crunch of metal against metal, machine against machine, and debris flying haphazardly through the air, smashing windshields and slashing tires, and cars rolling over or catching fire, and their drivers dashing for safety through the smoky, moving maze of the pockmarked field.

The insurance coverage must have been a nightmare.

And Dell was right, I did recognize a lot of the cars. Mrs. McRady's old Pinto was one of the first to burst into flames, so I figured maybe we had done her a favor after all. But I felt bad to see Red Robertson's little Toyota crushed between two big Oldsmobiles. I was sorry, too, when Miss Emily Reece's Chevette got totaled in a head-on with Doug Strong's Pontiac Catalina. And my heart sank when I recognized Alma's Omni limping timidly among much sturdier pieces of junk.

Still, there was Dell's assurance of a silver lining, no matter how faint. We were, after all, helping to raise money for the Jaycees so they could support some local worthy cause. New traffic lights at a dangerous intersection, maybe, or new textbooks for the high school. Something helpful, something useful. Something to balance out the sheer tonnage of so much pointless destruction.

"What're the Jaycees raising money for?" I asked.

Dell turned from the iron rail that fronted the improvised figure-eight track and cupped his hand behind his ear. We'd managed to squeeze ourselves through the standing mob of latecomers and drunks down to the very edge of the action, to the deafening middle ground where the roar of the derby echoed against the roar of the grandstand crowd.

"What're the Jaycees raising money for?" I repeated, louder this time so Dell could hear.

He smiled and nodded, then leaned in close to my face and told me the answer. "A new war memorial!" he yelled.

"What?" I said, though I knew I'd heard him right.

"A new war memorial!" he shouted again. "Some big bronze thing for the courthouse lawn!"

There was a sudden lull in the action as the half-dozen surviving cars idled down into more defensive maneuvers, circling slowly away from each other like careful predators searching out a weakness. The crowd quieted down, too, waiting to see what strategies the drivers would try next.

"Why the hell would the Jaycees do that?" I asked.

"The Gulf War," he said. "They want to get a jump on the rest of the state."

"But nobody from this county died in the Gulf War. We didn't even have anybody over there."

"Humpy Hawthorne was there," Dell corrected me. "You remember him—he was that goofy-looking batboy our last year in Pony League. And Butch Fuller's kid—what's his name? You know, the slow one—bald-headed fellow—works down at the feed warehouse."

"Arnett," I told him.

"Yeah, that's him," he said. "Well, Arnett and Humpy was both over there with some kind of medical reserve outfit. They was in charge of handing out the water."

So that was the story. Two local half-wits had been water boys in Desert Storm, and now we needed another war memorial.

Another goddamned war memorial.

Didn't they know what the real war was?

If the Jaycees truly wanted to get a jump on the rest of the state, they'd forget about Humpy and Arnett and put their money into something more original. Something innovative. An imaginary monument, maybe—a giant, invisible purple heart for all the casualties who never left the county, the ones who spent their whole unmilitary lives treading water right here in the deep end of the pool, praying for the next sour gulp of air. I could help with the list: a cousin with four fingers, a comatose grandmother still waiting for Jesus, a sister-in-law crippled by nightmares, a baby brother someone dropped in the delivery room, an alcoholic mother who finally swallowed the right pills. Maybe even a disappointed wife living unhappily in the broken-down shell of an uninsured house.

They were the ones who deserved a demolition derby.

"The Legion or the VFW probably should've been the people to back it," Dell added. "But you know how snobby those old game birds are about their wars. They ain't ever gonna empty their bank accounts to commemorate a handful of rear-guard noncombatants."

A sudden cheer went up from the crowd, and Dell and I both shifted our attention back to the field.

"Well, sonofabitch," Dell said. "I told you Steve Pitts would be easy enough to find."

It was Steve, all right. Even with the yellow blanket of dust still clouding the track, that much was obvious. He'd just rammed his company backhoe through the closed gate at the far end of the field and was now bearing down hard on a partly disabled Buick Skylark that had blundered across his path.

"What the hell's he doing?" I asked.

"Quitting his job, it looks like," Dell said. "Bill McDonald won't stand for having that backhoe tore up."

As he closed on the Skylark, Steve extended the backhoe's arm forward so the bucket rammed like a fist through the driver's window. The Skylark jolted to a stop, and we all held our breath, afraid the driver hadn't ducked in time. But a couple of seconds later, the passenger door swung open and Ricky Malone scrambled out onto the track.

The crowd cheered again, though it wasn't clear whether it was for Ricky or for Steve. Ricky gripped his thigh with both hands—I guess he'd taken some kind of blow in the collision—but instead of heading for the sidelines he limped angrily around the front end of his wreck to scream at Steve. Not a good move—apparently Steve had no interest in conversation. He carefully extracted the steel arm from the window of Ricky's Skylark and then turned the backhoe on Ricky himself.

When Ricky realized Steve was coming after him, he hobbled away toward the grandstand—toward me and Dell, in fact—but our guardrail was more than seventy yards away, and before he'd covered half the distance he had to take shelter behind a demolished Plymouth Fury. Steve rammed that car, too, punching through from the passenger side this time, and when the bucket got hung up for a moment under the steering column, Ricky broke again for the stands. He made it well ahead of the backhoe, but as he climbed up over the rail, a cluster of hostile drunks surged forward and shoved him back onto the track. He sprawled on his stomach in the dirt, and I could see his panicked face as he froze there, watching the backhoe accelerate toward him. But then he rolled to the side and clawed his way under the bottom rail just as Steve came rumbling past. The drunks hooted their disappointment as Ricky pulled himself up by a support post and struggled away through the crowd like a wounded animal.

Steve steered the backhoe in a slow circle before the grandstand, waving his green ball cap like a hero in a ticker-tape parade. Then he idled down for a moment and held up a Marine Corps flag. The mob thundered its approval, whistling and stomping and clapping until he finally veered toward the broken gate and puttered peacefully from the field. The remaining cars—Alma's frail Omni still among them—continued their cautious sparring, clipping each other's fenders in low-speed attacks. But the crowd hardly cared anymore. The real show was already over.

"What do you think that was all about?" I yelled.

Dell tilted his head closer to my ear. "Tump Wood, most likely," he shouted. "Steve and Tump was both in the Corps. Marines tend to stick up for each other. *Semper fi*." He stuck two fingers in his teeth and let out a long, shrill whistle. "That boy ain't changed a lick since high school!"

"None of us has," I said, though I don't think he heard me.

Dell turned away from the derby and we both began to watch the rowdy drunks who'd given Ricky such a hard time. They were younger than us, just baby-faced delinquents, mostly—grimy punks with scraggly beards and cigarettes and fake daredevil toughness, happy to threaten anybody who came along.

Same crops, different seasons.

In time, they'd learn to rein themselves in, just like we had. They'd learn to put on a better face for the public, not sneer so much. They'd take over their fathers' businesses, marry each other's sisters, and plan family trips to Disney World. They'd become active in the churches and the men's clubs. They'd coach Little League. They'd raise money for charity. They'd get invited to cut the ribbons for local grand openings. And they'd still be capable of just about anything.

"I need some french fries," Dell finally shouted, and we walked out of the grandstand before the derby was finished.

On the midway the atmosphere was a lot more cordial, and while Dell settled down to a pair of cheeseburgers and a plate of fries at a card table under the Masons' big dining canopy, I relaxed on a cool metal chair out front, enjoying the familiar background of carnival smells and colored lights and calliope tunes.

The human noises were different on the midway, too—less raucous than the catcall of the grandstand, where everybody was part of the same near-frantic sound. Here, I could pick out my father's voice from time to time as he called tonight's bingo game; and the false-friendly barkers luring those earnest 4-H-ers to their booths; and the roving packs of junior-high-school girls, shrieking out happy revelations about their current rotation of boyfriends. And underneath it all, faint but still recognizable, I could even hear Chet wailing hoarsely about salvation somewhere among the sideshows.

Then I noticed another distant sound: the periodic popping of balloons.

I looked back at Dell, who'd moved his plate to another table so he could eat with Rex Yearwood and Bobby Allen, two former repo men who now worked at Lincoln Savings and Loan. Bobby was the loan officer who'd financed my new family room, and since I'd missed my last two payments, I figured it might be best not to join them.

I got up and moved farther along the midway, beyond the food tents and the Scrambler and the Zipper, all the way down past Donna's Tilt-A-Whirl, where the sideshow attractions began. The sideshows were standard stuff, mostly—rip-off exhibits that promised all kinds of freaks and oddities but were usually just photo galleries or stunts rigged with mirrors. The fat man was real, but no fatter than my Great-Aunt Aggie. The bearded woman looked like a teenaged boy.

The skill booths along that row were sucker bets, too—lead milk bottles that wouldn't knock over, basketball rims too tight for even the most perfect shot, peach baskets angled forward to dump the softballs on the ground. Any carny hack could run those games—just take the money and pretend to be surprised and sympathetic when nobody won.

But the dart game was a different kind of con. Breaking the balloons was easy. The trick was collecting the prize. Pop a thousand in a row, and the barker would still keep pulling key chains and colored fuzz balls from beneath his counter, swearing all the time you were just three balloons away from that giant stuffed giraffe. It took a liar's liar to run a booth like that—somebody who could contradict himself without batting an eye and then claim you'd heard him wrong the first time. It took a fellow like Buddy Pilot.

But business looked slow at the moment. Because of the derby, traffic was light all over the midway, and Buddy was taking advantage of the lull, leaning against a clear space on his target wall, blowing up some replacement balloons. I guess he knew there'd be a fresh round of customers once the grandstand crowd emptied back onto the carnival, so he was trying to get a head start on the rush. Each small balloon took just half a breath, and then he'd tie off the neck and drop it into a big cardboard box against a side wall of his booth. The other side was lined with shelves where the un-winnable prizes were on display—clock radios and watches and gaudy cowboy boots and studded leather jackets and compact-disc players and all kinds of exotic stuffed animals, including big red bears.

Buddy wasn't off-duty, though. A few couples strolled by—teenage sweethearts who knew better than to squander their date in the chaos of the demolition derby—and Buddy would hold back at first, pretending to let them pass unaccosted. But as they came alongside his loudspeaker, which he'd hidden in the narrow grass alley between his dart booth and the penny-pitch next door, he'd hold a balloon to his barker's microphone and pop it. The amplified sound was startling, like a gunshot from the dark. Some of the kids laughed it off and some got angry—but all of them stopped. That's when Buddy would make his pitch, quiet and personal, without the microphone at all. I was too far away to hear what he was saying, but it must have been smooth because he managed to get into the wallet of just about everybody who stopped.

I wasn't the only one watching Buddy snag suckers from that thin parade of passersby. Frank Shelton had an eye on him, too. I liked Frank—we'd been on a bowling team together in tenth grade and had stayed friends, even though we hadn't seen each other much since graduation. Frank was a deputy sheriff now.

He was sitting on a spare electrical generator directly across from Buddy's booth, right next to the guess-your-weight guy. His arms were folded across his chest, and his deputy hat—which I guess they made him wear even on hot nights—was pulled down low over his eyes. I think he meant to look intimidating, but that kind of thing was wasted on Buddy, who'd known Frank just as long as I had. Finally, I walked over and said hello.

He frowned when he first glanced up—annoyed, I guess, to have his mean stare interrupted—but when he saw it was me, he dropped the hard-ass look and bobbed his head a few times—a trademark nod of approval left over from our bowling-team days.

"I see you're giving Buddy the old evil eye," I said.

"He needs it," Frank answered.

"No argument there," I agreed, and Frank went back to watching Buddy, who was blowing up more balloons. I propped my foot on the edge of the generator and leaned across my knee. "I guess you must know something."

"I know all kinds of things," he told me. "I even know who found Jerry Rathburn's body."

"Maybe you ought to write a book. Get yourself on some of those talk shows."

"Lose too many friends that way." He looked at me again. "Hey, how's Donna doing these days? Thought I saw y'all here the other night."

"Yeah, that was probably us. Donna's doing okay. She's got a pretty good job over there in Lynchburg taking tour groups through the distillery. But I guess she has her ups and downs, same as the rest of us."

"Ain't that the truth," he said. He shook his head. "I sure wish she'd move back to town. You know, I had a crush on that girl all through high school."

"She ain't living on the moon, Frank. She's just a half hour away."

"Yeah, I know," he said. "But she never had any real interest in me anyway. She never even knew my name until a couple of years after we graduated."

"Give it a shot," I told him. "She'd probably be glad to hear from you."

I meant that sincerely. Frank had always been a decent fellow, and while decency had never been the best way to attract girls in high school, it carried more weight now that we were older. I mean, sooner or later most women realized that jail time wasn't the best qualification in a boyfriend. Eventually the sociopaths got traded in for milder, more reliable types, the kind who bought life insurance. I saw a lot of that when I worked for my father.

Laney was an obvious exception—she still had that weakness for men with bad attitudes. But not Donna—Donna had already had her fill of outlaw bastards. She might just be ready for somebody like Frank.

"I honest-to-God wish that was the case, Nolan," he said, "but it ain't too likely. Her and me did kinda get together one time about six years ago. I thought it was a pretty big night. Most fun I've had at a carnival my whole life. But when I called her up later she just brushed me off. Acted like she didn't even know me."

A sudden line drive off the left-field wall.

I guess I could have asked the obvious question: was Frank's big night the same night Donna lost the pageant? But somehow I couldn't bring myself to do it. Paternity was a touchy subject for me right then and I felt skittish about pinning down any details, even if they weren't my own. Certain topics were just too volatile to settle with a quick yes or no, I knew that much. And for the first time I realized that, whatever might happen with me and Laney down the line, I'd probably never ask her for a straight answer on that point. Facts could be fatal in too large a dose.

So I didn't ask Frank anything. What I did instead was lift his hat off his head to look at him more closely. He grabbed the hat back and glanced around to see if anybody had witnessed my breach of his authority.

"Hey, don't be doing that, Nolan," he said, smoothing out the crease. "This hat's official."

It was a tough call either way. Maybe so, maybe not. But definitely possible. Anyway, I couldn't help but laugh. When the deck was this full of wild cards, almost anybody could draw a good hand.

"You might stand a better chance than you think," I said. "You know anything about Darwin?"

That seemed safe enough to ask, but Frank just looked confused. "I know a little bit, I guess. Survival of the fittest, right? And evolution—they had that famous monkey trial about it over in Dayton. My grandparents grew up there, said the whole town stayed on edge about it for years." He set the hat on his head and carefully adjusted it back into place. "Made a good movie, though."

"Not that Darwin," I said. "I'm talking about my nephew. Donna's kid."

Frank narrowed his eyes and nodded. "Oh, yeah, I know who you mean. I figured that little boy must be hers—I knew you and Laney didn't have kids yet. But Donna's divorced now, right?"

"She never got married," I told him.

"I sure cain't imagine that. A knockout like her."

"I'm telling you, Frank, she's waiting for you to pick up that phone."

"I appreciate the false encouragement," he said. "Maybe one of these days I'll give her a call."

I thumped the brim of Frank's hat, then stood up straight and stretched the sore muscles in my back. Buddy was still stockpiling balloons for the next wave of customers—the last wave, since this was closing night. He seemed totally preoccupied with his work, but I knew that was just an act. Buddy wasn't the kind of guy who could concentrate that long, especially with a deputy sheriff watching him. I knew he was keeping track of every move we made.

"I believe I'll step over there and try my hand at some darts," I told Frank. "I'm feeling pretty lucky right now."

"Holler if you need help," he said cheerfully. "I sure wouldn't mind shooting Buddy in the knee."

"Just don't hit me by mistake," I said, and walked across the lane to Buddy's booth.

Buddy didn't look up, but he knew I was there. He began to work with more style, more showmanship, knotting each neck with a snap and then shooting each oblong balloon into the air so it could drift down slowly onto the pile.

"Looks like you found something you're good at," I said.

Buddy gave me a tight, phony smile. "Three darts for a dollar," he announced, the robot tending to business. "Break three balloons, take home a prize."

"Okay." I took out a dollar and put it on the counter. "What can I win?"

Buddy slid three darts across to me and nodded toward the crowded shelves. "Just about anything you see on that wall," he lied.

"For just three darts?"

"Three darts'll win you a prize."

"One of those red bears, maybe?"

"A prize," he repeated. "You'll get a choice."

I faced the wall of balloons and measured out three careful throws.

"Nice going, champ," he said after the third balloon popped. "Here's your choice." He reached under the counter and brought out a rubber worm and a six-inch wooden ruler.

"What about that bear?"

"You're not up to that level yet," he said. "You'd have to break a few more balloons. Trade your way up."

"How many more?"

"A few," he answered. "I'll tell you when you get there."

"All right." I put a five-dollar bill on the counter. "Give me fifteen darts."

Buddy smiled and stuffed the money in his jeans pocket, then counted out the darts and shoved them toward me. I picked up the whole bundle, which completely filled my hand.

"By the way, you missed a good derby tonight," I said. "Steve Pitts tried to run down Ricky Malone."

Buddy didn't react, so I figured Ricky must have already limped through with the news.

"Yeah, lots of people get hurt in those derbies," Buddy said. "But Ricky's a big boy. He can take care of himself."

"I guess he can," I agreed. "I'm sure he'll figure out how to get Steve and everybody else off his back."

"And how's that?" he asked, the smirk spreading over his face.

"Just tell the sheriff what he knows about Tump Wood."

Buddy leaned across the counter and stared at me hard. "Look, asshole, I ain't worried about Ricky. I ain't worried about Steve Pitts, or you, or goddamn Deputy Dawg over there. And if I want to use some old fart's butt for target practice, I'll do it any goddamn time I feel like it. You got that?"

I was grateful to Buddy for his little speech, because a new light fell on the whole situation. Maybe it wasn't the kind of grand revelation my father came to after the war—my life's calling wasn't revealed to me, or anything like that. But I did have a sudden clear vision of the work at hand. After all this time, I'd finally been drafted.

"I don't know if you remember this, Buddy," I said, "but I never was a very good pitcher."

"What?"

"My slider kept getting away from me. Two years in a row I hit more batters than anybody else in Pony League."

"Yeah, you sucked," he said. "So what?"

"I'm going for fifteen balloons at once," I informed him, stepping back a couple of paces and squaring up to the target wall.

I could see the uncertainty on Buddy's face. That much was typical—he'd never had good reaction time. Hot grounders always made it past him to the outfield. I was already accelerating into the forward motion of the pitch before he even opened his mouth to form a question, and by then it was too late. His standard look of slack-jawed surprise had just barely begun to register as the darts left my hand, and as they hit, he stumbled sideways, his whole face wide with disbelief.

Three of the darts hit balloons.

Most of the others hit Buddy—five or six solid shots, maybe, strung out across his torso, plus a couple of shallow punctures up by one shoulder. I was pretty pleased with the percentage. I knew there'd be misses—I'd intentionally loosened my grip so the darts would sling wide. A tight pattern might have been something he could duck away from, and I didn't want to risk that. This wasn't meant to be a brush-back pitch. It was meant to take the sorry son-ofabitch out of the game.

Buddy stiffened up and started making little gasping noises, like somebody had just poured ice water down his back. I think maybe one of the darts had poked into a lung, but mostly he was just pan-icked and confused. Part of him wanted to climb over the counter and come after me, I was sure of that. But he also must have been worried about internal damage, because instead of scrambling out to fight, which I'd expected, he just stood there, rooted in place. For a few seconds he stared down at his chest, watching the rise and fall of his own shaky breaths, then he began frantically plucking darts from his T-shirt like he was snatching away hornets. When he'd cleared himself of the darts he pressed his hands over as many of the small blood spots as he could cover at once, and began to holler. Not words, really—just incoherent wailing. I guess I'd scared him pretty good.

Still, I was surprised at how fast he fell apart. When I let go of those darts, I thought sure I'd pushed us both across the line, that he'd come charging out with a rage as big as my own, and that one of us would be halfway dead even before Frank could cross the mid-way to stop it.

But there was no fight in him at all. He just stood there shaking, croaking out those sad animal noises. Maybe he thought I'd killed him, I don't know. But whatever the case, he looked like a ruin, and I felt bad for him. I also felt guilty. I'd imagined Buddy Pilot to be a true monster of the midway, and here he'd turned out to be just one more balloon in the gallery.

Frank gripped my shoulder. "Stay calm, you two." He stepped past me toward Buddy, who still looked dazed. "You all right there, Buddy?"

"I need a doctor," he said in a voice I hadn't heard him use since grade school.

"Lemme take a look," Frank said, and Buddy staggered to the counter and pulled up his shirt. His skin was pale, and blood still trickled from a few of the holes. Frank leaned forward and examined the holes. "Peppered you pretty good," he said. "But you'll be all right."

"I'm not all right," Buddy insisted. "You don't know nothing about it."

"Oh, hell, Buddy, get over it," Frank told him. "He didn't hit nothing but fat. My cousin Billy went through worse than this when they treated him for rabies."

He turned back to me. "So what's the story here, Nolan?"

"I don't know, Frank."

"He hit me with a handful of darts," Buddy whined. "You saw it, Frank. Arrest him."

"I cain't arrest him, Buddy," Frank said. His tone was purely reasonable, like he was explaining something to a five-year-old. "You just stepped in front of his throw. One of those freak accidents you always hear about. Personally, I think they ought to outlaw these carnival dart games before somebody gets hurt."

Buddy didn't argue—he saw justice would be a dead end for him this time around.

"I need a doctor," he repeated, more sullenly. "I might be stuck somewhere bad."

Frank sighed. "All right, come on, then. I'll take you up to the emergency room. Have 'em give you a tetanus shot."

Buddy hung his "Back in 5 Minutes" sign on the balloon wall and climbed awkwardly over the counter. He still looked like he might faint. Frank mumbled a few things into his walkie-talkie, then straightened his hat.

"I'm surprised at you, Nolan," Frank said, lowering his voice. "You could've put this redneck bastard's eye out, playing around like that."

"I wasn't playing," I told him.

Frank looked over at Buddy, who was still pressing his hands to his wounds. "You're also lucky he's drugged up right now. Buddy's a whole lot meaner when his head's clear."

"You think he's stoned?" I asked.

"Hell, just look at him," Frank said. "Not even Buddy's that dim-witted. Those pupils are big enough to ride the school bus."

"Might be a good time to talk to him about Tump Wood."

"Oh, yeah," Frank said, "we'll definitely take the scenic route. But you're the one I'm worried about. You think you can behave yourself while I'm gone?"

"Shouldn't be a problem," I told him, though I had my doubts. This was the last night of the carnival, after all, and sometimes things got rowdy.

"I want your word on that, Nolan."

My word. Hardly the best guarantee, when words could be taken so many ways.

"Sure," I told him. He bobbed his head a few times, accepting my answer, and then led Buddy away through the gathering crowd.

Maybe I should have gone with him. He could have dropped me off at home and we both could have stopped worrying. My house was safe enough tonight. Nothing there but broken beams and a broken desktop. And a dead lizard buried in the yard.

But I couldn't leave the game just yet, not with a runner still on base.

Anyway, it hadn't been dark but an hour. The midway was just now coming back to life. No harm in walking around a little more. I could treat myself to a corndog, maybe say hello to a few old friends. I could even try some of those other skill games. Trade my way up to bigger prizes.

Sure. I could slow myself down for a while.

I still had time to kill before the fireworks.

Revelations

THE FORTUNE-TELLER WOULDN'T COMMENT on my future. Both my palms, she said, were clever forgeries.

"What's that supposed to mean?" I asked.

The only light came from a red-paned kerosene lantern on the card table between us, so the atmosphere was murky at best. I could barely make out the patterns on the mock Persian rugs that hung from the tent walls. But she seemed to see everything clearly.

"Your hands are full of lies," she said, jabbing a blunt forefinger into my left palm. "Too many contradictions. I can't predict five minutes from hands like this. Nobody could."

"They're scratched up," I explained. "I've been doing fieldwork."

She peered closely at the joints of my fingers and shook her head. "No. You haven't. Anyway, your time's up. Sorry." She let go of my wrist and sat up straight in her seat.

"But I just got here," I objected.

"Some readings don't take very long," she said, turning the lantern down low. "Sometimes the future's illegible. Now beat it."

"I don't think you're the real Madame Zanzibar."

"Who is?" she replied, and extinguished the light.

It wasn't the best five bucks I'd ever spent.

As I felt my way through the darkness toward the exit flap, I tried to think what my next move ought to be. I'd already lost money at nearly every booth on the midway, and now that I had Madame Zanzibar's House of Mystery under my belt there wasn't much left to check out. I had no interest in letting The Great Gordo guess my weight, and I'd long ago learned to stop embarrassing myself with a sledgehammer at the Test-Your-Strength pole.

The only game left was Steve Pitts.

The midway crowd was noisier now, and with the closing-night clock ticking down, clueless gangs of high-school boys prowled more obnoxiously among the booths and rides, hoping to impress some girl, any girl, with crude remarks and dirty come-ons. I remembered what it was like—that desperate stretch of howling when nothing in the teenaged heart worked right. I probably started out that way with Laney, staging some ugly spectacle to make her slow down and look at me, the way gawkers might pause for wreckage on the highway.

But it wasn't Laney who stood waiting for me outside Madame Zanzibar's tent. It was Alma.

"I thought that was you," she said, smiling and reaching out to touch my arm.

"I did, too, until a minute ago," I answered.

She looked up at the ornately painted tent behind me. "I take it you didn't much like your fortune."

"Madame Zanzibar had some technical difficulties. Apparently my fortune's still in doubt."

"Sounds ominous. I like that."

Oh, Alma. If I were still a young punk menacing the midway crowds, I'd offer you my letter jacket. I'd buy you cotton candy by the pound.

"She's pretty professional, though. I mean, she seemed to take her work seriously. I got the impression I was a genuine disappointment to her."

"Oh, I can't believe that," she said, and I came within a sledgehammer of kissing her. I didn't, though. I just smiled blandly, like I barely knew she was there. In the Test-Your-Strength category, it was a new personal best.

"Why don't you give the old girl a try," I suggested. "Maybe you'll have better luck."

"Maybe I'll do that." She started toward the tent opening, but lingered for a moment against my side. "We can compare notes when I come out," she said, draping her arm loosely around my waist.

"Don't know for sure if I'll be here," I warned her. "I'm still the guy with the unforseeable future."

"I guess I can risk it," she said, giving me a slight squeeze. Then she disappeared into Madame Zanzibar's tent to bet five dollars on her fate. The old woman cackled at once and began to moan through her lengthy introduction about the spirits of the lost—the same speech she'd given me before discovering I had so much confusion on my hands.

Surely Alma's case would be different, and Madame Zanzibar would give her the future she wanted—something risky and wild, with a homemade zoo full of dangerous animals. That was my hope, anyway, as I hurried away through the crowd.

My plan, insofar as I had one, was to make my way down to the far end of the midway, duck through the field where most of the carnival big-rigs and freight trailers were parked, and follow the bypass around toward the old Stone Bridge, three-quarters of a mile away. For safety reasons, the larger fireworks displays were always staged from the floodplain just south of the bridge, where no people or houses or businesses could be hurt by misfired rockets. It was an isolated piece of flatland, a landscape broken only by the old Camp Blount marker commemorating General Jackson's campaign against the Creeks. Steve would be there now, overseeing the final preparations for the spectacle.

But as I came to the end of the long row of gambling booths and sideshow tents, the mob thickened unexpectedly, and I found myself blocked by a wall of people, 200 or more, all clumped together and pressing forward, trying to hear the words of the newest attraction on the midway.

Chet had found his congregation.

"And there appeared a great wonder in the heaven!" he was shouting. *"A woman clothed with the sun! And the moon under her*

feet, and upon her head a crown of twelve stars! And there were lightnings, and voices, and thunderings, and an earthquake, and great hail! And there was war in heaven!"

War in heaven. No wonder Chet had drawn a crowd—he'd tapped into the mother lode. Jesus and his do-gooding were all right for Sunday mornings, but when it came to holding a carnival mob on a hot summer night, nothing could beat the Book of Revelation. It was God's horror movie, the nightmare at the end of the world, filled with mechanical monsters and genetic mutations, rolling without mercy across the land in wave after wave of unstoppable slaughter. The Four Horsemen of the Apocalypse, the Seven-Headed Beast, the Whore of Babylon, devils in the bottomless pit— everything conjured up for one final Earth-destroying battle, winner take all.

Winner take all that was left, anyway: ashes and stones and the smell of burnt sulphur.

"And behold a pale horse!" Chet cried out, his voice rising on the breeze. A few literalist morons near the back actually looked around, thinking the horse must be there somewhere. *"And his name that sat on him was Death!"* Chet continued. *"And Hell followed with him!"*

Madame Zanzibar could definitely have taken a couple of lessons from Chet in the drama department. He knew what sold the tickets, all right. Armageddon. Bloodletting and terror on the grandest scale. The hopeless agony of souls writhing in liquid fire. Swords of retribution striking down the multitudes. A war story to end all war stories.

But I had other business to look after. Not on Alma's behalf, so much, not anymore. Now that I'd abandoned her to her fate, I knew there were other reasons for me to find Steve Pitts. Dynamite permits barely figured into it.

I circled around the rear of the crowd and climbed across a trailer hitch into the darkness. As I walked out into the open field, I was struck by how completely separate the carnival was from the world around it. The wall of parked semis dampened the sound and blocked most of the ground-level light, so passing through the outer ring was as distinct as quitting some wild blowout of a party and stumbling out, ten seconds later, onto an absolutely deserted street.

The pioneers must have known what that separation was like—leaving the huddled circle of the wagon train at night to carry out some chore in hostile territory.

I wondered if any of them had ever felt the way I did now: that hostile territory wasn't so bad, once you got used to it. I guess they must have, because eventually all of them left the flimsy protection of the wagon trains behind them. That's what happened when people finally got where they were going.

As it happened, part of my family came to this county by wagon train. That was 180 years ago, and they stopped here not because it was their planned destination, but because their wagons got burned and they had to bury their dead.

And here I was, the beneficiary of it all, the latest and last offspring of the calamity. I mean, surely we inherited more from our forebears than just big family Bibles and rolltop desks. Surely, somewhere bone-deep in my makeup, embedded in the very structure of my cells, I carried some ancestral remnant of that massacre, some hint of knowing what it was like to have my family hacked apart by enemies I'd never met.

According to my Great-Aunt Ethel, the enemies that night were Creek Indians—or, more precisely, they were displaced Hillabees, originally the most peaceful of the North Alabama tribes. They went to war only after an unprovoked attack by one of General Jackson's glory-seeking subordinates, who cut down even the women and children as they tried to surrender. General White was his name. Later he suffered the embarrassment of a court-martial, though of course he was acquitted.

Great-Aunt Ethel came from the Hillabee branch of the family, on my great-great-grandmother's side. So the kinship I shared with those hapless souls murdered in their bunks was no different from the kinship I shared with those who swung the hatchets and lit the flames.

Maybe that's the contradiction Madame Zanzibar thought she saw. Maybe the past was what made my future so indecipherable.

The highway was almost bright in the moonlight, though the ditch beside it was shadowed over so I had to step carefully until I'd climbed up to the raised gravel shoulder. The occasional stock trailer rumbled by as tired farmers set out for home with their show animals, and a few older cars chugged slowly past—civic leaders, I imagined, taking the grandkids home to bed. The frogs and cicadas grew louder as I rounded the last curve before the river, and before long the great ball of carnival noise had dwindled to a single, small sound, just one more cricket chirping on the highway behind me. It was a perfect country summer night, with cool air drifting up from the bottomland along the river. I could even see the Milky Way carpeting a path across the center of the sky. There was no sign at all of Chet's war in the heavens.

Not that that was any kind of excuse. I should have known better than to turn my back to the headlights on this particular stretch of road no matter how calm the moment might have seemed. Young kids had hot-rodded this highway since before I was born, and tonight there were sure to be more than a few drunks driving home from the fair. By the time it registered that skidding tires were kicking up shoulder gravel behind me, I had no time to do anything but glance back at the approaching car and then jump.

It was a strange feeling—that first moment of commitment when I leapt from the side of the highway into the bottomless dark. I mean, sure, I knew there was ground down there somewhere, but I couldn't see it, and I had no idea what kind of landing to expect. A blind fall could be crippling, or maybe fatal. Even my baby brother had learned that much about the world, and he was only around for two minutes.

I guess that was the moment when my whole shoddy life was supposed to flash before my eyes and fill me with some kind of life-changing revelation. But my mind wasn't quick enough for that—or maybe it was just too disinterested to sit through such uninspired reruns. In any case, the only bubble of thought my brain managed to pump out was a sort of vague *uh-oh*. After that, there wasn't much left to do but pay close attention and hope for the best.

As it turned out, I was lucky. It was maybe fifteen feet to the bottom of the drop, but the shoulder had been recently regraded, so when I hit the slope about halfway down, the loose dirt and fresh gravel cushioned my fall. From there I skimmed and skittered to the ditch bottom in a spray of quartz chips and granite, and except for having a few more contradictions carved into my palms on the rough slide down, I came away unharmed. The adrenaline rush left me shaking, though, so for a long moment I didn't move, but just breathed deeply and listened to the bad carburetor of the car idling above me.

When I looked up, I saw two teenage boys craning out the driver-side windows, peering down into the darkness. The side of the car was crumpled from some previous wreck, and I could smell the oil burning on the engine block. They'd crossed two lanes of highway to chase me into this ditch, apparently just for the hell of it. And I'd have bet five dollars they were uninsured.

"Hey, old man!" the driver called. "You all right down there?"

Old man. Another milestone in my life.

"Yeah," I called up. "I'm okay."

"Well, keep your bony ass off my road!" he yelled, and both boys erupted into rude laughter. The boy in the backseat leaned farther out his window and threw a beer bottle down at me, but it bounced harmlessly along the slope to my right. Then the driver floored his heap through the gravel, showering me with sand and grit, and the car squealed out a long trail of rubber down the highway.

I decided not to climb back up. I was almost to Sherman's Curve, anyway, where the road doubled back to the southwest and followed the river, and I needed to veer east.

Sherman's Curve was the spot where General William Tecumseh Sherman first laid eyes on the Stone Bridge and reversed his own order to have it destroyed. Sherman left the road here, too, and took the same path I now climbed, up the boulder-pocked rise to the high ground on the town side of the span.

Even now, so many years after the marks of that local war had faded, the bridge still looked impressive, though at night the stonework seemed more skeletal than massive. As I neared the north approach, the darkness thinned and I began to make out more of the details—grassy shadows where the white granite met the riverbank, and flickers of light rippling on the water down below. Most striking of all, a pale and bony shape rose from the center of the arc—Steve's backhoe shining in a flood of moonlight.

I didn't see Steve, though, or any of his fireworks crew. When I reached the apron of the bridge I stopped to listen for voices, but heard only the night sounds of the river—the slight burble of the shallows mixing with the rise-and-fall whir of the katydids. I also heard the occasional spray of sandy dirt leaking from the underside of the archway into the water below.

I walked up the hump to the backhoe and checked for the keys, thinking maybe I should move the heavy machine off the bridge before the strain got to be too much. The keys were in it, but as I climbed into the molded saddle seat, Steve's voice stopped me.

"You break it, you bought it," he said. He was sitting on the ground on the far side of the backhoe, just beneath the dredger, leaning against the large rear tire. He held what looked like a quart bottle of whiskey propped on his knee.

"The same goes for this bridge," I said. "It's not in any shape to be holding up this kind of equipment. You've got to get it off here."

Steve pushed himself to his feet and stepped around the side of the backhoe to face me.

"Well, looky here. It's Nolan Vann, come to tell me what I got to do." He took a swallow from his bottle and turned away. "God's got a sense of humor after all."

"I mean it, Steve. Sammy saw half the underside fall out when we crossed over here the other day."

"This bridge is already history," Steve said. He sat on the stone guard wall and patted it with his free hand. "Has been, from the day we started blasting the riverbed. Sucker's got no keystones to bear the weight when it shifts. Whoever built it was a moron."

"What about your backhoe, then? You don't want that dumped in the river."

"The backhoe stays where it is," he said flatly. He took another swallow, then leaned forward and looked at me. "What the hell are you doing here, anyway?"

"Somebody I work for wanted me to find out about dynamite permits," I said. "I figured you were the right person to ask."

"Yeah, I heard you was bush-hogging for some woman out in the county. So what's her problem—besides you, I mean."

"She's got some oak stumps to take out."

"They're easy," he said, waving the bottle in front of him. "Just strap a stick to the biggest root. But keep the hole small so the blast'll stay focused."

"I'm not asking how to use it," I told him. "I'm asking how to get it."

"That's easier yet," he said. He took a ring of keys from his pocket and jangled them in the moonlight. "Down yonder at the new bridge site. There's two boxes on the back wall of the equipment shed. Help yourself." He tossed the keys to me, and then swung his legs over the wall and vomited into the river. "I'm not supposed to drink anymore," he said. "It aggravates my condition."

"What condition?"

"My condition of unconditional surrender. That's what it is." He drew his legs back over the wall and flung the bottle downriver. I listened for the splash, but it never came. "At first I thought about lining up all the fireworks to bombard the hospital," he went on. "But Tump Wood's still up there, so I couldn't do it. Brothers in arms, and all that." He stood up and walked over to the backhoe. "But I bet you'd rather talk about Laney."

"Yeah," I told him. "I think it's time we did."

"You just about waited too long," he said, and though I couldn't make out his face with the moon at his back, I got the impression he was smiling. "Lemme ask you something, Nolan. What was the worst game we ever won?"

"What?"

"In Pony League. Out of all our victories, which one was the biggest letdown?"

"I don't have any idea."

"Shelbyville," he said, smacking the side of the oversized tire. "Our senior year. Remember?"

"Yeah, I do. Their bus broke down. They had to forfeit."

"Damn straight," he said. "Our biggest rivals, and we didn't even get to play the game. Shit, I'd rather get beat than win by forfeit."

"I want you to back off from Laney," I told him. "I don't know what's liable to happen between her and me, but it's gonna happen without you figuring into it."

He started to laugh. "This must be your lucky day, Nolan. I've already called that one quits. Home team wins again."

"I mean it."

"I reckon you do." There was a weariness in his voice that made me think of Buddy Pilot. He reached out and patted the steering wheel. "Now get off my horse."

I climbed down on the opposite side and watched Steve hoist himself up to the seat. He stared out across the floodplain toward the Wal-Mart parking lot, where scores of cars were beginning to gather to watch the fireworks.

"I'd have been good in a war," he said. "I'm that kind of person." He leaned back and propped his feet on the engine casing. "Instead I got *peacetime*—nothing but *peacetime* my whole stinking hitch." He settled into a silence, and for a second I thought he'd fallen asleep.

"I thought you were in charge of the fireworks display," I said.

He turned and looked at me. "That's me, all right." Then he slapped his hand to his chest and began to sing:

> *And the rockets' red glare.*
> *The bombs bursting in air,*
> *Gave proof through the night*
> *It's the end of the fair.*

He slid farther down in his seat and began to laugh uncontrollably, so hard that he finally had to gasp for breath. "Oh, man," he said. "I better ease up some. I'm liable to puke again."

"Where's your crew?"

"Gave 'em the night off. Turned out to be a one-man job this year." He reached forward and groped along the side of the casing, then lifted up one end of a thin cord, or maybe a wire. Even in the dark, I could trace the line of it against the night sky: the other end stretched past the engine and disappeared into the hollow of the dredger bucket. "I'm trying out the single-fuse approach," he said. "Figure it might be more efficient."

I stepped around to the arm of the dredger and felt along the raised rim with my hand. The whole bucket was packed tight with fat, paper-covered tubes—the fireworks he should have already rigged for the show.

"Steve, what the hell are you doing?"

He swiveled on the seat to face me. "I'll tell you, Nolan, since you and me used to be teammates. I'm fixing to blow myself to Kingdom Come."

My first thought was Laney—that she'd dumped him and he couldn't take the loss. I can't say I felt entirely bad.

"With a bunch of Roman candles?" I asked. "You'll probably just set yourself on fire and have to jump in the river."

"Hey, give me a little credit, boy," he said. "I do this kind of thing for a living."

"You can't be serious."

"There's eight sticks of dynamite in the bottom of that bucket," he said cheerfully. "How serious is that? And then there's all the fancy Fourth of July type stuff on top of it—but that part's just for show. Crowd pleasers. Something for the kids."

"It's not a good idea to play around like this."

He laughed. "No offense, Nolan, but you ain't exactly the local guru on good ideas."

"I don't have to be. This one's a no-brainer."

"That's the way I see it," he agreed. "Hell, don't get me wrong—

this ain't something I'm happy about. But what can I tell you? Sometimes the bus breaks down."

"Laney's not the only woman in Lincoln," I said.

He cleared his throat and spit over the front of the backhoe. "Laney? Well, goddamn, son—you think I'd kill myself over some woman? I ain't never been that big a fool." He tapped his forefinger against his temple. "It's the head, Nolan. Not the heart."

"I don't know what the hell you're talking about."

"I'm talking about a brain that's going into business for itself—starting to grow its own spare parts."

"You mean a tumor?"

He nodded. "Three inches back of my right eyeball. Sprouting like it had plans. Supposed to be a pretty rare thing, but I don't think it is. I knew a guy in the Service who died of it just last March." He rubbed his palms against his eyes like he was wiping away a long night's sleep. "I worked around a lot of weird chemicals in the Corps," he said quietly. "Demolition ain't just gunpowder, you know. Maybe I stepped in something I shouldn't have on a cleanup detail. 'Course the VA says I probably just used the wrong brand of toothpaste. So who the hell knows?"

"What do the doctors say?"

"They say I've got a great shot at full-time vegetable. That's if they can dig it all out okay. Somehow the option don't appeal to me."

I thought of my grandmother curled in her bed at the hospital. Maybe she'd have wanted to end things, too, if she'd seen where she was going.

"My mother killed herself," I told him. "She made an awful lot of people unhappy doing that."

"Well, tough luck for them. If she wanted to go, she had every right to, that's the way I see it. Anyway, nobody's about to lose much sleep over me. I been out of line for way too long." He shook the fuse in his fist. "But by-God they'll remember who I was. Nobody ever went out like this before. Hell, the Legion might even put up a plaque."

"You seem okay now," I said. "You might still have a lot of good time left. What do you want to throw it away for?"

"Yeah, that's a trade-off," he admitted. "But I won't never have a chance like this again. Look over yonder." He pointed to the Wal-Mart, where the cars were now flashing their lights and honking their horns, impatient for the show to start. "I don't want to rot away in some easy chair like Jerry Rathburn did. I want to go fast. And I want witnesses. I want the bleachers filled."

"What about—" I wanted to ask about Laney's baby, but I didn't have the words.

"Don't forget who you're talking to, bud," he said. "You ought to be tickled pink about this. Hell, you ought to be handing me the matches."

"I know. But it's more complicated than just you and me."

"Then here's something you might be interested in," he said. "Laney ain't at her sister's—she went up to Nashville. And she ain't there for the Grand Ole Opry."

Going up to Nashville. That was the euphemism we'd used in high school. There were plenty of clinics in Nashville, and it was far enough from home that people weren't as likely to find out.

I didn't know what to say.

Steve and I just stared at each other for what must have been half a minute, neither one of us really able to see the other, I guess, in that darkness. Finally he took a lighter out of his pocket and flicked on the flame between us.

"Believe I'll be going now," he said. His face looked ghostly above the lighter, full of wavering shadows. There was a grimy redness around his eyes, the same redness I'd sometimes seen after bad ball games, the games we'd squandered in the bottom of the ninth.

"All right then," I said. "If that's the way you want it." I stepped away from the backhoe. "Guess I'll be seeing you."

"Everywhere you look," he laughed, and, for the moment, clicked out the flame.

I turned away and crossed down to the other side of the river.

When I reached the far bank I kept on walking, straight out onto the southern floodplain that my grandfather had once dreamed of as a tourist attraction, straight toward the Andrew Jackson monument, straight toward the Wal-Mart parking lot and the drunken, blaring crowd.

For a long time I considered not looking back. Steve would be watching for that, for my shape to stop moving on the dark field, and it occurred to me that if I never turned around at all but just kept on walking, maybe he'd lose his nerve and go on home to sleep it off.

Maybe that's what would have happened. But about 200 yards out, I stopped—maybe because I realized that I still had Steve's keys in my hand. At first I just stood there, halfway between the bridge and the Wal-Mart, wondering about the right thing to do. Then I dropped the keys into the dirt—a war relic for some future tourist scouring the land with a metal detector. When I did finally turn around to face it, the show had already begun. The fuse was trailing sparks along the backhoe.

The blast still caught me by surprise. The flash came first, obviously, riding on the speed of light, but what stunned me was the way it lit the scene before disturbing it, like a camera clicking off a souvenir snapshot before the molecules got blown apart. What I think I saw in that sliver of a second, flashing by like a subliminal message on a television screen, was Steve Pitts lounging on the seat of the backhoe, calm as the night air. But maybe not. When time splits down to a hair that thin, it's hard to know what's real.

The rest of it was almost slow. The explosion ballooned out from the dredger, obliterating the backhoe in a pure, white ball of power, and as the machine rose in pieces from the bridge, the sound of mass disintegration cracked across the field in its own bone-rattling wind, booming in my head and shoving me backward. Bright streaks of color spewed across the sky, showering sparks into the river, and soon the secondary sounds of falling debris and collapsing stone pillars rumbled along the banks and echoed out across the field—gently, it seemed, like the falling pulse of the cicadas. The beat of a thousand startled wings rose from the northern bank, and a blue halo of smoke hovered above the cut where the bridge no longer stood.

Then the quiet came down, and after a small space of wonder, when my eyes had readjusted to the night, I turned again toward the highway, guessing it was time to go home.

That Angle at Which Montgomery Fell

WHILE LANEY LIMPED BACK TO the Visitors' Center to use the rest room again, I dragged our broken cooler out to an open spot on the battlefield to set up lunch. Except for the hornets and Laney's cracked ankle, everything was going pretty well. Neither one of us had said anything meaningful all morning.

Baby steps, that was the only way to make it. Any tightrope walker knew that much.

The newspaper had called Steve's death a tragic accident. I don't know if Laney believed that or not, but I wasn't about to ask her. Sometimes it was better to leave a scarred landscape undisturbed. Digging around for keepsakes could turn up a land mine.

For three days now Laney and I had been civil, but we'd also kept to ourselves. I didn't even know if she'd gone to the funeral, because I was out job hunting that day.

I also didn't know the story on her trip to Nashville, if in fact she went. She still acted pregnant—peeing every fifteen minutes and eating more sardines than a trained seal—but I was sure no expert on the subject. The first-aid section of the *Boy Scout Handbook* didn't have a lot to say about pregnancy, so there were sizeable gaps in my knowledge.

Maybe we needed to take one of those birthing classes together. That might bring me up to speed.

If she were still pregnant.

If we weren't getting a divorce.

I spread our blanket on the ground and opened the cooler. The inside was a mess. Most of the ice had melted during the morning drive, so the sandwiches were all soggy. Also, Laney hadn't tightened the lid on the tomato juice, so the water inside the chest looked like it had been run through rusty pipes.

I held my hand under the cold reddish water to numb the pain, but apparently that's not the right treatment for hornet stings because the burning only got worse. I pulled my hand out of the chest and carefully dried it on the blanket. My palm had puffed up like a catcher's mitt. I could barely move my fingers.

Twenty yards away, the hornets still swarmed around the base of the white marker post, the one I'd stumbled against when the handle on the cooler snapped. At least two had got me on the hand, and I was surprised how much it hurt.

I barely mentioned it to Laney, though, because she had her own crisis to deal with. The heavy chest had swung down hard into the side of her foot. I told her the ankle was only bruised and that she just needed to walk it off, but I really had no idea. I was just repeating what I'd always heard from coaches: *You'll be okay, son. Just walk it off.* It didn't matter what the problem was—a fastball to the temple, a line drive in the groin—just walk it off. That was the only medical advice I'd ever heard on a ball field.

This place had been a ball field once, two hundred years ago, back before the battle turned it into something else. The Creeks used to play a kind of lacrosse here. It was a rough sport, and sometimes people even got killed. But that was the point. The game was a substitute for war between rival towns.

I didn't know the point of our games.

I salvaged what I could from the cooler—a wet box of raisins, two Cokes, and a bag of carrot sticks. Not much of a picnic, but that didn't matter. Laney and I hadn't had much appetite around each other for a while now.

There was nobody else on the battlefield, probably because of the heat, which was in the high-90s, and the suffocating river-country humidity. I hadn't paid enough attention back at the Visitors'

Center, so I didn't know what the weather had been like for the actual battle, but it must have been cooler than this. The air was muggy enough to parboil an egg—way too thick to keep up any kind of fight. Even the animals had given up for the afternoon. This place was pretty deep in the backcountry, so I knew there was plenty of wildlife around, but the woods bordering the field had no movement at all, not a bird or a squirrel or a chipmunk. The trees along the horseshoe curve of the riverbank were so still they looked painted in place, and even the river, which showed through in murky green patches between the bramble thickets, looked stale as old soup, stagnant in the pot.

But I was glad to be here, given the alternatives. At least there was no major appliance strapped to my back. At least I wasn't chopping out stumps.

I'd left my hat in the car, and since I didn't need another heat-stroke, I grabbed one of the chilled Coke cans to hold against my forehead and started up the grassy slope toward the parking lot. It was a long hike, nearly a quarter of a mile, and as I trudged through the brittle yellow weeds I began to worry about Laney. This kind of weather had to put a strain on her. Maybe we shouldn't have gone so far downhill for our picnic. From the crest it had seemed like an easy stroll, but the distance was deceptive and the climb back was harder than it looked.

General Jackson's men had probably found that out, too. Natural momentum must have carried them easily down the long sweep to the barricade, but the inevitable slow retreat of tired and wounded soldiers back up the open hillside—that trek must have seemed endless.

The barricade line—that's how far Laney and I had made it. There wasn't much to it now, just a skeleton fence of bone white posts strung across the 300-yard gap of the horseshoe. But when Jackson had thrown his troops against it, it had been a zigzag wall of logs stacked ten feet high. Most of his casualties had come trying to cross that line. But there'd been no choice, as far as he was concerned. The Tallapoosa River looped around the other three sides, so if he truly wanted to destroy the Creek Nation, he had to come at them head-on.

Well, not him personally. He stayed at the top of the slope all day, behind the cannon.

As I reached the bench at the top of the hill, Laney was just coming up the other side from the parking lot. She walked slowly, but her limp was nearly gone. She waved when she saw me, and as she got closer I realized she had my ball cap in her hand.

"Thought you might need this," she said, tossing it to me across the back of the bench. "It'll keep the sun off that bald spot."

"Thanks," I said, and tossed her the Coke can in trade. "I was just coming up to get it. How's the foot?"

"Not bad," she said, holding the can to the side of her face. "I guess the walk got the kinks worked out." She moved around the side of the bench and sat down. "Felt good to get back to that air-conditioned building, too. Got my second wind." She reached down and clawed at a red welt on her calf. "But you'd think they'd take better care of the grounds. I must have half a dozen chigger bites already. Land worth dying for ought to be worth mowing."

"Glad you're feeling better," I said. I sat beside her and we both stared for a while out at the battlefield.

"I found out some things," she said. "I told a park ranger about the hornets, and he had me show him where it was on a map. Turns out you got stung at a real historic spot."

She took a yellow envelope from the back pocket of her shorts and handed it to me. "The Battle of Tehopiska" was printed in bold letters across the top, and beneath that, in smaller type, was the full promo:

General Andrew Jackson's Map & Description
of the Battle of Horseshoe Bend
March 27, 1814
Reproduced on antiqued parchment that looks
and feels authentically old.
$.75

"The ranger gave it to me for being such a good citizen," Laney said. "Or maybe he was just worried about a lawsuit."

"We might have a case." I held out my hand, the same one Madame Zanzibar had found so annoying.

"Jesus, Nolan," she said, examining it more closely. "That looks pretty bad."

"It's better than it was," I said. "The swelling's already gone down a little."

"You must be allergic or something."

"Don't write me off just yet," I said. "I'm sturdier than my mother."

She didn't seem to know what to say to that, and I worried for a second that I might have sounded hostile. But she smiled and took the envelope from my hand. "Then let me help you with that," she said. She pulled out the fake parchment and unfolded it on the bench between us.

It was a crude sketch—presumably penned by Jackson himself—of the horseshoe bend in the Tallapoosa, with all the strategic locations marked. The zigzag line inked across the gap of the horseshoe was labeled "Breast Works," and Laney pointed to a tiny circle at one of the corners on that line, the very place our cooler handle had snapped.

"See this?" she asked, tapping the spot on the map.

I looked at the mark, then scanned the identification key above the drawing. There it was, the last item on the list, carefully lettered in Jackson's own hand:

That angle at which Montgomery fell.

"Who was Montgomery?" I asked.

"The first man over the barricade," Laney answered. "It wasn't much of an accomplishment, though. They shot him in the head before he made it down the other side."

"He must have been an officer."

Laney looked at me over the top of her sunglasses. "What makes you say that?"

"Generals don't keep track of dead privates. Only officers have names. That's how history works."

"Well, you're right," she said, pushing her sunglasses back into place. "He was a major."

"Probably a good one, too," I added. "Guys with that much rank didn't usually go out and get killed with their men. I bet he was pretty popular with the troops."

Laney folded her arms over her breasts and faced out toward the battlefield. "Just because he made a suicide charge doesn't mean anybody liked him. For all you know, he might have been a total jerk. He might have been one of those psychotic lunatics who just wanted to be a war hero."

There was a slight tension in her voice, and I suddenly knew there was one bet we both would have been willing to take: Steve Pitts would have made it over that wall—and probably well ahead of Major Montgomery.

"Yeah, you're right," I admitted. "I've got no clue what any-body's like in a war. All my battlefields have had souvenir stands and Porta Potties."

She reached over and hooked her arm in mine. "That's fine with me. I'm glad you never went into the army. People turn it into too big a deal."

"I do feel a little left out sometimes, though," I told her. "I'm probably the only guy in town who's never been on a committee to raise money for a war memorial."

Laney laughed. "God, those things are stupid. Especially the ones with cannonballs. They look like big bowling trophies."

She was right, of course, that's exactly what they were—trophies for the winners, as if war were just some grand team sport and dying was a way to help the score. But I didn't think they were stu-pid at all. Memorials told us a lot of interesting things about who and what we were—or at least that's the way it seemed to me. Whenever I saw some bronze or marble soldier, I couldn't help but think how lucky we were to have made it even this far.

"But if you really do feel left out," Laney went on, "maybe you ought to join the Rotary or the Elks. Let 'em teach you the secret handshake. Make you one of the boys."

She was being sarcastic, I knew, but it was still something to think about. The Rotary and the Elks both sponsored baseball teams in the summer youth leagues. And so did the Masons, and the Lions, and Kiwanis, and Moose, and Oddfellows, and Jaycees, and even the Knights of Columbus. Maybe I could coach for one of them next year.

"So what else did you learn from the ranger?" I asked.

"More than I meant to," she said. "I made some crappy comment about the weather and that opened up a whole crate of cheerful tidbits about Creek superstitions and religious beliefs. Then he went off on some riff about rabid skunks and what a headache that's been for the Park Service. I never saw anybody so determined to be informative. He was like a Jehovah's Witness with a day job."

"Blame it on the uniform," I told her. "I bet his wife can't get two words out of him at home."

"Yeah, I know what that's like," Laney said, and we both went quiet. A red-tailed hawk glided out from the woods behind us and banked a long slow circle above our picnic spot, above that angle at which Montgomery fell.

"There was a cloud," Laney said at last. "Just when the Creeks were about to surrender, some rain cloud drifted out over the battlefield. The Creek holy men decided it was a good omen, so they told everybody they had to keep fighting. That's why it turned into such a slaughter—the goddamned fanatics wouldn't let anybody quit."

I believed in omens myself, so I understood the problem. The good ones always looked pretty much the same as the bad. The only sure way to peg them was in hindsight, and that kind of defeated the whole purpose.

"Yeah, religion can be an ugly dance partner," I said. "But Jackson's men weren't much better off. They couldn't quit either. Old Hickory was always ready to shoot deserters."

Laney shook her head. "That's so sick." She gave the Coke can a quick shake and then popped it open, spraying brown foam across the grass in front of us.

"Still, that cloud really was a good omen," I told her. "For me, anyway. I had ancestors here on both sides. If the Creeks hadn't lost all their men in battle, the women wouldn't have had to move into the white settlements. My great-grandmother never would have met my great-grandfather."

"Well, that's pretty creepy," Laney said.

And it was, in a way—to think that my very existence had hinged on something as flimsy as a cloud floating in a spring sky four life-times ago.

"That's destiny for you," I said, smiling. "It's like Mr. Yarbor-ough used to tell us in history class—we're all just the natural prod-uct of the last ten thousand years of tribal warfare."

"He meant that as a criticism," she reminded me. "Mr. Yar-borough thought people were crap."

"Yeah, but the idea still holds. I think everything leads up to what it's supposed to."

"How about getting fired by your father?" she asked. "Was that just destiny's way of helping you find exciting new opportunities in repo work?"

"I'm out of the repo business," I told her. "Dell took a job at the Savings and Loan."

"Oh, great," she said. "So we're even worse off than I thought."

"Not really. I got a new job."

She took a few methodical sips from the can. "And you had to drive us all the way down here to break the news? Oh, God, it must be something awful. Please don't tell me you have to wear one of those sandwich boards."

"Store manager," I told her.

She took a moment to turn that over in her mind. "Okay. What store?"

"Salvation Army."

She laughed again, then looked at me closely. "Really?"

"I start Monday. Turns out my background in paperwork and junk furniture was just what they were looking for."

She reached down and squeezed my knee. "Way to go, sweetheart."

Sweetheart. She hadn't called me that since before she took up with Steve Pitts. Hell, it was longer ago than that—before she even took up with Randall.

She set the drink aside and began to rummage through her purse. "I bought one of those disposable cameras at the gift shop," she said, pulling out the small yellow box. She stood up from the bench and took off her sunglasses. "Take my picture. I want proof that I've been here." She handed me the cardboard camera and moved a few steps away so I could fit her in the viewfinder. "Get as much of the battlefield as you can."

I stood on the bench for a better angle and framed her in the shot with the gentle roll of the hillside falling away behind her, all the way down to the line of white posts and our neglected picnic lunch.

"Uh-oh," I said, and caught Laney's frown as I snapped the picture.

"What's the matter?" she asked.

"Uninvited guest." I pointed down the slope to where a large brown dog was pawing through the food in our cooler.

"You shouldn't have left the top open," she scolded me.

I stepped down from the bench. "It's no real loss," I told her. "The sandwiches didn't survive the trip."

"Neither will that blanket."

We watched as the dog knocked the cooler over and began scattering the contents across the grass. I couldn't tell if it was even eating anything—it just seemed to be tearing things up, shaking each Baggie in its jaws until the food flew out, as if every sandwich had to be killed separately. Then it suddenly flopped onto its back and began to squirm around through the mess.

"Not the best table manners," Laney said.

"Maybe it got stung," I suggested.

The dog sprang to its feet and began to drag the blanket away from the cooler, stopping every few steps to give it a vicious shake. I stuck two fingers between my teeth and let out a shrill whistle. The dog dropped the blanket and looked up.

"I don't think you should have done that," Laney said. "The ranger was serious about the rabies problem around here. And that's no house dog."

"I just wanted to get him off our blanket," I said, but she was right, he was either wild or a longtime stray. Dogs like that were unpredictable. Sometimes rabid.

"So what's the plan now?" Laney asked as the animal bounded up the hill toward us.

"We might want to get to the car."

"Shit," she answered, and began to hobble quickly down toward the parking lot on her bad ankle. Running wasn't always the best tactic—sometimes even a good dog would give chase if you acted like prey, and in those cases the smart thing was to move slowly or else just stand your ground. But that didn't work for mad dogs, and with Laney probably still pregnant I figured it might be best just to go ahead and make a break for it. But I hung back a little to see to it she had enough time.

As it turned out, we needn't have worried—the battlefield itself was all the rescue either of us needed. It was a long run up from that barricade, and by the time the poor animal staggered across the crest to the bench, Laney and I were fifty yards away, safe in our car with the windows rolled. Laney had even locked her door.

"He can't use the handle," I teased her. "He's got no thumbs."

"You don't know what that dog can do," she said. "For all you know, he could come right through this windshield."

He had the size for it, all right—part shepherd, maybe, with a few larger breeds mixed in. But he was too winded right now to be that aggressive. He just stood there, panting and drooling, with his large head drooped between his shoulders.

"Look at that," Laney went on. "I think he's foaming at the mouth."

"I'd expect he would be," I laughed. "He just ran a quarter of a mile uphill in hundred-degree heat. He's probably fighting off a heart attack."

Laney picked up an old paper napkin from the floor mat and tried to rub away some of the oily windshield grime, but that just made the view more blurry. "I'm still glad we're not out there on that bench," she said, tossing the wadded napkin back to the floor. She shifted uncomfortably on the hot plastic seat. "Now start this thing up, Nolan. Get that air conditioner on."

"All right." I tucked her camera in my shirt pocket and took out my keys. "But we can't leave yet."

"Why not?" she asked. "We've pretty much seen everything. And lunch got canceled."

As the engine caught, a rush of hot air hissed from the dashboard vents, and Laney covered the flow with her hands, waiting for it to cool down.

"All our stuff's out there," I reminded her.

"Just junk and garbage," she said. "A broken cooler and a chewed-up army surplus blanket. I'm sure as hell not going back out there for that—not with a rabid dog on the loose."

"You can't litter on federal land," I told her. "There's fines."

"Nothing's got our name on it," she argued.

"I wouldn't feel right about it."

It surprised me to say that. I'd broken so many laws lately I'd lost count—fraud, forgery, theft, breaking and entering, criminal trespass, aggravated assault, and who knew what else. Now suddenly the prospect of littering stopped me dead in my tracks. What the hell was wrong with me?

"God, that is just like you," she said, dropping her head back against the seat. She turned her face away and angrily cleared her throat. "You've always got to color inside the lines, don't you? Follow all the goddamned rules, like some kind of citizen robot."

Inside the lines—that was rich. I couldn't remember the last time I'd colored anything inside the lines. For the most part I'd been off the page entirely.

Apparently, she'd confused me with my father.

"Maybe you've got me wrong," I said.

"After twelve years? I don't think so."

She had a point. Twelve years of marriage was a lot of history to refute in one conversation, no matter what I might think of to say. But that was my only shot.

The problem, as I saw it, was the same for both of us. We knew way too much about each other without really knowing anything at all. And talking that out would be like swapping our coffin-nail collections.

Still, other things might happen. Maybe it was time for another blind leap from the highway.

"I'm not Steve Pitts," I said. "And I wouldn't want to be."

That caught her like a slap.

"Steve has nothing to do with this," she said. Her jaw was locked so tight she could barely growl out the words.

"Not anymore he doesn't."

She turned around and glared at me. "Steve's dead. Don't you dare say another word about him."

"Yeah, right." I knew my attitude was ugly and that I was probably pushing her too far, but I couldn't help it anymore. "Look, Laney, we've obviously got problems. And we both know why."

"You don't know anything," she said savagely. "Not about me or anybody else. You want to know what's wrong?" She leaned her face closer to mine. "There's no life in it. We used to do all kinds of wild things together. You remember that? Back in high school? We used to have fun. Now we just sit. You're the most boring man I know."

That pretty well summed it up, all right.

I opened the car door and stepped out into the noon sun.

"What do you think you're doing?" Laney said.

I started to tell her, but my throat had closed up so much I couldn't speak. I gestured toward the battlefield, over the hill where our picnic wreckage would be.

"Nolan, you get back in this car right now," she said, but I closed the door and began to walk slowly up the back side of the slope. My legs were a little wobbly and my forehead felt prickly, like it had that day in Alma's field. But this wasn't heatstroke. This was just the general collapse of my life.

I veered off toward the bench, realizing that I'd have to sit for a minute before starting the long walk downhill. The dog had already perked up, and now he took a few cautious steps toward me, warning me with a low snarl. But I felt too drained to care.

As I got closer, I remembered Laney's camera in my shirt pocket. I stopped about ten feet from the snarling dog and framed him in the viewfinder. Laney had it right—we needed proof that we were here.

"Good dog," I said, and snapped the picture. He growled half-heartedly, but didn't move, so I took a couple of steps closer. He sniffed at me across the remaining distance, then raised his head slightly and took a step back, confused by the smell of my apathy. I circled past him and sat down heavily on the bench.

Laney gunned the engine a couple of times to announce her intentions, but I didn't look around. I heard the tires skid on the asphalt as she backed out of the parking space, then she rumbled away down the narrow park road toward Route 49. A few shaky breaths later, everything was quiet.

"Good boy," I said, trying to keep up the conversation. The dog walked wearily out in front of me and began another growl, but slipped instead into a wide and noisy yawn. Aparently Laney had been right about how boring I was. I couldn't even hold the attention of a rabid dog.

Not that I truly believed he was rabid. From a distance, those jerky movements and wild lunges had brought him under suspicion, but up close I could see that he was really just an enormous pup, maybe a year old, still frisky enough to turn everything into a game. His coat was mangy and matted, so I knew he'd been on his own for a while, and it wasn't hard to spell out his future. Sooner or later some semi would catch him unawares, and he'd be the next dead lump along the highway.

I took another picture, then patted my thigh a couple of times and stuck out my good hand. He stepped up and sniffed it thoroughly, then snorted a tired sigh and sprawled in the grass at my feet. He still kept an eye on me, though—in case I turned out to be rabid.

After a few minutes a slight breeze kicked up, and that revived me enough to get going again. I stood up slowly so as not to spook the dog, and started down toward that angle at which Montgomery fell, retracing, I imagined, the very path he'd followed on his unlucky day. The dog stood up, too, and trailed along after me as I made my way down through the long yellow field.

He'd made a complete mess of the picnic site, but when we reached the spot he sniffed everything again, like he thought some key ingredient might have been tampered with. The hornets, for the most part, had settled back into their nest, though a couple still buzzed around the ravaged box of raisins. I put the trash and most of the remaining food back into the cooler, then stuffed the blanket in on top and snapped the lid shut. The cooler was hollow plastic, so without the ice it was light enough to carry like a suitcase. I grabbed it by the good handle and started back up the hill. Again, the dog trotted along behind.

I watched the ground as I walked, pacing myself against the heat of the afternoon and wondering what to do next. I was almost to the crest before I realized Laney was sitting there on the government bench waiting for me. She wasn't smiling. But still she was there.

I stopped in front of her, and the dog ambled up by my side.

"Who's your friend?" she asked. Her voice was even and noncommittal.

"This is Jerry," I told her. "He's not rabid. He's just young."

"Looks like he's had a hard time."

"A dog's life," I said, and sat down carefully beside her.

We sat quietly for a while, watching Jerry follow his nose along the row of thistles and bramble-berries that bordered the woods on our left. Then Laney took off her sunglasses, and while she cleaned the lenses with the shirttail of her blouse, I looked at her face. Her eyes were red and swollen, and in full sunlight I could see that age was finally settling in, etching new lines that makeup wouldn't hide.

She looked better than ever.

But I understood now why fortune-tellers had to work with palms. The face had too many futures to wear. The hand was a far safer map.

She put her glasses back on and draped her arms along the back of the bench. "Maybe I could work there, too," she said.

"Maybe so," I told her. "It's a big store. I'm sure there'll be openings. But what about the baby?"

"People can do both." She drew her foot up onto the edge of the bench and rubbed her sore ankle. "I almost didn't keep it," she said quietly.

"What stopped you?"

She shrugged. "I don't know." She rested her chin against her knee and sighed. "I don't know why I do anything."

"That's common ground."

I took her hand and rubbed my fingers across her palm. Life lines. Love lines. Family lines. They were all there, somewhere, spelling things out, and as Laney gave my own unread hand a squeeze, a possible future glimmered from some distant place in my mind:

Laney and me at the Salvation Army.
A rebuilt family room.
A dog named Jerry.
A son named Thomas Winston Vann.

Hell of an unlikely long shot, given my career stats. I'd never been the guy people looked to for that bases-loaded homer in the bottom of the ninth. But I did have a good eye. In a tight spot, I could check my swing and draw the walk. I could at least keep the inning alive.

So we sat there together, sunning ourselves on the fringe of the battlefield, while the dog scoured the hillside for clues and a bank of dark clouds drifted in over the treetops.

But these clouds were no omen. Just a natural change in the weather.

And change didn't bother me much anymore. I'd learned a lot lately about the way things come and go. The way uncertainty marries itself into every breath we take. The way the guesswork keeps us moving. I'd grown to like the unhinged balance of it all. The way a storm spends itself in a downpour. The way blue repossesses the sky.

Clint McCown was born in Fayetteville, Tennessee, and grew up in the South. He currently chairs the creative writing program at Beloit College and has twice won the American Fiction Prize for his short stories, which have been widely published. His first book of poems, *Sidetracks,* received the Germaine Bree Book Award. As a journalist, he received the AP Award for Documentary Excellence for his investigations of organized crime and election fraud in Alabama. The author of a previous novel, *The Member-Guest,* he has also been a screenwriter for Warner Brothers. He lives in Beloit, Wisconsin, with his wife and two daughters.